SUCKERS

SUCKERS

LeeSha Shay

HODDER CHILDREN'S BOOKS

First published in Great Britain in 2025 by Hodder & Stoughton Limited

1 3 5 7 9 10 8 6 4 2

Text copyright © LeeSha Shay, 2025
Cover illustration copyright © Charlie Bowater, 2025

The moral right of the author has been asserted.

*All characters and events in this publication, other than those clearly
in the public domain, are fictitious and any resemblance to
real persons, living or dead, is purely coincidental.*

All rights reserved.
No part of this publication may be reproduced, stored in
a retrieval system, or transmitted, in any form or by any means, without
the prior permission in writing of the publisher, nor be otherwise circulated
in any form of binding or cover other than that in which it is published
and without a similar condition including this condition being
imposed on the subsequent purchaser.

A CIP catalogue record for this book
is available from the British Library.

ISBN 978 1 444 98189 6

Printed and bound in Great Britain by
Clays Ltd, Elcograf S.p.A.

The paper and board used in this book
are made from wood from responsible sources.

Hodder Children's Books
An imprint of
Hachette Children's Group
Part of Hodder & Stoughton Limited
Carmelite House
50 Victoria Embankment
London EC4Y 0DZ

The authorised representative in the EEA is Hachette Ireland, 8 Castlecourt Centre, Dublin 15,
D15 XTP3, Ireland (email: info@hbgi.ie)

An Hachette UK Company
www.hachette.co.uk

www.hachettechildrens.co.uk

For my babies, Leshaylia, Tadaicia, Kesharia and Keontay, for brightening my days and always cheering me on.

My incredible mother, Lynda, for always believing in me, no matter how much I doubt myself.

My diamonds, Anuwara, Peter and Henry, for always listening without judgement, making me feel seen, and loving me the way you do.

My readers, for all your words of encouragement and being the reason I do what I do.

Thank you all. I love you so much.

Chapter One

'Any last requests?' I yell at the cheering crowd in front of me.

This gig at the Underworld in Camden is the last my bandmates and I are playing for two weeks and, so far, it's been one of our best performances to date. The tickets for this grungy venue sold out days ago, but judging by how tightly squeezed together everyone looks, I'm sure a few extra people snuck in.

'"The Less I Know the Better"!' is screamed back at us, but we expected it. Our version of the Tame Impala hit has been requested at almost every gig we've played since the beginning of last year.

Fallon, our lead singer, wipes his face with the towel that lives on his shoulder, then lifts his free hand to grab the beam above the stage. 'Sorry, what was that?'

'"The Less I Know the Better"! "The Less I Know the Better"!'

The crowd moves as one, punching their hands in the air while they throw themselves up and down. They chant Fallon's name too — mostly the girls, which he revels in.

'All right, all right . . .' He drops his hand, smirking at the rest of us. 'Let's goooo!'

I tighten the hair tie around my locs before teasing the first few chords on my bass guitar, enjoying my own moment of hype. Once I start for real, though, and Kyle hits the drums, everyone sings along with Fallon, and the pillars holding up the roof begin to shake.

Playing here is always a vibe but tonight has been especially *wild*.

I'm deafened by screams as Fallon seduces his mic, softly singing half of the first verse, until Kyle picks up the tempo on the drums, and his harsh, guttural growls arrive.

I lose myself with the crowd, miming along with Fallon as I caress my bass strings. Beads of my sweat join theirs on the floor with each jerk of my head, adding to the well-used, musky scent in here. And with each inhale, the more aroused my senses become.

This is what I live for: the high that comes with the rush of adrenaline in my blood. These moments have gotten so much better since I turned eighteen a few months ago, so . . . *intense*.

But before I begin to dwell on all the other strange things that have been happening to me, I block it from my mind and encourage the crowd to clap their hands in time with Kyle's drums.

Since I picked up my first instrument — a keyboard — when I was seven, playing music has come naturally to me. Same went for my transition to a guitar at ten and, eventually, my first bass at fourteen. Then, it just became a part of who I was.

Playing bass always saved me in one way or another too, whether it was how learning new music or techniques soothed my loneliness, or how certain melodies would lift my mood. The deep sounds spoke to me in a way that no other instrument could. And even more so now.

I'm as buzzed as our audience is when we finish the song, but once Fallon thanks everyone, I make my usual excuses to leave. Now that I don't have the distraction of playing my guitar, it's a struggle to keep the overthinking at bay.

Particularly about Kyle.

'Oh, come on, Gabby,' our guitarist, Mads, complains when I tell her my plan to head home. 'We're not gonna see each other for two weeks. You can't kick it with us for one night?'

I clip my bass case closed. 'It's not that I don't want to . . .' Of course I want to party at Freddie's place. It's always a good time when we chill there, but it wouldn't be a good idea with how I currently feel.

'Boring,' Kyle sings, coming over with Fallon. 'One drink, and I'll pay for your taxi home. You haven't hung with us outside of these gigs for ages.'

Kyle's tanned skin looks so good against all that black he's wearing . . .

It used to be so easy to see him only as my bandmate, regardless of how cute I thought he was but, recently, I've found it pretty much impossible to keep my thoughts about him professional. Not only does he always smell good, but he's been growing his hair out, and I've often wondered what it would feel like to run my—

Stop.

'That's not been on purpose,' I retort, feeling conflicted. 'I've had a lot going on.'

He rolls his hazel eyes. 'So you keep saying.'

Fallon, though, he's suspicious. 'Have we done something to upset you? Is the next step you quitting on us?'

'Not at all.' It hurts he would think that, but I don't blame him.

I can't exactly tell them about all the crazy things I've been feeling – hell, I can't make sense of them half the time. But I also can't keep lying – my well of lies has run empty.

'So, come for one drink,' Mads says, grinning like I've already conceded.

I roll my eyes. 'Just one.'

I have to force myself to breathe deeper so I can settle my pounding heart and the sudden rush of desire caused by Kyle smiling at me.

He playfully punches my arm, oblivious to my torment. 'Now that's more like it.'

Despite giving in, the band didn't seem convinced that I wouldn't back out of going to the party at the last moment. Kyle even insisted on driving me home and waiting for me to get ready. He might not have said anything directly to my face, but it's obvious he's feeling some kind of way about me not hanging out with him and the others anymore.

Kyle and I would spend a lot of time together outside the band before my birthday, but he was the first thing I had to cut out when the . . . weirdness started happening. But it didn't stop my attraction towards him.

I try to remember the last party I'd been to – or raves or music festivals, all the things I'd be first in line for – and can't. Now all I seem to do is worry about the next lie I'll feed to the people I care about. My parents are still suspicious after I skipped Metal Fest this year, and I know they didn't believe it was because I 'couldn't get tickets'.

I have a quick shower and change into a black, oversized hoodie and ripped jeans, but I wear the same boots because they're my favourite. They're leather with a two-inch platform, and they're super comfortable. I'd bought them to match a dress I had with huge cut-out slits that would show the ink on my arms and back, but I don't wear things like that any more.

Being a gothic black girl always makes me stand out, as do a few of my more unorthodox facial piercings. That doesn't bother me, though. My parents have always made me feel comfortable with expressing my alternative style. However, being different means attention — and that *is* currently a problem.

'All good?' Kyle asks, once I've got back into his Sprinter van.

'Yeah, I'm fine.' I feign being cold when he glances at my outfit. 'Thanks for waiting on me.'

'I wanted to.'

He's quiet for a little while he drives, but he fiddles with the chain on his jeans' pocket. 'The gig was wild tonight, huh?'

I smile as I remember it. 'It was. Nice that the fans showed up for us, though, especially as it was the last one for a few weeks.'

'Right . . .' He glances my way. 'Got any plans for the time off?'

I shake my head before staring out of the window, my heart racing after meeting those hazel eyes. *Don't be weird . . .* 'Nah. What about you? Have you planned anything?'

'Spending some time in the studio, might hit the skate park.' He gestures at the stereo, nudging me to play some music for the drive. 'Apart from that, I guess I'll just go with the flow.'

'Sounds good.' I connect my phone and play 'Raining Blood' by Slayer. We both like this band, and soon we're both nodding our heads along to it. It helps me relax, too, and I actually start looking forward to the party we're on our way to.

Freddie's parties are always epic because he knows a lot of people and his parents' place is huge. He lives in a cul-de-sac called Grange

Gardens, which is a stark contrast to the rough council estate I've grown up on. It has, like, seven bedrooms, a handful of bathrooms and a heated pool out the back.

When we arrive, there is a ton of people out front and whatever calm I'd felt dissipates. It's weird given how much time I've spent at Freddie's. Kyle and Freddie have been friends for years and the rest of us became friends with him too, since this is where we'd practice when we were first setting up the band. Freddie makes his own music too, so he has an in-house studio that became a second home for the rest of us.

'Come on,' Kyle says, once he manages to find somewhere to park his van. 'Let's get you that drink.'

He leads me into the house, helping me squeeze past couples making out and groups drinking and dancing in the crowded hallways. The music isn't my preference: pop music is playing currently, and the further inside we get, the more I regret my decision to come.

Kyle eyes me when we arrive at the drinks table in the kitchen. 'Rum? Vodka?' He looks me up and down and raises an eyebrow. 'Cider?'

I roll my eyes. Last summer, we ended up getting drunk on cider in the park. I drank way too much of it and threw up on my minidress – something he's never let me forget. 'Vodka and Coke would be good.'

He smirks, reaching for a cup. 'You sure? Freddie should have some around here—'

'I can leave.'

His expression falters. 'I'm just kidding. Damn, you're so stressed these days.' He hands me my cup. 'Wanna talk about it?'

'Nah, I'm good.' I sip my drink, but it doesn't relax me at all. If anything, it makes me more jittery and I think he can tell.

He leans closer. 'I recorded that new track I told you about. Wanna hear it?'

'Hell yeah.' That switches my entire mood. Not only can I finally hear this 'masterpiece' he's been banging on about, but it means I can get away from all these bodies.

All these scents are making me—

'Come on, then.'

I follow him upstairs to the studio, away from the thumping music and confined spaces. To my relief, I finally begin to chill the hell out.

'This better be good after you've hyped it up so much,' I tease.

He chuckles as he leans over the chair to make a few clicks on his laptop. 'It is.' Then he straightens when an intro heavy with cymbals plays, quickly joined by the bass drum.

Wow . . . He wasn't lying . . .

I nod my head as soon as the full beat kicks in, and then I'm smiling up at him. 'I love this.'

'Really?'

'Really.' I'm already imagining my own contribution to it.

His eyes light up. 'You should come over one day next week and jam with me.'

'Yeah . . .' I do miss chilling with him here, and it's been obvious he's missed it too. I just wish I knew why I've suddenly started to feel so differently about him.

No one told me I'd suddenly have a bunch of intense emotions to deal with when I turned eighteen. Emotions I don't have names for.

Don't go there.

I think back to how good I felt at the Underworld earlier instead, to take my mind off the confused emotions, then I start visualising the chords I'd play while strumming my air bass. 'We should play this at our next gig.'

That makes him laugh. 'Yeah?'

I screw my face up and strum my imaginary strings with more enthusiasm. 'Definitely.' But when he just stares back at me, with that cute-ass grin, I start wishing my bass really was between us.

His lips look so soft.

His gaze drops to my mouth and my insides clench with the way he licks his lips, and then the thirst I've been pushing down for months suddenly makes a reappearance with a vengeance.

Just one taste . . .

'Gab,' he says quietly, but that's all that is said, because then we're kissing, and even when my surprise passes, I still honestly have no idea who started it.

He pulls me closer, clutching the waist of my hoodie in his hands while slipping his tongue between my parted lips. I gasp and hold him back just as fervently, because the taste of him makes me ravenous.

So much so, I experience a sharp pang in my stomach.

More.

Our teeth clash when he starts walking me backwards, but amongst me almost tripping, I taste something coppery on my tongue.

Oh god . . .

I gasp as a warm shudder ripples up my spine, and it's as if every cell in my body ignites before it explodes to awaken something within me that only compares to lust. The thirst that's been tormenting me escalates with it and, before I know what's happening, my gums are tingling and I'm sinking my teeth deeply into his juicy bottom lip.

A part of me is shocked, but I can't stop, especially after my mouth is flooded with his blood. What I experience with it is better than any high I've ever had. The metallic, slightly bitter taste, the sickly-sweet smell, and the way my body reacts, leaves me with no doubt that I've been irrevocably changed.

I choke on a moan as I desperately suck to get more. It's the most incredible thing I've ever tasted and beyond the feeling of pure ecstasy, there's also a wave of relief. The craving that has tortured me for months *finally* feels like it's being quenched.

But no faster am I satiated than I'm served a harsh dose of sobering reality when my right mind returns, and I realise what I've done. All the sound I'd been blocking out floods back in and Kyle is . . . screaming.

I release my grip on him and he's holding his mouth and yelling. His eyes are wild, and he's backing away . . . like he's scared of me.

'Kyle—' The tip of my tongue catches two sharp points when I speak, and then my eyes are drawn to the red liquid dripping from his hand as he attempts to stop the bleeding.

'What the hell is wrong with you?' he screams, and with that, I'm fully snapped back into my body.

Oh god, what have I done?

I wipe my mouth with the back of my hand and it comes away covered in blood. 'I-I'm sorry. I don't . . . I didn't—'

I sob as I bolt from the room, barely remaining upright when I rush through the crowded hall. I crash into a girl coming up the stairs, but I don't even stop to apologise before leaping down them two at a time.

The front of the house is a little quieter now, but I can still hear Kyle's screams, so I sprint past everyone into the street.

My lungs burn with each desperate stride, bringing a wave of light-headedness, but even when I trip over an uneven dip in the path, I daren't stop.

My mind is playing out all kinds of scenarios about the mess I've just gotten myself into, and all the questions I'll be asked . . .

Why the hell did I do that?

My heartbeat is deafening as I think about everyone at the party rushing to Kyle, learning what I've done. When my palms begin to get clammy and my hands tremble, the panic becomes unbearable.

Breathe . . .

But I can't.

I gasp for my next breath, but no relief comes; and with the next attempt, a sudden heat spreads across my arms and legs. I'm forced to stop then, because my skin warms, and then my staggered whimper is silenced by amber clouding my eyes.

What the—?

A shrill scream is ripped from my throat as I'm thrust into the air, so high above the street that my heart attempts its own escape. I reach my hands out to grab something – a tree, a lamp post – but I'm swiftly silenced when I see flames dancing across my arms.

I turn and catch my reflection in the windows of the houses as I hurtle past, and even though I frantically slap the flames to put them out, they don't so much as flicker.

How can this be?

None of my clothes are burning, and although my skin is hot, the fire doesn't hurt . . .

What the hell is happening to me?

I continue to fight myself past the rest of the houses on the street, lighting up the night sky more than the moon the harder I try to pat down the flames.

I'm going to die . . .

SUCKERS

Mum and Dad will be heartbroken, and so ashamed. They'll forever be known as the parents of the freak who bit her bandmate to drink his blood and then went and set herself on fire.

I'm so sorry.

The flames on my arms splutter and spark as my chest aches, until I'm jolted to the right and start hurtling above entire housing estates. Across parks, fields, and busy, illuminated roads, until I realise I'm headed in the direction of home.

It barely takes a few moments before I see my bedroom window through my amber vision, but I can't slow down, let alone stop, so I squeeze my eyes shut.

I'm gonna crash—

Glass shattering all around me makes me wince with how I'm going to explain this to Mum and Dad, but when I land on the carpet and open my eyes, I'm more relieved that I'm no longer a flying human inferno.

I scramble up from the floor to check myself in the mirror, thankful that whatever just happened to me is over. *Thank god, I still have my locs, and no burns, no pain anywhere . . .* Just the scent of smoke in the back of my throat, and the faintest tingling over my skin.

But I'm alive . . .

However, the relief is short-lived, because I hear my parents rush out of their room.

'Gabby?' Mum blinds me with the light when she switches it on, and then I feel sick to the point of vomiting when her and Dad look down at the carpet at a burn mark there.

It appears that although I wasn't harmed by the flames that covered me, nothing else is immune.

I follow Dad's gaze to the busted window.

How the hell am I going to explain this?

Chapter Two

I've read plenty of books on strange and questionable subjects, and had a curious mind about esoteric topics since I was a young girl, but even I didn't think that it was really possible to wake up in an alternate reality.

Nothing seems real anymore.

Mum and Dad have just sat me down at the kitchen table now that I've finally managed to drag myself out of bed. It's late afternoon and I'm exhausted, which they seem to sympathise with when I yawn.

They're almost, *almost*, acting as if last night didn't happen.

But it did.

My boarded-up window greeted me with glimpses of light the moment I opened my eyes, and when I tried to will it away by rolling over, I was met with the ugly scorched ring etched into the carpet. The melted, crispy fibres scratched beneath my nails when I sat on the floor beside it, bringing back every tiny detail—

SUCKERS

'There was no trace of your bag,' Dad says. 'I'm sorry, love.'

'Don't worry.' I didn't expect him to find it when he said he'd go and look for it last night, and truthfully, I'm relieved he didn't. Ordering a new bank card is easy. Ignoring phone calls and texts – not so much. I hate to think what kind of abuse I would've woken up to. 'Thanks, though.'

He nods before looking to Mum, beside him. 'Do you want me to—'

'No.' Mum closes her eyes briefly when she shakes her head. 'Gabrielle, sweetheart . . . we need to talk about last night.'

'What about it?' I ask, hoping that by some miracle she tells me a different version of events. *I mean, I have always had vivid dreams . . . Maybe I drank more than I thought . . .*

Dad reaches across the table to hold my hand. 'You know what, love.'

The confirmation of my life being over hits hard, but so does something else when I look between the two of them.

Something about how calm they're being doesn't sit right. They didn't even ask questions about what happened when they found me last night. All they did was make sure I wasn't physically hurt, while giving each other knowing glances that they thought I couldn't see while Dad boarded up the window.

'Do you know what happened to me last night?' I ask.

There's that look between them again.

'Yes,' Mum answers.

'*What?*'

'Why hadn't you told us that you'd been struggling?' Mum asks, appearing upset. 'It started on your birthday, right?'

I scoff. 'Um, well, maybe because I didn't wanna be labelled a freak and be locked up in a mental institute!' Then it hits me. This means they've known how tormented I've been. That I'd be catching fire and thrown through the air, and they didn't warn me. 'I can't believe you knew . . .'

My chest aches with that realisation.

'We didn't,' Dad insists. 'Well, not really. We didn't notice any of the signs.'

'Can you stop being so calm about this?' I ask, irritated by how normal they're acting. 'You *do* know what happened to me isn't normal, right? My entire body was covered in . . .' I grimace. 'I can't even say it.'

Dad tries reaching across the table to hold my hand, but I tuck it into my lap. 'We understand how you must feel, love, but there's nothing wrong with you.'

I laugh bitterly. 'Are you kidding? I caught *fire.*' *Have they lost their minds?* 'I was flying through the sky!'

'We're sorry,' Mum says, remorseful now. 'We know you must have been so scared.'

'Scared?' I scoot my chair back from the table in disgust. 'I thought I was gonna *die*. Why am I like this?' I gape at them both. 'Does it happen to you, too?'

Dad shakes his head. 'No, but we knew there was a chance that you might . . . have the gift.'

'Gift?' I frown. 'Hold on . . . who else is like this?'

Mum sinks back in her chair. 'My mother.'

That knocks the wind right out of me. 'Grandma's like this?' *No way.*

She nods. 'I'm sorry we didn't tell you, sweetheart, but after I turned eighteen and didn't feel any different, we honestly thought she was the last one in our family . . .'

'Last one of what?'

Her eyes soften. 'A soucouyant.'

'That doesn't even sound like a real word,' I mutter, deep in my thoughts. 'And I've never seen her do what I did.'

It would explain why Grandma rarely visits us, though.

'She has learnt to control that side of her,' Mum says, cautiously, 'and you will, too.'

'How? What is a soucouyant exactly?'

Mum's and Dad's faces pale. 'It's a shape-shifting creature from our Caribbean culture,' Mum explains while regarding me closely. 'The ones in our family have been a little different to what is traditionally written, but the presence of fire and bloodsucking behaviour is—'

'So I'm a vampire?' I shriek. 'Please tell me you're not serious?'

Mum shakes her head. 'No. Some have labelled soucouyants as a *type* of vampire to simplify what it is, but as you will learn, it's not as simple as that.'

I'm so confused. 'None of this makes sense.'

'The gene shows itself around your eighteenth birthday,' Mum continues, her tone softer. 'I'm so sorry – you must have been feeling so alone. And you didn't go to any festivals this year . . . it all makes sense now.'

She keeps talking, but all I can focus on is the dread inside me that's suddenly multiplied. *That's what I've been craving . . . The thirst I could never put my finger on, or quench . . .*

Until last night.

A sob slips out as I accept my fate. 'I'm a freak.'

My parents gasp. 'No, you're not.'

'Yes, I am.' I'm suddenly furious with them. 'All this time I've been suffering! You should have told me this might happen.' I wipe my eyes when angry tears burn my cheeks. 'My life is ruined!'

'It's not,' Dad says, adamantly. 'You can learn to control the thirst and the shift.'

'I can't.' I try to catch my breath but it's hard to when my chest feels like it's caving in on itself. 'I don't want to be like this. I . . .' I close my eyes, guilt crushing me when I face the fact that what happened last night is even worse than I thought.

I could have killed Kyle.

'I bit someone last night,' I confess, but I keep my face covered because I'm ashamed.

'What?' they ask in unison. 'Who?'

'Kyle.' I'm met with their horror when I lift my head. 'It was an accident, I swear. One minute we were kissing, the next . . . I bit him. And everyone must know what I did by now. My life is over.'

I bury my head in my hands and begin to mourn life as I know it. Including my spot in the band, knowing I'll never be able to play with them again. I've literally lost everything. My friends, my passion, my life.

What the hell am I gonna do now?

Mum and Dad get up to come and rub my back and comfort me, but when they tell me everything is going to be okay, I lose it.

They both startle when I jump up, and that hurts my heart because I can see the fear in their eyes before they mask it.

I can't even blame them for being scared of me.

I'm scared of me, too.

'How is *this* going to be okay?' I ask, trying to catch my breath. 'I saw it in your eyes, even *you're* scared of me, and you should be. What happens when the craving comes back and I can't ignore it? What happens when I burst into flames in here?' The image I get of that last sentence kills me inside. 'I could burn the house down.'

SUCKERS

I could kill *them*.

I could've killed them last night.

'You won't,' Mum insists. 'Please, calm down—'

'Stop telling me to calm down!' I scream, but instead of telling me off for yelling at them, they try to comfort me again, so I pull away. 'I can't do this.'

'Gabby,' Dad calls after me as I head back to my room.

The sun has set by the time I wake up yet, surprisingly, I can still see quite well in here. I can read the titles of the books on my bookcase, and all the labels on my lotions and make-up.

These visual enhancements would be cool if my life was a film and I was some kind of superhero, but this is real life and, unfortunately, I'm a bloodsucking monster with pyromania tendencies towards myself. I messed up big-time and googled 'soucouyant' on my laptop after I came up here, and even though I know you can't trust everything you read on the internet, I really wish I hadn't gone looking for answers. I fell into a rabbit hole, almost had another panic attack, and then after I'd obsessed over everything I learnt, cried myself to sleep.

Soucouyants have many different names across the Caribbean and are supposed to be old women who shed their skin and turn into balls of fire. Although some of the descriptions I read are different to what I experienced – like mum said – the fire part and how I feel about blood are the same.

I don't want a lifelong addiction that could be triggered by the littlest thing. I don't want to live in fear of catching fire either, or outing myself at any given moment. Perhaps my parents were right when they said I can learn to control it, but I already miss my old life, and what if I end up being a complete recluse like Grandma Noemie?

Soucouyants are supposed to belong in folklore, not real life. And if I exist . . . what other monsters are out there?

I sit up in bed when I hear Mum and Dad downstairs in the kitchen and instinctively reach for my phone to check the time, forgetting that I don't own one right now.

Instead, all I can do is think about the past twenty-four hours.

I've never spoken to my parents the way I did earlier. The three of us have always been close, and they've always been supportive, yet I took my anger out on them when this isn't their fault.

They weren't to know, not really. Mum said they thought this 'gene' ended with Grandma, which is why they didn't tell me. And I guess there wouldn't be any point telling me something that might never affect me.

I know I hid those 'symptoms' well, too.

'Gabby?' Mum says softly, after there's a knock on my door. 'Are you awake, sweetheart?'

I almost tell her 'no' until I smell food, and then I feel bad all over again. 'Yeah, I'm awake.' I sigh. 'You can come in.'

Mum appears first, followed by Dad, who's holding a plate, but they linger by the door.

'You haven't eaten,' Mum says, sending a glance to the plate in Dad's hands. 'Are you hungry?'

'A little,' I reply, but it's all the words I can get out before I'm consumed with guilt.

Dad smiles weakly. 'We made fish. It's good.'

'I'm sorry.' I burst into tears but before I can get up to hug them, they surround me on the bed and hold me. 'I didn't mean to talk to you like that.'

'You don't have to apologise,' Mum says, wrapping her arms around me. 'We understand why you were upset. You were right, and so was my mother. We should have told you regardless.' She strokes my locs before resting them behind my shoulder. 'We put you in danger, and for that, we're deeply sorry, sweetheart.'

I wipe my eyes, but the tears keep coming. 'I just don't know what I'm going to do . . . Nothing feels real one minute, and then it's all too real the next . . . My life is definitely over, though, isn't it? What if what I've done spreads around and I'm taken away?'

'We'd never let that happen,' Dad says firmly. 'And your life isn't over, you just have to learn how to control your gift.'

'But how? Are you going to teach me?'

'No,' Mum says, 'but my mother can, and we think you should go and stay—'

I pull my hand away from her grasp. 'You want to send me away?'

'Of course not,' Dad says, unmistakeably hurt. 'We don't want you to go anywhere, but we can't teach you what you need to know. Noemie can.'

Mum agrees. 'You can learn everything you need to know from her, and then you can come back home. She'd love to have you stay with her.'

'Have you told her?'

Mum nods. 'I called her, yes, so she knows.'

'Oh god . . .'

'Please don't worry, sweetheart. She knows what you're going through, what it's like. You need support that we can't give you. Think about it.'

They're right.

And with Gran, no one will know me.

They won't know what I did.

Chapter Three

It's obvious that I've landed in the deadest place on earth when I get off the train at Whitby railway station. Here, there is no underground, no need for an Oyster card, and the station itself only has one single platform that looks like it was built in the eighteen hundreds.

It's also eerily quiet. Only a handful of other passengers got off with me, which is the complete opposite of what I'm used to. The hustle and bustle and barging your way on and off the train isn't going to be needed at all up here. No bruised shoulders either, or being cussed at for pushing ahead.

It smells a lot fresher here, though, and that *is* a welcome change. I'm greeted by the salty warm air and I'm excited to see if I can spot the sea as I look for my cab.

As I walk through an arched alley to a car park, I'm halted in my tracks.

BLOODSUCKERS BEWARE! ENTER AT YOUR OWN RISK. SUCKERS STAY OUT.

The walls are covered with fresh graffiti and weathered posters warning visitors about the existence of vampires living amongst humans in town.

What? People know about vampires in Whitby?

Why the hell would my parents send me here?

My stomach twists. It seems there's a group that actively seeks them out, too.

NEXT MEETING TO BE HELD AT THE TOWN HALL

I'm hurried through the alley by other visitors behind me, who don't give the walls a second glance as we exit. Me, though, I can't get the images out of my head while I wait on the cobbles for a cab.

I thought this would be the most uneventful place on the planet.

Am I the only one who didn't know vampires existed?

It only takes five minutes for the cab to show up, and I'm relieved that I'm almost at Grandma's. The train journey took hours, and there were so many people; at least now I only have to deal with one more person.

Thank G—— I immediately regret closing the door after I get in the back of the car. *I can smell blood.* Of all the drivers I could be given, I get one who's cut himself shaving.

He smiles as he eyes me in his rearview mirror. 'Alright, lass. Where we going?'

'Um . . .' I drag my eyes away from the cut on his jaw to read out the address Grandma sent me. 'Apparently it's not that far—?'

He chuckles. 'This is Whitby. Nowhere is far. Where you from? That accent isn't from around 'ere, is it?'

'No.' I lick my suddenly dry lips before swallowing hard and looking out of my window. 'I'm visiting from London.'

'Ah, I see. Got family up 'ere, 'ave yer?'

'Yeah . . . Mind if I open this window a little? I get travel sick.'

'Help yourself.'

I immediately wind it down and inhale as deeply as I can. It offers some reprieve from the scent of this guy's blood, but it's not much, so I have to pull on what Mum told me before I left.

'*Take steady, even breaths, and try not to let your heart beat too fast . . .*'

But that's easier said than done when that coppery scent triggers flashbacks of tasting Kyle's blood. How the tang made me shudder, how it quenched the thirst – and how it was the most delicious thing I'd ever tasted.

I counter the desire and current temptation to experience that again by remembering that it's the reason I'm here. I hadn't wanted to come when Mum and Dad first suggested it, and I still don't know if I'm doing the right thing. Part of me feels like a coward for running away and avoiding the consequences of what I've done, but a bigger part of me doesn't know how else to handle the situation, so I figure this is for the best.

My plan was to take a break from gigs and enjoy the summer before starting university in September, and that's what I focus on. *Get through this nightmare, learn to control this . . . thing, and head off to uni.*

I sigh hopelessly as I close my messages on my new phone – Dad got me it so they could call me while I'm away. I've been so tempted to download my numbers or scroll my friends' socials so I can find out what's being said about me. Every time I almost do, though, I'm terrified of what I might find and chicken out.

SUCKERS

This is a fresh start.

Or perhaps not.

I see more graffiti before we head out of town. 'What's all this stuff about vampires graffitied on everything?' I ask the cab driver.

He chuckles. 'Not 'eard of Dracula before?'

'Yeah, but he wasn't real.'

'Well, quite a few people around 'ere think otherwise. Oliver, our mayor, especially.'

My eyes almost escape my head. 'The mayor?'

He nods. 'Been trying to convince people for years.' He glances back at me. 'Warn people about them. There have been incidences,' he mutters. 'Apparently.'

Is that why Grandma chose to settle down here, after all her years of travelling? To be around people who are different like us?

'Don't pay it any attention,' the cab driver says, sensing my unease. 'I don't believe it . . .'

'Yeah . . .' *Neither had I.*

I occupy my mind by looking back out of the window, appreciating the mixture of green trees and hills in the distance, instead of nothing but red London brick. There are a handful of shops dotted amongst red and white houses, and some older-looking buildings that appear medieval.

I still can't believe I'm going to be staying in a three-hundred-year-old manor for the next six weeks. The way Mum described it, though, it sounds more like a castle. My grandma, Noemie, used to be a glorified house-sitter for mega rich people all over the UK, but five years ago she decided to make Whitby her permanent home. I was surprised when I found out she'd chosen this place, and I know my parents were, too, but I suppose that makes sense now, if other bloodsuckers have made this place their home too.

I recall the graffiti and posters and wonder how Gran feels about them, and whether the mayor's apparent rantings about vampires are more serious than what the cab drivers made them out to be.

'There we are.'

I blink when I realise the cab driver's pulled up on a wide drive. 'Already?'

'I told you, no where's that far around 'ere. That'll be five-fifty, please.'

I hand him six pounds and tell him to keep the change before insisting on getting my suitcase out of the boot on my own.

I'm relieved when he drives away. And then, when I turn around, my jaw hits the ground because of how epic this place is.

Wow.

Grandma lives here?

I experience an array of emotions as I wrestle my suitcase wheels through the gravel towards the towering, dark, stone manor house. I count three floors, but it seems there is another level peeking out from the back. It even has two towers either side with coned roofs, although the charm is slightly ruined by the scaffolding around it.

As I get closer, it appears there's a lot of work being done on the building. The faint sound of hammering and sawing echoes around the place, and several of the dark stones are missing on the lower floors. There are countless cracks in the structure as well as parts of the main roof, and trees and shrubs close by have managed to weave themselves inside.

There even seems to be a raven's nest in the right-hand tower.

It's giving spooky vibes, and when I get inside, it feels it, too. Two chandeliers high above me have broken chains and cobwebs hanging off them, the wooden ceilings themselves are in a drastic state of disrepair, and dust sheets cover various pieces of furniture.

SUCKERS

The smell in here tickles my nose, and it takes a few seconds to get used to that. It's musky and damp, and I shiver as a result, although it's summertime. Being in here speaks to my soul, though, and although it's far from visually appearing homely, it feels it.

'Hello?' I call out, smiling when the chipped, unpainted walls echo it back to me almost immediately. 'Grandma?'

There's no reply, so I leave my suitcase by what looks like a covered dresser and venture further inside, following noises I can hear coming from the back.

I pop my head into several rooms on the way. A study, I think, and a few larders. This place is huge; it's like I need a map.

This place would be the perfect venue for a gig. The thought reminds me of the band and Kyle, and my heart sinks as I remember why I'm here.

'Can I help you?'

I spin around, clutching my chest. 'Yes, actually—' I blink a few times, because I was expecting to see an old guy from the tone of his voice, but he looks to be around my age. 'I'm looking for my grandmother. Noemie?'

'Ah . . .' His smile reaches his slightly monolid, dark brown eyes. 'Gabrielle, right?'

'Yeah.' My cheeks warm. 'Well, I go by Gabby.'

'Nice to meet you, Gabby.' He dusts his hand off behind his back to shake mine, and the smile he gives me this time makes my heart beat faster.

Control your heart beat.

'Nice to meet you, too.' I chew my lip while assessing his sawdust-covered overalls. It's even in his hair, which he's just ruffled with his fingers. It's a warm chestnut colour that reminds me of my first guitar. *Not too long, not too short . . .* I imagine how it would look if he rocked out to some heavy metal, but that visual is ripped away when he smirks.

'Noemie's out the back, in the gardens. I can show you the way—?'

I nod up at him. *This guy is* fine. 'Thanks.'

'Don't mention it.' He leads me back the way I came. 'My name's Ethan, by the way,' he says, making me feel rude that I didn't ask. 'I'm helping with the renovations on this place.'

'Oh, cool.' I assess the cracks in the walls in this hallway. 'How long's it going to take?'

He glances down at me. 'As you can probably tell, a while. Renovating these places are slow-going because of all the red tape. Listed buildings, y'know?'

'Yeah, I can imagine. It's still incredible, though.'

'It is. How was the trip up from London?'

'Long,' I answer honestly, wondering where his parents are from. If I had to guess, I'd say he's of mixed black heritage. However, I'm not sure which part of Asia the other part is from . . .

He chuckles. 'I haven't been that far south, but I can't imagine five hours on a train is fun.'

I thank him when he holds a door open for me. 'It's not. I don't recommend it.'

'Noted.' He holds another door to outside, and then he points out a middle-aged guy wearing similar overalls. He's currently halfway up a ladder. 'That's my boss, Josh. He's a good guy. A hard worker.'

'Are you here every day?' I ask, as we step onto the lawn.

'Eight till five. Except Sundays. So if you're used to sleeping in, I apologise in advance.'

I chuckle. 'It's fine. I'm usually up early.'

He nods before stopping and pointing to a greenhouse peeking out of an overgrown area at the end of the garden. 'She'll be over there. See you around, Gabby.'

'Yeah, thanks.' I watch him disappear inside.

At least there's someone my age around here.

'Hello?' I shout when I reach the mini forest at the end of the garden. 'Grandma?'

'Over here!' I hear her yell back.

I have to duck under a few branches before the greenhouse comes into view. On a bench beside it, I spot Grandma dressed in a floral dress, hair tied up in a scarf, just closing a book on her lap.

I last saw her at Christmas, so six months ago, but we've never spent any long periods of time together, so I won't say I'm not a little nervous about what she'll truly be like while living with her. Knowing she's like me does make me feel a little easier, though.

'Hello, Grandma.'

'Gabrielle . . .' She gets up to walk towards me, arms spread wide. 'Sweet Gabby. Oh, it's so good to see you.' Her Spanish accent is thick, but it always is when she's emotional. 'Are you well?'

'Yes.' I hug her tightly, and she holds both my hands as she steps back. 'Thank you for having me here. I met the builders. You must be busy.'

'*They* are. I'm the lady of leisure.'

That makes me laugh. 'This place is incredible.'

'It is.' Her next look is knowing. 'And peaceful.'

I look around us. *Like a sanctuary*. 'I see that.'

She releases my hands. 'How was your trip? Are you hungry?'

'A little. I ate a few of the sweet breads mum sent me up here with on the train, but I could definitely eat some proper food.'

'And you must, to keep your strength up.' She links her arm with mine as we walk back towards the manor.

Chapter Four

After Grandma shows me the kitchen that's already been renovated and that I'm to use in the manor, she warms me a plate of leftover chicken, rice and beans. Mum doesn't make Guatemalan food that often because my dad is from France and cooks a lot of dishes from his homeland, so eating like this will be a change I'm definitely here for.

Grandma's cooking is so, so good.

She eats too, while she tells me more about how she ended up here. 'After leaving my previous house-sit in Berkshire, this manor house came up.'

'So you took care of this place before you bought it?'

'I did, for almost a year. When I found out they were selling, that was that.' She looks around the room, smiling. 'I'd long fallen in love with the place, and truthfully, I'd grown tired of always moving.'

SUCKERS

'It makes sense now, why you travelled so much,' I whisper. 'Didn't you ever get lonely?'

She chuckles. 'No. I didn't only look after houses when I travelled: I researched, became a sort of historian, if you like. I met many people along the way, some I'm still in contact with now. People like us.'

I quickly swallow my mouthful. 'I knew it. When I arrived, at the station, I saw loads of posters and graffiti about vampires. I had no idea people actually believed in them. Is what they say true? Have vampire attacks happened here?'

I hadn't realised quite how much the posters had filled me with unease. The whole point of this trip is to be somewhere where I can learn to control this thing, but how can I do that if there are people out there actively hunting down people like me?

What *were* my parents thinking?

'Whitby's always attracted others like us because of the history of Dracula. People like their legends.'

She hasn't answered my question, but I decide not to push her.

'I did a bit of googling last night.'

Her eyes widen. 'Oh, no, you didn't.'

'Mum said the same when I told her. She said a lot of what I read should be taken lightly.'

'Hmm,' she muses. 'Not everything on there is incorrect, but our history is a little complicated. And as you can see, we're not old hags, are we?'

'Definitely not.' Grandma may be in her late fifties, but she still looks good and could easily pass for my mum. Black women almost always age well, though. That's a fact.

'We will have plenty of time to talk but, right now, we're about to have company.'

At first, I have no idea what she's talking about but it's only a few seconds later that Ethan and Josh make an appearance in the kitchen.

'We smelled heaven,' Josh says, chuckling to himself. 'Did we arrive at the right time?'

Grandma nods. 'You did. The pot's on the stove, help yourself.'

She gets up to make them a cold drink made from cinnamon and cranberry while I'm introduced to Josh, who swiftly begins asking me about myself.

'Eighteen, eh?' he comments, with a mouthful. 'Same age as my apprentice, Ethan, here.'

Ethan shoots him a look before smiling at me. 'I'm not really an apprentice any more. I've worked with him since I was fifteen.'

'That young?'

'Josh and my dad were best friends.'

Were?

He must notice the question on my face. 'My dad passed last year,' he explains, and continues before I can say anything else. 'It's fine. But, yeah, that's how I ended up working with Josh. He took me to work with him at the weekends, showed me how to fix little things at first. He's kind of like a second dad to me now.' He smirks. 'Bangs on at me like one, too.'

I smile when Josh mutters under his breath.

'Your mum's Noemi's daughter, right?' Ethan asks, after gulping down some of his drink.

I nod.

Grandma sits back down with us. 'Ethan can speak some French, too.'

'Is French the only other language you speak?'

He shakes his head at his plate before looking up at me. 'Nah, I speak a few. Chinese and Shona. Heard of that one before?'

'Never, actually.'

He chuckles. 'My dad was Chinese and my mum's Zimbabwean.' Then he speaks a language I've never heard before. 'I said, "Thanks for the delicious food, Noemie," in Shona.'

That amuses her. 'He's a sweet boy,' she says to me. 'Kind and considerate. That's what we like.'

Josh pretends to be offended. 'Oh, so you're saying I'm not?'

Grandma waves his comment off. 'I didn't say anything of the sort. You've come to that conclusion all by yourself.'

I catch Ethan's gaze and we both laugh. It makes my heart flutter a little, which makes me uneasy. *I can't be getting mixed up with any guys.* Especially as it's the reason I'm here in the first place.

Ethan offered to bring my suitcase up to my room on the third floor when I told Grandma I'd left it in the lobby.

After he leaves, she shows me the room. It's got to be at least four times bigger than my bedroom back home, but regardless of its size, it does feel cosy in here. It has its own fireplace, albeit covered in a few cobwebs, and it has heaps of character. Creaky wooden floorboards that have recently been sanded and revarnished, bare walls with only a few small visible cracks, and this part of the roof is rainproof, so at least I won't have any leaks to contend with.

I think the window is my favourite part, though, because it's bay style with a cushioned seat, and the view is of the back garden where I'd found Grandma earlier.

'I'll let you get settled in up here,' she says, after showing me the empty wardrobe and dresser to put my clothes in. 'The boys will be around for a few more hours yet so there isn't any rush. Come down when you're ready, or rest. Just . . . make yourself at home.'

'I will. Thanks, Grandma.'

She rests a kiss on my forehead before she leaves, pulling the door closed behind her, and then I collapse on to the bed and stare at the ceiling.

So far so good.

Being here is gonna take some getting used to, though. The town looked seriously small, and I didn't see one drive thru, so God knows if they even have any here. What happens when I need my locs refreshed? I hate doing it myself, and I don't know if Grandma can do it.

I barely saw anyone on the way here either and no one my age, other than Ethan. Not that it matters. I'm only here for one reason – to learn to control my 'gift' – and I don't need any distractions.

How long will it take, anyway? Will I pick it up quickly or will it take me weeks to master even the basics? I can't risk looking like a weirdo in front of new people. I mean, I've heard Yorkshire people are friendly, but I doubt they would be if I accidently bit someone, or worse.

I need to stay under the radar, at least for now.

I get up from the bed to open my suitcase, but as I unpack my clothes, I'm reminded again that I chose to leave my bass at home. After what happened, it didn't seem right to use her to take my mind off what I did.

That window seat would have been the perfect place to play her as well.

I imagine sitting in the nook, rain hitting the window and the weight of my bass in my hands, and I sigh.

CHAPTER FIVE

After dinner, when the guys have left and Grandma and I are finally alone, I sit with her in one of the living rooms on the second floor. None of the furniture is covered or dusty, there are plush burgundy velvet curtains over the windows, and the fire's lit, so it's warm in here.

Over mugs of creamy hot chocolate, she's been telling me stories about the famous one hundred and ninety-nine steps to the abbey, more about the legend of Dracula being from Whitby, and how the book by Bram Stoker shaped the gothic buildings and atmosphere of the seaside town.

Still, she doesn't mention anything about the attacks here.

'So you can see, people's minds are capable of creating the most fantastical stories, which is why it is best to learn the facts.'

I nod, knowing that was direct disapproval of my Googling what we are. 'So, can you tell me then? What is a soucouyant?'

She tucks her legs up underneath her at the opposite end of the couch. 'The parts about us being shapeshifters and craving blood are true, but we do not dabble in black magic or attack people in their sleep. We're not savages.'

'I read that each Caribbean country has their own idea of what a soucouyant is, though. Do you think they do those things and that's why they've been written?'

'Perhaps,' she muses. 'I've always believed that some type of magic was involved at some point, to aid in our evolution, so to speak.'

'So we didn't look like old hags or get caught by grains of rice outside people's front doors?'

She chuckles. 'Exactly that. Could you imagine having an obsession with picking up rice grains on top of everything else we have going on? And with the amount of rice *we* cook? We wouldn't stand a chance of staying hidden.'

She's not wrong. 'Do you not worry about being here, though? With all the rumours, do you not worry that someone will find you out?'

'Sometimes it's good to hide in plain sight.' She suddenly looks concerned. 'As you've mentioned, there are threats you should be aware of.'

My stomach turns when she finally addresses my question from earlier. 'Those vampire hunters.'

'Yes. The group was harmless when I first arrived here, but there have been several attacks recently which has fuelled unrest in the community.'

My anxiety skyrockets. 'How many are there?'

'Their numbers are growing, so I can't be sure.' She sighs. 'Our local mayor seems to have a personal vendetta against our kind,' she mutters. 'He was mostly ignored when the rumoured attacks began, but now he leads others in seeking us out.'

'Oh god . . . So we're *hunted*?'

She's hesitant to answer. 'Only the ones hurting others. There is also a group in town led by a woman that actively protects those like us, and she and others are working to find the real monsters responsible.' She reaches across to hold my hand. 'Do not concern yourself over this, Gabby. Your time will be much better spent on working on your discipline. As long as you master that, you have nothing to fear.'

I nod, but inside, the thought of there being vampire hunters in town is terrifying, whether only some people believe their theories or not.

I need to get this under control.

'What do I need to work on first?'

'Firstly, I'd like you to tell me what happened on Saturday night.'

My stomach sinks. 'I thought Mum told you what happened—?'

'Only partly.' She briefly rests a reassuring hand on my arm. 'I won't judge you, if that is what you think.'

'I don't . . .' I sigh. 'I'd started feeling weird after my birthday . . .'

I tell her everything that's happened: the extreme hunger, my spiralling emotions, the intense sense of smell, the cravings. 'I stopped going out, especially around large groups of people.'

'That must have been hard for you. Does that mean that you didn't go to your favourite festival? And what about your band performances?'

'I skipped the festivals, but I kept going to the gigs. It was difficult . . . my bandmates could tell something was wrong. I'd stopped hanging out with them and would go home straight after a gig. The feelings were just so *overwhelming*.'

I tell her about the party and what happened afterwards, but she stays true to her word and doesn't judge me. If anything, she seems upset for me.

'I remember my first time like it was yesterday,' she says, sympathetically. 'I knew about the women in my family, which also meant I knew the signs. However, as much as I knew, I didn't want to believe it. I convinced myself that it was my mind playing tricks on me.'

'Were you scared?'

She hands me a handkerchief, and I realise I'm crying.

'I was terrified. Your mother and I disagreed many times about her decision not to tell you. Although she didn't carry the gene, I knew there was still a chance you might. She said you were angry with her.'

'I was, but I understand her reasons. If I wasn't one, there was no reason for me to know . . . It's just, I wish I could've been prepared. What happened on Saturday . . . I'm terrified,' I confess. 'And everything seems so hopeless now. I just wish I could turn it all off.'

She shuffles closer so she can wrap an arm around me. 'I want you to listen to me carefully. The fact you managed to drag yourself away from that boy when it was your first taste of blood is no small feat. Not many are strong enough to stop once they start, at least not until there's nothing left.'

'Really?'

She nods encouragingly. 'Really. The taste of blood is something quite delectable and offers a quench of thirst like nothing else in the world.'

'The feeling – the thirst – comes and goes,' I say, taking her openness as a chance to be honest. 'I don't get the cravings around everyone, or at least it doesn't feel the same around everyone. Why is that?'

'It's similar to attraction,' she explains. 'And scent plays a part also.'

'Okay . . .' *That makes sense, I guess.* I take another sip of hot chocolate and let the quiet fall, the only sound being the crackling of the fire.

Fire.

'Why did I burst into flames?'

'You felt threatened, and that triggered your ability to transform, which enabled you to escape.'

I blink back at her in surprise. 'So, it's like a defence mechanism?'

'Yes, pretty much. You said you got home after the initial fright of what happened to you. Did you think of home before that happened?'

'I don't know . . . Yes? I remember thinking I might never see my parents again.' I inhale sharply when I realise something. 'Wait, so does that mean I can control where I go when I'm like that?'

'Yes, with time,' she said, with a small smile. 'And it's the most efficient way to travel, if I do say so myself.'

I laugh, imagining Grandma bursting into flames and heading down to the local farmers' market.

'See, it is not all bad, is it?' She gets up to retrieve a small, gold box from beside the fireplace. 'The first thing you must master, Gabby, and the most important, is your craving for blood.'

She opens the box, and my entire body tenses when several vial necklaces of red liquid come into view.

I glance up at her. 'Are those—?'

'Filled with blood, yes.' She lifts one of the necklaces out of the box and turns her hand so the liquid flows back and forth within the glass. 'I'm going to let you smell each of these until there is one that piques your interest.'

My nerves rise. 'What if none of them do?'

Her eyes alight. 'One will.'

'How will I know?'

'You'll know, and so will I.' She turns slightly towards me while keeping hold of the vial. 'Are you ready to scent the first?'

I shake my head, remembering how I felt in the cab earlier today. If a small cut had me almost losing control, what would an entire vial do? What happens if one of these reminds me of Kyle? 'I don't think—'

But it's too late, she's already removed the cap, and the coppery scent immediately floods my senses.

I focus on the glass, my pulse quickening, but I manage to resist the urge to take it from her. I do lick my lips, though, and I can almost taste the blood on them. My gums have begun to throb, too.

'Not this one,' she mutters, replacing the lid. She tries another one. 'Not this one either . . .' She continues to open the vials, but none seem to provoke the reaction she's looking for.

Until . . .

I inhale, my lungs cramping from how sharply I do, and then a sudden wave of euphoria rushes through me, causing my eyes to snap shut. With a groan, I lick my lips, which is when I feel the same two sharp tips in my mouth that I felt right after I bit Kyle.

'This is the one.'

I open my eyes when Grandma's statement pulls me from my trance, but my attention goes to the necklace in her hand, which I hastily attempt to snatch from her.

Grandma holds it out of reach and quickly closes it, but although

SUCKERS

I'm confused and want to question the point of this, I can't take my eyes off the now-swirling liquid inside the glass.

'How do you feel?' she asks, holding it clenched in her fist.

My stomach cramps with need as I look up at her. 'Frustrated, annoyed . . . confused.'

'This is the first lesson.' She glances down at her hand. 'There are many safe ways to enjoy blood, Gabby, with another intimately or with donor blood if you should so desire, but before you can, you must learn to resist it, even when every part of you is telling you to give in.'

I gape at her. 'Wait, I'm *allowed* to drink blood? I thought I'd have to stay away from it forever.'

She seems alarmed by that comment. 'Not at all. Your desire for it is a part of who you are, and this lesson isn't about making it go away. It's about *control*, so that when you do indulge, no one gets hurt. Understand?'

I nod thoughtfully to myself, torn over how I feel about this newfound information. We may not technically be vampires but there is no ignoring the similarities.

Grandma notices me skimming my fangs with the tip of my tongue, so I decide that now is a good time to ask her about them.

'They'll appear when your thirst hits its peak or when you will them to come,' she explains, lifting her top lip to show me hers. 'You'll learn to control them, too, but know that they're a tool to obtain what we crave most.'

I groan in torment. 'Another thing to grasp.'

'Which you are more than capable of doing.' She holds up the necklace again, appearing more determined. 'Now, you will wear this around your neck and use it to teach yourself self-control. At first, you will merely admire the blood within the vial. Remember its allure and scent, and then, once you can hold it, look at it, and still remain of sound mind, you will begin to open it at random and learn the same.'

My entire being rejects her request. 'But surely that's torture! You saw how I just reacted to it. I can't do that. If you give me that vial—'

'You won't drink it.'

I can't help but laugh. 'You have way too much faith in me.'

'No, I have just enough. You can do this, Gabrielle. I believe in you, and you must believe in yourself. Controlling your thirst and craving is something you must master. You *must*.'

Her tone frightens me. There is undoubtedly a warning there, too, and it subdues my lingering desire.

'Are you ready for me to give this to you now?' she asks, holding it out to me.

'I'm ready.' I take it, wanting to believe I can do this, but I'm scared I'll let her down.

She closes my fingers around it. 'I trust you, but you have to also learn to trust yourself.'

My exhale is shaky. 'I'll try my hardest.'

Chapter Six

When I finish getting dressed, I look at the bedside table where the necklace Grandma gave me last night sits. I may not be able to smell its contents, but the remembered scent still taunts me, whispering promises of taking me to a place of bliss if I just have a little taste . . .

One drop . . .

I skim the tip of my tongue between my fangs that have partially begun to appear, still wondering why I hadn't noticed them when I bit Kyle. I thought about that for a long time before I fell asleep last night. Would I have run away from him sooner if I had? Or was what happened inevitable?

Regardless, having this vial is tearing me apart inside. Every moment in its presence is a constant reminder of what I am. That I'll forever have a longing for a forbidden nectar that could hurt or even kill someone if I'm not careful.

And that's with the vial across the room.

How am I going to wear it around my neck?

It makes me scared of what the future might bring. Will I ever be able to fully enjoy myself again? What happens if I'm exhausted or I drink too much alcohol on a night out and end up losing control, even after doing all the work to train my thirst? Am I destined to hurt the people I care about? Will I ever have a family of my own, or will I forever be a shadow of my former self?

I just need to get a grip on my thirst.

I try to shake off the sadness as I pick up the vial to hide it in the back of my drawer, but even as I leave my room to seek out Grandma, I realise what she told me last night is true.

'*Whether it is with you or you are far from it, the desire for it will be inescapable. That knowledge will help you do the work to tame the thirst. Merely knowing it is there and you cannot have it, will be enough . . .*'

By the time I reach the kitchen and find her at the stove, my mood is low, and frankly, unpredictable.

Grandma is talking in low, hushed tones and I realise she has a phone pressed between her ear and shoulder. 'You're right, it *is* worrying . . .'

I sit down at the table to text Mum and Dad, but I'm distracted by Grandma's conversation and wonder what's happened.

'Yes, we will keep an eye on it. I've mentioned it . . . Not fully . . . I plan to today. Yes, I will . . .'

I finish sending the text to the group chat with my parents, and wait for Grandma to end the call before I ask if everything is okay.

'It will be,' she says, turning to me. 'Good morning. How did you sleep?'

'Not great, as you probably expected.'

Her eyes soften. 'I did predict that, yes, but do you still have it?'

I nod. 'Not on me, though. I've hidden it in my dresser for now.' I couldn't bring myself to put it around my neck. Not yet, anyway.

'And you haven't . . .?'

I shake my head. 'No, it's still all there.'

Her eyes widen. 'You've managed your first task better than most. See, you can do this.'

'It doesn't feel like it.' I could easily run back up there and gulp it down. I'm starting to think this is what withdrawal feels like. 'How long is this going to last?'

'Every day, it will get a little easier.' She turns back to the stove. 'Perhaps you need a distraction. Filling your time and keeping your mind busy will help.'

'Well, I'm open to suggestions.' I'm not going to lie and say I'm not bored. All I have is time to think about that blood.

'I noticed you didn't bring your bass.'

I sigh at her back. 'I left it at home.'

She turns, seemingly confused. 'Why?'

The memory of the last night I played it borderline makes me sick. 'I didn't want the constant reminder of what I did the last time I played it.'

'But playing your music brings you joy, dear. I've *seen* how happy you look when you play. You must be missing it terribly.'

'I do. So much. And if I'm honest, I wish I did bring her. But I don't deserve her.'

Grandma sits in the chair beside me, but it's a while before she speaks. 'You can't punish yourself, Gabrielle. What is done is done, but do not bring more anguish to yourself.'

'How can I not?' I bite my lip. 'I could've killed someone.'

'But you didn't.' She holds my hand firmly.

I tear my eyes away from her. 'Have you spoken to Mum and Dad? Did they say anything about . . .'

'Your friend is fine,' Grandma says, immediately understanding. 'From what I was told, he required a couple of stitches.'

The guilt in my stomach grows heavier but there's also some relief. There had been so much blood . . . what if he had died? Because of *me*.

'I don't need my bass, it'll just be a distraction from what I'm doing here,' I say.

'Your bass is a part of who you are. I think you should consider letting your parents bring it up when they visit, all right?'

'I'll think about it,' I lie.

She smiles. 'Good. Would you like something to eat? I've made porridge.'

She dishes some out for me, but when she brings me the bowl, she also hands me two thick journals wrapped in worn mahogany leather.

I trace the embossed gold flame on the front of the top one with my finger. 'What are these?'

'Many of the women in our family kept journals, and I have chosen two that I think will help you greatly. They each had their own triggers and difficulties that they had to overcome, and they helped me no end when I was your age.'

Wow. 'Thank you. I can't wait to read them.'

'Good, because I believe they will serve you well. They speak of techniques – some that are different to the ones I will teach you. But it is my hope that between us, you can find the ones that will help you. We may be the same in name, but as you will find out for yourself, our journeys are very different.'

'Do you have a journal?'

She smiles. 'I do, and you don't have to begin one yourself, but I strongly encourage you to. Documenting your experiences is important for not only yourself, but possibly for another woman in your future family.'

'I'll think about it.'

'Perhaps we can pop to town later. There is a lovely little shop that you can choose one from. And maybe we could get something to eat?'

I smile. 'That would be nice. Thanks.'

After breakfast, I take some time to explore the manor alone, hoping to clear my head. I find myself in the library and remember Grandma said there are some books about vampires in here that she picked up during her travels.

I stand in the middle of the room and begin scanning the top shelves, using my enhanced vision to read the spines. *Mythology, giants, astrology . . . vampires.*

I bring the ladder over from the opposite shelves and climb up to reach it, surprised by how thick it is.

How many different types of vampires could there possibly be?

'Good morning,' Ethan says, startling me.

He rushes over to help me pick up the books I've dropped, but I quickly take them from him and hold them tight against my chest.

'I'm sorry, I didn't mean to scare you. You must have been in your own world.'

'I was.' *My heart is thumping.*

He schools his expression but I get the feeling he wants to laugh.

I roll my eyes before chuckling. 'How scared did I look?'

'It was more how high you jumped.' He eyes the ceiling. 'Is your head okay?'

'Ha ha.'

'Just checking.' He laughs, but then he eyes the books in my arms again. 'You settling in all right?'

'So far so good.' I glance down at his lips but look straight back up when my cheeks begin to warm. *Calm your breathing.* He smells good and it puts me on edge. 'I was just looking for something to read.'

'What did you pick?'

'Uh, astrology.' *Ugh.*

He seems impressed, though. 'Nice choice. Do you always read, or are you bored?'

'Bit of both. Are you a reader?'

'I don't get much time to be,' he says, his attention flickering between my nose and lip piercings. 'But I always had a book in my hand when I was younger. I liked thrillers and fiction, mostly. How about you?'

'I mostly choose books from the blurbs. I like books that make you ask questions, y'know?'

His eyes soften. 'Yeah.'

I smile and walk past him to the door after he gives me a look that makes me nervous. He was staring at my piercings so hard. *I wonder what he thinks . . .*

He follows me to the end of the corridor and then holds the door for me. 'You planning on spending all your time in this manor, or will you be doing some sightseeing?'

I smile. 'I definitely want to check out the sights.'

'Well, there's a group of us that hang out down by the water sometimes, if you wanna come along. The people are cool, and we always have a good time.'

'Really?' I look up at him. 'Are they our age?'

SUCKERS

'Mostly. Some are a little older. No pressure, but the offer's there.'

I'm grateful for the invite but I think of the conversation with Grandma, and the vial that's tucked into my drawer upstairs but still at the forefront of my mind. 'All right, I'll let you know,' I lie.

He nods. 'Cool. I'd better get back to work.'

I smile and we go our separate ways.

I spend the warm morning sprawled out on a blanket beside Grandma's bench, hidden away from the world, lost in my great grandmother Helene's journal.

Date: July 7th, 1946

I do not wish to write this entry, as once I do, there will forever be a record of what I have done. But for days upon days, I have been sick. Sick with overwhelming guilt and remorse because of what I have done.

However, to say I did not mean it would only be a half truth, for a large part of me surely did. The insatiable side. The side of me that holds no regard for the lives of others and unceasingly longs to give in to my most grave and darkest desires.

My faith becomes weaker by the day, and I have questioned it and the Lord every night since. Why he made me this way, why he would make anyone this way, and what His purpose for me is.

Perhaps I am not the child of God I have been led

to believe I was by my Catholic faith, regardless of my mother insisting that He makes no mistakes. What if I am indeed a child of the Devil, and it is his work that I have been born to carry out?

I weep as I write this, wishing I could turn back the hands on the clock. Wishing I had never left my house that fateful night. However, the scent I caught from my bedroom window was too overpowering for me to resist, and so I snuck out in the dead of night to follow it.

The young woman was startled when she first turned, but once she saw me under the orange glow of the streetlamp, she visibly relaxed. She believed she was safe. She was not. And now I know that no one is safe from me.

She fought hard, but I was much stronger, and once I had her pinned beneath me, a hand firmly pressed to her mouth, I drank. I took it all, leaving a mere empty shell in my wake. I would bet that not even a drop was left.

Initially, I basked in the bliss, feeling more satiated than I ever have in my life. Until, all too soon, the delusion left me, and I was made to face the consequences of my despicable actions.

I am a murderer.

I cry silently, feeling her remorse like it's my own. It could have been *me* experiencing that right now. I can't imagine how she must have felt, especially back then.

'I reacted the same way when I read that part.'

I look up at Grandma when she sits down on the bench. 'I feel so bad for her.'

'So do I.' She sighs, and it's a heavy one. 'I think her story is the most heartbreaking. But it does get better and, actually, her words gave me the most hope out of them all.'

I'm relieved to know that it isn't all bad, but the feeling of melancholy doesn't go away.

'Accidents happen, Gabrielle, but they are preventable as long as we do the work to learn self-control. That story is why you must try your very best to get your urges under control, and I hope it helps you understand why I may sometimes be hard on you.'

I glance down at the journal. 'I understand.' I think I even *want* her to be hard on me, because I don't think I could live after doing something like that.

'What's that other book there?'

I sit up to hand the book about vampires over to her, and she smiles knowingly.

'Have you read any of this yet?'

'No, only skimmed the pages. How many different ones have you met?'

'Plenty,' she says, unmoving.

'Really?'

'You did not think that we were the only kind to exist, did you? When you were doing your googling did it not point to other 'tales' of beings?'

'Yeah, but there are *so* many mentioned in the back of this book.' I think about the long list of different types of vampires I had glimpsed, before becoming overwhelmed and turning back to Helene's journal.

'I think it's time to take your first trip to town.'

Chapter Seven

Grandma takes me to a quirky little gift shop on the parade when we get to town. It sells all sorts, from sticks of rock to Dracula trinkets and toys. She insists on me picking up a notebook, just in case I do decide to journal. There aren't many that stand out, so I choose a plain beige one and grab some glitter gel pens I spotted on the way in. It's been a while since I was creative in this way, so I figure it won't only keep my restless hands busy, but it will help to kill time.

I might even forget about that vial of blood for longer than a few minutes.

The path is busy, so we wait a moment before continuing up the street. For such a small town, it gets some heavy footfall.

This place is, without a doubt, alternative. We've barely been here twenty minutes and so far I've seen a handful of tattoo parlours and fancy dress, occult and goth shops. However, as nice as it is that no one so much as bats an eye at me or my style, and that this could be a home away from home, the vandalised walls continue to unsettle me.

'There's so much graffiti,' I say quietly, staring at the words **VAMPS NOT WELCOME HERE** on the wall beside the harbour.

Grandma follows my line of sight. 'People are upset. Scared.' She keeps her voice low, too. 'As I said, not everyone is like us.'

'Yeah, I get that.'

I know not everyone is good, even when they're human, but why bring attention to yourself when it could put you in serious danger? I mean, I get craving blood and wanting to drink it, but if there are safe ways to do so, why risk getting caught?

Unless it's more about the thrill of hunting someone down.

I shudder but quickly frown when a dark green building catches my eye. The door has a picture of a cauldron on it, and from the outside, it looks quite big inside.

I laugh at the name. 'The Coven?'

Grandma quickly looks at me. 'We don't go in there.'

'Why?'

She appears uncomfortable. 'I don't want you falling in with the wrong crowd.'

'Oh . . . is that where the not-so-good ones hang out?'

She nods. 'Our world, as you will discover, Gabby, is full of surprises.'

There's something in her tone that makes my stomach knot, but when I turn my head to focus on something else, my eyes latch on to a blood-red poster.

NEXT SUCKER PROTEST THIS SUNDAY.

Grandma rests a hand on my arm. 'Let's get something to eat.'

Grandma treats me to steak pie and mashed potatoes, which is actually pretty good. I'd been expecting fish and chips considering it's what Whitby's most known for, but she reminded me that hearty meals will always serve me better, especially while I'm learning 'the ropes'.

Soon, though, we're back in her royal blue Honda Jazz on our way home. I've been quiet most of the way, taking in the views while trying not to think about earlier.

Now that I know other types of vampires exist, I wonder how many I've unknowingly passed on the streets in London. Do vampires recognise each other? By scent, maybe? Or perhaps just an inner feeling when around each other?

I turn a little in my seat to look at Grandma. 'Have vampires ever hunted each other?'

She sends a short glance my way. 'Not that I'm aware of, no. Why?'

That's good to know, but . . . 'Well . . .'

'Go on,' she encourages gently.

'I was just wondering, if vampires exist, does that mean other creatures exist. Like, werewolves?'

'Ah,' she says, nodding knowingly. 'I can't tell you yes or no for sure, but as far as I'm aware, no one in our family has encountered one.'

That's a relief, but I remember how on edge she'd been when we walked past The Coven. 'What *can* hurt us?'

She pulls up to the manor and turns to face me. 'Garlic, holy water, and the rest of those kinds of things are all nonsense. And now that you are eighteen, you will heal from all wounds much quicker.'

'That's so cool,' I breathe, looking down at my hands as if they've suddenly changed.

'That doesn't mean we're indestructible,' she continues grimly. 'There is only one way to kill a vampire and that way *can* be found on the internet.'

'A stake through the heart?'

She nods.

I exhale deeply. 'Okay.'

She rests a hand briefly on mine. 'You have no reason to be afraid, Gabby. Ask me all the questions you need, by all means, but do try not to dwell on things that don't affect you.'

'I won't.'

Or at least, I'll try not to.

I check in with Mum and Dad when I go up to my room, but once I'm off the phone, my mind almost immediately goes back to those vampire hunters and the rogue vampires causing trouble in the town.

It only makes me feel an urge to learn faster. If I can master my gift, it'll mean I'll be able to not only prevent outing myself, but I'll be able to defend myself, too.

One good thing about all this worrying, though, is that I haven't thought about that blood all day.

I lie back on my bed and close my eyes.

Without social media, my friends and my bass, life feels still in a way that it hasn't for a long time. I can't say I've really missed the constant scrolling, but it's different with my bass. If I had her, my mind would be able to switch off.

It would be quiet.

Playing her always gave me an escape.

There's a knock at my bedroom door and Grandma comes in. I know it's her, because who else would it be? But also because my sense of smell has heightened, and I can smell the sweetness of her perfume.

I've just finished getting dressed and the sun's only just rising over the manor. I'm exhausted after a night of more tossing and turning than actual sleep.

In my latest attempt at mastering my thirst for blood, I'd had the crazy and, frankly, sadistic idea to sleep with the necklace under my pillow.

Huuuge mistake.

I swear I could hear it calling out to me.

Just a drop.

'Good morning.' Grandma's as cheerful as the yellow dress she's wearing today. 'I heard the shower and gathered you were up for the day, so I thought I would catch you now before Josh and Ethan arrive. You went to bed so early last night. Are you okay?'

'A little tired, but I'm fine.' I'm more concerned with what she's going to tell me now. Maybe werewolves *do* exist and she's here to tell me the truth. Or maybe there's been another attack. Oh god.

'Don't look so worried, dear,' she says, closing the door behind her. 'I'd like to show you something, that's all.'

I immediately glance down at her hands. 'It's not more blood, is it? I don't think I can handle being around any more of that.' I shoot a glare at my pillow. 'Babysitting that one is hard enough.'

She chuckles. 'Ah, decided to get straight into it, I see. No wonder you look fed up.'

I sigh. 'Just a little, but it's not all bad. I'm finally managing to keep the fangs hidden.'

'Very good. I'm impressed.' And she looks it, until . . . 'We've talked at length about blood and controlling your desires, but we haven't talked much about the other exciting part. The part that protects us.'

That switches my entire mood. 'The fire part?'

She nods. 'I thought it was about time I showed you some of what I can do.'

I recoil slightly. 'You want to set yourself on fire?' I look around my room. 'Now?'

'I won't burn anything, don't worry.'

'Are you sure? There's a lot of wood in here.'

She stands in the centre of the room, between the bed and my dresser, and rolls her eyes playfully. 'Yes, Gabrielle, I am quite sure, thank you.'

The moment makes me smile.

'All right.' She clasps her hands together in front of her. 'Ready?'

Not entirely, but I nod anyway.

She lifts her hands, palms facing up, inhaling deeply and closing her eyes. Then, as she begins to levitate a few inches from the floorboards, her dark skin begins to illuminate.

I gasp when the glow becomes a blinding flash that ignites into fire. 'No way . . .' The flames don't burn anything on her. Her dress, her short curls that are dancing amongst the flames – all of it is encased within the fire that surrounds her entire body.

However, the tips of the flames do crackle and spit, causing small sparks to jump off her like embers. None make it to the floor still glowing, but I still find myself looking down every few seconds to check.

'Was this the form you took?' she asks, when I return my attention to her face.

I nod, hypnotised by her eyes that are burning so hot, they appear white. 'Yeah, why? A-are there other forms?'

'There are.' She shrinks to an orb the size of a basketball, and I'm stunned. The centre burns like the sun, and I can only look at it for short periods of time before I'm momentarily blinded, but the outside looks just how her skin did.

And it's *really* warm in here all of a sudden.

'We can take different forms when in our fire state,' Grandma says from within the orb. 'This is one, and if you let me come to you like this, I can show you another.'

'Okay.' I definitely want to see this. I'm still trying to adjust my vision, so I don't lose the ability to see. I can make out golden swirls inside the orb now, and although it hurts my eyes when I look at them too long, it's hard to look away.

It's mesmerising.

'Hold out your hands,' she says, and I hesitate.

'Won't it burn me?' I ask, holding my hands against my chest.

'No, I promise. Just watch. And when you cup your hands, lift them as high as you can. Fingers spread wide.'

I reluctantly do as she asks, preparing myself for impending pain.

But none comes.

Only awe.

'We can't hurt each other with our fire,' she says, resting herself on my hands above me.

It's the strangest thing. There's definitely a weight to her, and a warmth, but the flames on my palms tickle instead of hurt, almost as if they're gentle caresses.

'Now, watch this.'

I gape when the sphere that is Grandma collapses and begins to flow through my parted fingers, like she's become sand.

'That is wild . . .' I shake my head when she returns to her fireball beneath my hands.

SUCKERS

'Using that technique, we can fit through the tiniest of gaps.'

My mind imagines all sorts. Sneaking into places, slipping through locks, cracks . . . 'Like we were made to be able to escape.'

'Possibly.'

She circles my room a few times afterwards, but then she shifts back to her normal self and sits on my bed.

'That was incredible, Grandma,' I say quietly, still not quite believing what I've just seen.

She taps my hand, which is still warm. 'I'm glad you think so.'

'I thought it was only possible when we're scared or triggered. I had no idea that we could do it on command.'

'We can, but you *do* need your strength for it. Why do you think I have been feeding you so? The first shift always takes the most out of you. After that, you need to be mentally and physically strong in order for you to be able to control it.'

'Will I know when I can? Like, I'll sense when I can do it?'

'Yes. At first, you'll begin to notice a small flame deep inside your spirit.' She puts a hand briefly to my chest. 'The stronger you grow, the stronger the fire will be, until it is a constant that waits to be unleashed.'

'I don't feel anything yet,' I say, disappointed.

Her eyes alight. 'Oh, you will.'

Chapter Eight

A few days have passed since Grandma shifted in front of me, but it's still constantly on my mind, because her shifting has made this all too real. This is now my reality.

I really did turn into fire that night at the party.

I really am a soucouyant.

After the initial excitement of what Grandma did, I felt myself sink into a dark, hopeless place.

Nothing would ever truly be the same again.

I've had no choice but to let go of the world I knew. I've had to accept that not all fantastical stories are made up, and that, most likely, a lot of them are based on some truth. Which also means there are thousands of unrealised dangers in the world that I still don't know about . . .

'Morning, dear,' Grandma says, when I join her for breakfast.

I'm not sure what she's cooking but it smells good and the aroma of it lures me downstairs.

'Morning,' I mumble, unable to match her upbeat attitude. I'm not tired as the blood isn't even keeping me awake any more, and I'm managing to forget about it for longer periods. I should be pleased but no matter what I try, I can't seem to pull myself out of this pit.

'Want to talk about it?' she asks, after I accept her offer of a mug of fruit tea.

'Not really. There's nothing you can do about it, anyway.'

Grandma visibly saddens and I feel another tug of guilt for dampening her mood.

'I've made liver for breakfast,' she says, and then begins to tell me how good it is for us. 'The iron can also help tame the thirst and keep the hunger at bay.'

I stare into my mug, blowing clouds of steam from the top with my constant sighing. She'd commented on my quietness the other day, and it made me feel bad, but what am I supposed to say?

'Sorry, Grandma, it's just that it's finally dawned on me that this isn't all a dream and I'm a bloodsucking potential murderer who can burst into flames and that my life is well and truly over. But I'm sure I'll get over it, eventually.'

We eat mostly in silence, and then I wash up. I keep noticing her looking at me, like she's going to say something, but she never does.

'What are your plans for today?' she asks, as I try to quietly leave the kitchen.

I hover in the doorway. 'I don't know. Maybe I'll go for a walk.' She keeps suggesting it. Says the rest of the grounds are really beautiful and more interesting than my bedroom's four walls.

She rests her knife and fork on her empty plate and leans back in her chair. 'There's a group that meets on Saturdays. I think you should go.'

I recoil. 'With other bloodsuckers?'

She nods. 'The woman who runs it is a very dear friend of mine. I told her you were staying with me, and she would love for you to go along.'

'Do you go?'

'I did when I first moved here.'

My mind reels, not only because someone else – someone that isn't my parents or her – knows what I am, but also at the idea that there are vampires who actively meet up to hang out.

She gets up from the table, determined. 'It will be good for you. You won't have to hide who you are there.'

She does have a point with that.

But still, the thought makes me nervous.

I straighten as she approaches. 'I don't think so,' I say. 'I don't want to hang out with other freaks when I haven't even come to terms with being one myself.'

She frowns. 'So, you think I'm a freak?'

I wince. 'Of course not. That's not what I meant.'

But she doesn't look convinced.

'Ugh.' I cross my arms. 'You don't understand.'

'Then help me to. If this is about you mourning your old life, it's okay—'

'Fine! I'll go,' I say, unable to bear another one of her lectures right now.

I'm so *not* in the mood.

'We're here,' Grandma announces as she parks outside what can only be described as an abandoned daycare centre – or so it looks, at least from the outside. The windows are boarded up, the yellow paint covering the brick has faded, and there's a girl with long, curly hair pulling really, really hard on a vape right beside the entrance.

'It might not look like much, but I think you'll be pleasantly surprised.'

I doubt that.

I mean, I'm fully aware that people like us can't be meeting up in Costa or Caffè Nero, but *here*?

Grandma rests a hand on my arm. 'You'll be fine.'

I attempt to disappear into my seat. 'Do I really have to go?'

'No, but what else are you going to do?' she asks in Spanish. 'Spend the entire summer hiding away from the world with me? You're a young girl, so you must do young girl things. Socialise, have fun.'

'But do I have to do that with . . .'

Other freaks.

I turn to look at her when she stays silent, but it's obvious she's filled in the blanks to my last sentence.

She glances out of the window. 'I'll pick you up in a few hours.'

Whatever. I undo my seat belt. 'What's the woman's name again?'

'Sanse. She's expecting you.'

'Great.'

I guess doing a runner is out of the question.

Grandma says goodbye when I get out of the car, and I'm surprised when she drives away without making sure I go inside.

As much as I'm tempted to wait out the two hours for her to return, when I look up and down the street, I see there's no point. There's not a soul to be seen and all the buildings look abandoned, so I guess I might as well see what this is all about.

The girl vaping at the door assesses me when I walk over. She looks normal, dressed in a white denim jacket and a pair of blue jeans, but the closer I get, the more I sense that she's different.

I wonder if she thinks the same about me.

'Hey,' she says, giving me a nod. Her eyes are dark and inquisitive, and she smells musky. At least, I think it's her that smells that way. My heightened sense of smell means I'm still trying to learn to pick out individual scents, especially when there are so many new smells around.

Gosh, I sound like some kind of hound.

I say 'Hi,' back to her, but that's all she gets. Since I don't know what kind of vampire *she* is, I figure it's good to be cautious.

'Coming in?' she asks, tucking her vape into her pocket.

'Um, yeah.'

She gives me a sympathetic smile and holds the door open. 'It's really not that bad.'

'Sure.' I follow her inside.

Wow.

The inside looks nothing like the out. There's artwork all over the walls; some drawings, but mostly paintings of various creatures. Snakes, dragons, something that looks like a giant with bloodied eyes . . . angels and demons with wings . . . I even spot werewolves on my way through the hallway.

Grandma said I'd be the only soucouyant attending and I don't see any fireballs or flaming humans in the artwork.

Eventually, we find ourselves in a room with about fifteen men and women of all ages sitting in a circle, and when their attention falls on me, I get the feeling that this is going to be like an AA meeting, but with an F and an A.

Freaks Anonymous.

Maybe I should have practised my introduction . . .

SUCKERS

An older woman in a dreamcatcher dress with a septum piercing stands up. 'Gabrielle?'

I nod.

'I'm Sanse.' She looks exactly how I'd imagined her. Her long, flowy dress makes her look like she's floating around all the chairs when she comes to greet me. 'Welcome.'

She turns to everyone else and leads me to an empty chair beside the girl I'd followed in.

'Everyone, please welcome Gabrielle to the group,' Sanse says, before going around and introducing everyone by name. I only manage to remember one.

Maria. *Vaper girl*.

'How are you finding Whitby so far?' Sanse asks me, returning to her seat.

'Quiet,' I answer, deciding not to start this all off with a lie. 'Pretty, though.'

'Yes, Whitby has quite the history.'

'I've heard,' I say, eyeing the pale-skinned, slightly greying guy across from me who looks a lot like— 'Dracula, right?'

She smiles knowingly. 'That's right.' She turns her attention to everyone then. 'Anyone else have something they wish to talk about?'

I figure by that question that I've missed some of the session, but after everyone says no, Sanse comes over to give me a tour and explain how these groups work.

'There are many support groups like ours in the UK, so no matter where any type of vampire resides, there is help available to them.'

'I had no idea.'

'You had no need to before now.' She smiles as we walk through the hall. 'They all run pretty much the same. We take the first few minutes to ask how everyone is. If no one needs to talk about anything, everyone is free to spend their time here how they like.' She shows me the art room, a music room, and then we end up in a room with a pottery wheel. 'People like us are creative, and I like to encourage that. It offers an escape for the mind.'

She's not wrong about that.

'Your grandmother said you play bass in a band?'

'I did. You're right about it being an escape.' *Shame it's not a cure.*

'We have a few musicians in the group, but maybe you'd like to try something different while you're here?'

Grandma must have told her about what happened. 'Sure.'

She leads me back into the art room, to where Maria, the guy who looks like Dracula, and a few others are. 'Maria, here, has lived in Whitby her entire life. She also enjoys learning about different cultures and "beings".'

Maria smirks. 'I like feeding my mind with knowledge, that's all. I find it interesting.'

'I think the two of you will get along,' Sanse says with a smile, before disappearing.

Maria watches Sanse leave. 'I'm always the one she dumps newbies on. Not everyone else is as welcoming as I am.'

Lorenzo – I think that's his name – peers at us from around his easel. He gave me a nod earlier when I first arrived, and I immediately liked him. I did think that maybe he was around my age when I first saw him, but now seeing his deep smile lines, I'm not so sure. He's wearing traditional South African dress and some kind of bird pendant around his neck, which makes me curious of what type of being *he* is.

'Not all of us are *unwelcoming*, either,' he says with an accent, and then he offers me his fist. 'Nice to meet you.'

SUCKERS

I return his greeting and smile. 'You too.'

Maria rolls her eyes at Lorenzo. 'I didn't say you were.' She starts setting me up an easel of my own and offers to share her paints with me. 'So, what are you in for?'

'Uh, I'm a soucouyant.' God, I don't think I'll ever feel comfortable saying that.

Her eyes widen. 'Wow.'

'Yeah,' I say, dipping my paintbrush into the blue paint. I'm not sure exactly how she meant that, but before she asks any more questions . . . 'What about you?'

'A peuchen,' she says, like I should know.

'Not to sound ignorant, but I have no idea what that is.'

She chuckles at her painting. 'Not many people do.' She gives me her full attention then. 'I can shift into a snake. Wanna see?'

'I, um . . . okay?'

She steps around me, closer to the door, and everyone in there starts chuckling.

'Here she goes,' Lorenzo says. 'Mind your feet. And don't look into her eyes too long.'

'My feet?' I ask, but a sharp hiss draws my attention back to Maria, whose legs are now joined as one, and covered in turquoise scales, as her face morphs to resemble a serpent's.

I step back, hitting my hip on my easel when her slitted tongue flicks at me, and that leads to another flurry of chuckles behind me.

'Uh . . .'

Maria's eyes grow bigger in her head as it elongates, her arms disappearing into her tail, too, and then her pearlescent scales shimmer as she tightly coils the lower end of her body beneath her.

The musky scent I smelled on her earlier intensifies once she's fully shifted, and I have to look up to meet her eyes now, because she's at least three feet taller than she was ten seconds ago.

'Does she still know it's me?' I ask the others, panicked by how close she's getting. I look into her green, glowing eyes, hoping she sees how unsettled I am, but I remember the warning from Lorenzo and bring my attention down to her pointed tail.

What does that vibrating mean?

'Maria, cut the shit,' Lorenzo chastens her. 'Can't you see you're scaring the girl? For goodness' sake.'

I startle when a loud clap of thunder sounds behind me, and I almost fall over my easel as I spin around.

There's a huge, increscent bird with a long beak and narrow head where Lorenzo had just been, as tall as I am, and with black, razor-sharp talons bigger than my face.

I shriek. 'What the—?'

The bird doesn't pay any attention to my obvious horror, though: its focus is on Maria, eyes as dark as night.

Until they suddenly spark bright white, and I hear Maria hiss.

I turn around to see Maria back in her human form, rubbing her head. She glares at Lorenzo, who has also shifted back to his human form. '*That* hurt.'

Lorenzo narrows his eyes back at her. 'One of us had to pull you out of your trance. You were about to give the poor girl a heart attack.'

She rolls her eyes, something telling me this isn't the first time this has happened. 'Sorry, girl. Sometimes my serpent mind gets a little carried away when she's in control.'

'Yeah, I noticed.' I give Lorenzo a look, thanking him before he returns to his easel. 'That was pretty cool, though.' Even if my heart is hammering in my chest.

My life cannot be real.

SUCKERS

Maria shrugs it off. 'There are a lot cooler shifts here than ours. You just wait till you see those. And the things they can do . . .' Her eyes widen. 'You couldn't make it up.'

'I couldn't make *those* up,' I tell her, thinking of her and Lorenzo's shifts.

I grimace at my sorry attempt of the sky on my canvas while my mind attempts to comprehend what I saw. I'm still struggling to come to terms with my own transformation, and now seeing theirs . . .

Do I really want to see anyone else's?

'So how did you hear about this place?' Maria asks, and I'm relieved she hasn't asked me about my shift.

'My grandma thought it would be good for me to come.'

'Ohhh, I see. Not what you expected, right?'

'What do you mean?' I ask.

'I saw the way you were looking at the place when you got here. Looks like a dump from the outside, right?'

'Not to be rude, but yeah. I suppose you have to stay hidden, though.'

She frowns. 'Not always. We don't always meet here. Sometimes we go to the caves, or the beach.' Her next smile is a mischievous one. 'The woods are fun, too, especially at night. It's safe to shift out there.'

I rest my paintbrush down. 'So do you all shift often?'

'All the time. As long as you can control yourself and don't get caught, there's no harm in having fun with your gift.'

'Yeah, well, I think I'm a little way away from that yet. Being what I am has ruined my life.'

Her smile slips. 'Oh, I'm sorry to hear that.'

'Yeah,' I say, but then I feel bad because I think I might have upset her. 'Maybe once I learn how to control everything, I might feel different.'

'Maybe . . . I agree that it's not always easy.' She's quiet for a while after that. 'I still struggle, too. Believe me.'

I want to ask her if *she*'s ever hurt anyone, but I keep my mouth shut because I'm not sure what I'm more afraid of.

Finding out she has and we're all monsters, or learning she hasn't and I'm the worst person here.

CHAPTER NINE

'So, what did you think?' Grandma asks cautiously when I get in the car.

I give a quick wave back to Maria who's waiting outside the building for her dad to pick her up. He's who she got her gift from. I also found out that she's a year older than me, and her parents are from Chile.

And, so far, she seems really nice.

'I think you were right. It was really good to get out.' I was so tempted to go back to that music room at the end, though: my fingers were literally itching to. 'Sanse was really welcoming. I don't think I'll be using the word "freaks" any more.'

Although, I won't say I wasn't freaked out after hearing from Maria what other types of beings were in the group. When I found out Sanse is a cihuateteo, a type of demon that originated in Mexico, I was stunned into silence.

She can cause madness in people . . .

Grandma's smile reaches her eyes. 'Oh, I'm so pleased to hear that. What about everyone else? Were you introduced to the whole group?'

'Yeah, they were cool. You were right about the history of this place attracting all the different types of vampires. There were people there from all over the world. I did miss most of the group talk at the beginning, though.'

'Never mind that,' she says, as she starts the engine. 'You'll catch it next week, won't you?'

'I'll think about it.' I didn't think I'd want to come again, but after the initial fright of Maria and Lorenzo shifting, I actually had fun. 'I saw someone turn into a serpent, and a giant bird.' Lorenzo is an impundulu, or a lightning bird, as Maria calls him. He can summon thunder and lightning.

Grandma chuckles. 'Maria and Lorenzo?'

'Yeah. I'm assuming it's a regular thing for them to do? Maria showing the newbie her shift and Lorenzo striking her with lightning to stop her terrifying them?'

'You could say that. Sanse always gets Maria to welcome the new members. She's a sweet girl. Sociable.' Her expression saddens briefly before she masks it. 'What did you think of the inside? Was it what you expected in there?'

'Not at all. The artwork is incredible.' I remember how free I felt in there, and how almost-normal again.

'Yes, this is a different world to the one you once knew,' Grandma says, driving through the busy town centre, 'but in *both*, there are things to be afraid of, until you learn how to protect yourself.'

She's right. If I'd constantly worried about the dangers in London, I never would have left my house, but I navigated those just fine.

SUCKERS

'Grandma?'

'Hmm?'

'I'm sorry for calling us freaks,' I whisper.

'New things always feel scary until you come to understand them.' Her face softens. '"Anyway, "normal" is overrated.'

I always used to say that when people questioned my look.

'Maria gave me her number and invited me to hang out sometime.'

She'd asked me if I'd met anyone here yet, and after I told her about Josh and Ethan, she mentioned she and Ethan had gone to the same secondary school but moved in different circles, so barely interacted.

'I'm not surprised,' Grandma says, when I tell her. 'Everyone knows everyone in a small town like this. Do you think you'll take her up on her offer?'

'I'm not sure. I don't know if it's safe for me yet, especially because we won't just be around people like us,' I say, knowing she'll understand.

'There's no rush, and I'm sure she'll understand if you don't want to quite yet, but you can't hide away forever. Besides, it would be a good opportunity to start learning how to be around groups of people again, and with someone who'll take care of you.'

Grandma's right, of course. And if I have any hope of going to uni, I really need to get comfortable being in larger groups again. 'I did get the vibe she'd look out for me.'

'They all will.' She gives me her full attention while we wait at a red light. 'Think of the group as extended family. They may not have the same gifts as you, but they're all trying to live a normal life, too. It's okay to have fun. Like I said, you don't need to punish yourself. Everyone makes mistakes — what matters is that we learn from them. And, as far as I can see, dear, you are.'

Hell, I'm trying.

'How are you getting on with your vial?' she asks when she accelerates away from the traffic lights.

'Good. I'm sleeping better, and it's not constantly on my mind.'

She nods with approval. 'Perhaps then, you should think about taking the next step with it.'

My stomach lurches. 'I don't know if I'm ready for that yet.'

'But are we ever truly ready for anything?'

I roll my eyes but end up laughing. 'I guess not.'

'There you go then.'

I smile out of the window, appreciating her lecture this time. Today seems to have shifted something inside me, and I think I might have found some hope at that group.

A tiny, sliver of hope that my life might not be over, after all.

I spend a little while in my room journalling about the group when we get home, and then as soon as I'm done I text Mum and ask her to bring my bass with her next weekend. I miss holding her in my arms, the deep sound of her strings, and I want her back. I miss music in general actually and, while I was journalling, I played some of my favourite songs on my laptop.

But now I'm bored, so I decide to take that walk Grandma's been suggesting since I got here. Part of me also hopes to see Ethan now that I'm in a better mood. I've barely even said 'hi' and 'bye' to him the past few days.

I mouth the lyrics to 'Retribution' by Black Death while I play air bass down the hallway, bopping my head with each step, becoming a little unsettled by the lyrics that now hold a new meaning. I'd never really paid much attention to them before . . .

The feeling doesn't last long before it's replaced with a

lightness inside, and I'm rocking out, intermittently closing my eyes.

This has got to be the longest time I've gone without playing since I first started, and my god, do I miss it.

I switch to play Arch Enemy's 'We Will Rise', shuffling my feet along the dulled, uneven carpet to the beat of the drums in my head, remembering when I played this with the band at The Black Heart in Camden. The crowd was unruly from start to finish, and the moshing got so out of control at one point that the owner cut the sound and made us take a ten-minute break.

Not that it did much to tame anyone.

That night was one of the best of my early gigs.

A chuckling at the entrance to the main hall momentarily stops me in my tracks, causing a flaming heat to creep up my cheeks.

Ethan's there with his arms crossed, leaning against the wall.

Oh god. How long has he been watching?

'*That* bored, huh?' he asks. His overalls are covered in grass stains today, and I can smell them too. They must be working on pulling that ivy out of the cracks in the walls.

'I have no idea what you're talking about.' I try to scoot past him but he doesn't move much.

He wriggles his fingers on a pretend guitar of his own. 'Do you take requests?'

I blush harder, but can't help but smile. 'Depends on the genre.'

His eyes widen. 'Oh, yeah?'

I notice how clear his eyes are. They are gorgeous and he is undeniably good looking.

'Do you really play?'

'Yeah, I play the bass.'

'Nice.' He sounds impressed. 'Can't say I've met anyone that plays that before. You played long?'

'Since I was fourteen. I played the guitar before that, though.'

'Cool.' But then he frowns. 'I haven't heard you playing.'

'I left her at home. I, uh, didn't wanna risk her getting damaged on the train up here.'

'Oh, that sucks.'

'Yeah . . .' My gaze lowers to his neck, to where his pulse is fluttering away.

Control your breaths.

I slip past him and make my way to the kitchen.

He follows. 'So, what genres?'

'Metal, mostly,' I say, practising my coping techniques. I name a few of my favourite bands.

'Can't say I've heard of them.'

I glance at him behind me, and I'm relieved to see there's a bigger gap between us. 'They're mostly indie bands.'

'Do you play in one? A band?'

'I used to,' I answer, finally able to breathe easier. 'Not at the moment, though.'

'I'd love to hear you play something,' he says, as the kitchen comes into view ahead. 'I've always wanted to learn an instrument. Dad played piano.'

I stop walking and turn to face him, curious. 'What instrument would you play?'

He shrugs. 'I hadn't thought of one in particular.' His eyes light up. 'You wanna teach me the bass?'

I smile. 'I could teach you a few chords, but the bass isn't for everyone. Are there any music shops in town?'

'I know of one . . .' He steps closer, engulfing me with the mixed scent of grass and his skin while he smirks down at me. 'Want me to save you from your boredom by showing you around?' He imitates me playing while chuckling. 'You could strum some real strings.'

That makes me laugh. 'I *have* real strings to play, thank you, but I wouldn't mind checking out the shop. Who knows, maybe you can try out a few instruments and pick one?'

'Sounds good,' he says straight away. 'You free tomorrow around one?'

I roll my eyes. 'You really need to ask me that?'

'You might've been busy putting on a show again.' He laughs and holds his hands up when I throw him daggers. 'I'll pick you up. Is that cool?'

I have to try so hard to tame my smile. 'I'll be ready.'

Chapter Ten

I don't know what I expected Ethan to look like out of his work clothes, but he's wearing those dark jeans and that oversized grey T-shirt so well.

He checks out my ripped shorts and vest before he smiles back at me. 'Ready for some sightseeing?'

'Yep.' I distract myself with my seatbelt while fighting a mental battle. I've been counting down the hours since our chat yesterday, but Ethan's scent hit me the moment I climbed into his car. It's on everything. And not only does he smell good, he looks it. I find myself doubting all the work I've been putting in to learning that damned discipline . . .

I tame my next breath while skimming my tongue over my front teeth.

Okay, we're safe, for now.

'Where did you go when you came to town with Noemie?' he

asks, and I'm grateful for the distraction. I fan myself and lower the window, hoping the salty sea air will cut through his scent.

'A few trinket shops, and we went for lunch. I saw a few goth shops I'd like to check out at some point, but I won't bore you with those.'

He chuckles. 'I don't mind.'

Good to know. 'What do you usually do on your day off?'

He makes a right turn into town. 'See Mum, hang out with friends.' He exhales. 'Rest.'

I'm not surprised to hear that last thing. He's always working hard around the manor and you can tell from a single glance at him that he does. That T-shirt he's wearing might be loose everywhere else on his body, but not around his arms. The way they flex while he steers is getting me heated.

Breathe . . .

'Do you not live with your mum?'

'Nah, I haven't for a few months now.' He glances at me. 'I have my own place. Josh might work me hard, but he pays well. Are you missing your parents?'

'A little, but we text all the time. I know they're missing me a lot, though.'

'Is this your first time away from home for this long?' he asks, as we find a parking spot close to the harbour.

'Yep.'

He nods knowingly while reversing into a space. 'Mum was like that. She wouldn't stop blowing up my phone when I first moved out.' He turns off the engine and pats my hand. 'They'll be okay.'

'Thanks. I hope so.' I follow him out of the car, thankful for the sea breeze. 'How far is the shop from here?'

'Not far.' He points up the hill to the right. 'Why? Bored already?'

'No!' I laugh, following him across the street. I like his company, regardless of how easily he can trigger me. He's got this aura around him that makes me feel at ease.

'You going to that?' he asks, pointing to a banner above a vintage record shop.

Book your tickets for GothFest here!

'You have a goth festival here?' I gush. 'I had no idea.'

'Every year,' he says. 'It's over two days. Town is always rammed for it.'

'I believe it. I love festivals and usually go to as many as I can.'

'A few of us usually go. You should come with us,' he suggests.

'Yeah, I might,' I say noncommittally. Even though I would love to, I'm not sure yet how I feel about the idea of crowds. Even now, all the different scents and sounds fill my mind, and I have to keep reminding myself to breathe evenly.

We take a turn, and I spot The Coven, so I ask him what he knows about it.

'The woman who owns it practises Chinese medicine. It was an acupuncture place when I was younger. The last few years, though, it's more out-of-towners that go there.'

'Really?' I'm not sure what I'd been expecting, but from Grandma's reaction it was definitely something more sinister.

'Yeah. It's where the self-proclaimed witches, healers and shamans hang out.' He leans into my side. 'Vampires, too, apparently. I've also heard there's a secret nightclub under it.'

I tense slightly at the mention of vampires and laugh nervously. 'This town has its fingers in a lot of pies.'

SUCKERS

He laughs. 'You ain't lying.' But then his smile slips. 'You heard about the vampire attacks around here?'

'All the "sucker" hate was the first thing that greeted me at the station when I arrived.' I glance sideways at him, trying to gauge his response.

'Yeah, that stuff's always been around, but Oliver's followers have grown like mad over the past few months.'

'Oliver? That's the mayor, right?'

'Uh-huh. Most of the town thought he was crazy, and I definitely did when I was growing up.'

I swallow down my unease. 'What about now? Do you think vampires exist?'

He looks down at me and shrugs. 'I've never seen anything myself, but the way things are going, it's hard not to think there's something in it, even if it's some crazy pretending to be one. What do you think?'

I exhale deeply. 'I have no idea.'

He gets the door for the music shop, ushering me in. 'Would be kinda cool if it was true. Not the people getting hurt part; but if vamps exist, imagine what else does.'

I laugh off his comment as I walk over to a wall of guitars. 'Is that your love of thriller books talking?'

He smiles at the guitars. 'What can I say? I have a vivid imagination.'

'Clearly.'

'What bass do you play? The four or the six string?'

'Four.' I point to one that looks like mine, and he asks me if I want to play it.

I shake my head. 'I don't want to hurt my bass's feelings.'

He laughs. 'Loyal, nice.' He takes an electric guitar down from the wall and strums it. 'Think I'd be reaching if I wanted to learn this?'

I chuckle. 'No. Every musician started somewhere. You just need to make sure you have a passion for it, because learning isn't easy. And you should probably start by holding it properly. Here.'

Without thinking, I reach over to adjust his grip. The moment my skin touches his, a shiver ripples up my spine, igniting all of my senses with it. I can practically taste his scent at the back of my throat, and is that his heart I hear humming away, or mine?

I pull my hand away as I'm quickly overwhelmed by thirst, but Ethan holds my wrist to pull it back.

'Show me.'

My heart races along with my thoughts while I try to focus on positioning his hands and tell him why he needs to hold it a certain way. 'You'll have better access to the strings if you position it like this.'

He strums the strings as he looks at me, his gaze soft before it falls to my lips. 'That feels much better.'

I exhale deeply. 'Good.'

I wish *I* did.

'Can I help you?' a shop assistant asks, interrupting us, and I jump away from Ethan like I've been electrocuted.

'Uh, my friend wants to play an instrument,' I tell him, my voice sounding strangely breathy. 'Could you maybe give him some suggestions?'

'Sure.'

Ethan doesn't find anything he likes by the time we leave the shop, and I'm now convinced the trip was more for me than it was for him.

I can no longer ignore that there's something between us, but there's no way I can act on it. Not only am I not ready for it, but I actually like Ethan and think we could be friends. He makes me laugh, and right now, he's my *only* friend.

SUCKERS

It also helps to know that he doesn't *hate* the idea of vampires . . .

'This is the best café in town,' Ethan says, stopping outside a mint-green building called Mr Cooper's Coffee House. 'Come on, I'll treat you.'

However, when we get inside, it's clear to see we won't be able to eat in here.

'Well, let's get it to go,' he says, noticing how busy it is for himself. 'What do you fancy?'

'Um . . .' I scan the menu boards and the cakes in the cases in front of us. 'I'm not sure. Everything looks good.'

'The jam and cream scones are the best. I always get one.'

'I'll have that then.'

He rests a brief hand against my lower back when the queue moves. 'Tea or coffee?'

'Uh, tea.'

He orders for both of us, while I remain beside him in some kind of silent hell with my temperamental feelings. However, I do remember my manners when we leave.

'Thank you. I'm excited to try it.'

'It's good, trust me.'

We take a short walk to Whalebone Arch to sit on one of the many benches that look over the water. Ethan points out the abbey in the distance and explains how the arch of the whale's jawbone behind us is a replica of the original.

'It's huge.'

He chuckles while passing me my scone from the bag he's carried here. 'Whales usually are.'

I roll my eyes at him but I'm interrupted by the burst of jam in my mouth. Ethan was right. 'Damn, this *is* good.'

'I told you.' He takes another bite of his. 'They're the best.'

While we enjoy the view, I ask him if he has any brothers or sisters.

'Nah, just me. What about you?'

'My parents were one and done, too. I've never felt lonely, though. We're all close.'

'I never felt lonely either,' Ethan says. 'But I do worry about Mum sometimes, as much as she tells me not to.'

'Because she doesn't have your dad?' I ask tentatively.

He glances at me and nods. 'We knew it was coming. Dad had been having chemo a while, but still . . . They spent all their time together, and I know as much as she tries to hide it, she struggles not having him here.'

Briefly, I rest a hand on his arm in comfort. 'You all must.'

'Yeah . . .'

'I can't even imagine,' I say, feeling sad for him. 'Are you going to see her today?'

'Yeah, once I drop you home.' He rests his paper cup of tea beside him and then gives me a long look. 'I've had a good time today, Gabby.'

I smile. 'So have I. Thanks for bringing me out. You were right, I've been *so* bored.'

Today wasn't as hard as I initially thought it might be. There were times, yes, where my heart raced and I thought my fangs might make an appearance because of the way he looked at me, but overall, I'm proud of how well I've coped.

He looks down at my hand, but he doesn't hold it like I think he's going to. 'Well, if you ever want to hang out again, I'm up for it. Be bored no more,' he announces playfully.

I laugh. 'We will definitely hang out again.'

Chapter Eleven

Don't be weird . . . You've got this . . . They're just people . . . You used to be around people all the time . . . Maria will look after you . . .

I'm nervous to the point of almost throwing up while I get ready to meet Maria, and I barely touched my dinner.

When Maria texted me asking if I wanted to hang out with her and some friends Wednesday night, I was still feeling light and positive from going to town with Ethan. However, since last night, I've been seriously regretting my decision.

Maybe I should just text to say I can't come.

No, I can't cancel on her.

Ugh.

I try on four different outfits before I give up and wear my comfort outfit of ripped jeans, a vest, my leather jacket and my favourite boots. I almost wore a dress that felt more 'normal' and like the stuff I'd seen the girls my age wearing around the harbour but I felt weird, like I was pretending to be someone else. One thing I've never done is try to fit in, and regardless of what secrets I'm hiding, I'm not going to start now.

They either like me for who I really am, or they don't.

Maria said the group we'd be chilling with are cool, but I'm still a little on edge about shifting or acting weird around strangers. I'm the new girl, too, which means the attention will inevitably be on me, at least for a little while.

'Are you ready to go?' Grandma calls from outside my door. 'You don't want to be late.'

I press a brief hand to my stomach before grabbing my phone and shoving it into my pocket. 'I'm ready.'

Grandma smiles when I open the door. 'You look lovely, but won't you be hot in that jacket?'

'No, I'll be fine.' I shrug it closed a little more while I follow her down the stairs, but the inked thorns that link my sleeve to the base of my neck are still visible.

Grandma turns when we reach the bottom of the stairs and holds my hands, so I have to stop. 'Relax. You're going to have fun.'

I breathe out some of my anxiety. 'I hope so.'

'If it gets too much, call me and I'll pick you up. But you've done well with your coping skills, so believe in yourself. You'll be fine.'

'Okay.' *I wish I had as much faith in me as she does.*

'I'll have to dig out some pictures from when I was your age,' she says, once we're in the car. 'Your outfits are tame compared to the things I wore.'

'Oh, yeah?' *This is tea . . .* 'What things?'

'Romanticism just hit, so imagine mini-skirts, fishnet clothing, bright hair, half a tube of eyeliner on a night out.' She smiles wistfully as she pulls away. 'Those were the days.'

I gape at her. 'You wore fishnets? Like tights?'

She glances at me. 'And the rest, dear. Vests — if you can call them that — jumpers, shorts . . .'

'Wow, you sounded so cool.'

She clears her throat disapprovingly. 'I still am, thank you.'

'I didn't mean it like that. I just mean, I didn't think you'd dress like that.'

'Ah, well, maybe that's why you shouldn't make assumptions, eh?'

I hold my hands up and chuckle. 'Excuse *me*. I'd love to see those pictures if you do find them.'

Maybe she's where I got my alternative style from, because Mum doesn't dress even slightly quirkily. Her and Dad are as prim and proper as they come.

Grandma seems happy during the drive, and I wonder if it's because I've triggered some fond memories for her. As much as I miss my parents, it has been good to get to know Grandma better. Yeah, her preaching can get a little annoying, but she does give good advice, and a part of me thinks she's enjoying having me around, too.

'Right,' she says, parking outside Whitby Abbey. 'Let me know if you need picking up. And remember, if it gets too much . . .'

'Thanks, Grandma.'

She looks past me and waves. 'Your friend is waiting. Have fun.'

Once out of the car, I join Maria beside a path leading into a field with woods in the far distance. Her outfit isn't too different to my own, which immediately puts me at ease, and so does the huge smile she has on her face.

'Hey, girl,' she says, surprising me with a brief hug. 'I'm so glad you came. You look good.'

'Thanks, so do you.' I'd wear those washed-out ripped jeans she has on myself. The matching, oversized denim jacket too.

She brushes my compliment off. 'Feeling okay? I got the impression you weren't fully up for coming when you texted back earlier. You didn't have to, honestly. I would've understood.'

This girl is *super* observant. 'To be honest, I kinda wasn't, but I'm good now.'

'All right, well, the place we're going is a half-hour walk from here.' She motions to the path, and we both begin to follow it. 'Most is through the woods, but the cove is quiet, and private. Far enough from the oldies that like to complain about loud music.'

'That's fine by me.'

'Cool. So, what did you *really* think of the group on Saturday? And I'm sorry again for scaring you with . . . y'know.'

I chuckle. 'To be honest, it was a lot better than I'd expected. And it's fine, I've thought about it a few times, actually. Your shift is pretty epic.'

'Good. Are *you* learning how to shift? Have you done it yet?'

'Um, kinda. Only once, by accident.' I pray she changes the subject, fast, before the next question comes.

She gives me a look, one that tells me she might know that it didn't end well. 'Oh . . . Sanse said your grandmother's shift is incredible, so I hope I see yours one day. A few people have learnt how to at the group.'

Good to know. I give her a look then. 'What was that between you and Lorenzo?'

She laughs. 'Him striking me with lightning?'

'Yeah, that.'

SUCKERS

'He's done it a few times when I've shifted to settle the newbies in. It doesn't hurt as much as you think, don't worry. I'm tougher than I look, especially in that form.'

'He gave the impression that he's used to your antics.'

Her eyes light up. 'He is. He's been at the group for a while now.'

'The people there seem nice, so I can see why . . . I'm not in a rush to learn my shift, but I hope I do soon . . . The stress of it happening when I don't want it to is very real.'

She nods thoughtfully. 'I feel you on that. Just . . . make sure you learn the most important thing first. Things can get really messy if you don't.'

I read between the lines. 'Are you talking about the thirst?'

'Yeah.' We both step over a fallen tree to enter the woods. 'There is help if you ever need it, but if you can get a hold over that yourself, things will be a lot easier for you. Believe me.'

The warning in her advice doesn't escape me. 'Thanks, I'll keep that in mind.'

Maria and I are both carrying our jackets after our trek through the woods. Most of the way here was walkable along a track trodden in by previous visits, but we also had to climb over fallen trees and fight overgrown thorn bushes, which made me glad I wore my boots.

'We're here,' she huffs out, leading me out of an opening that joins a dirt track to the beach.

'Thank God.' *I really should've walked more in London.*

We take a second to catch our breath when we reach the top of some dunes, and I admire the view of the small cove and the waves rushing up the beach below. The sand is a muted beige but the water is sparkling clear, reflecting the sun. It's completely opposite to the beach nearest to London, where dirty water, rubbish and pebbles are all you get.

There's no unpleasant smell either; just fresh air, tinged with the mild scent of salty seaweed.

The gusts of wind come and go as we make our way down closer to the water, but it doesn't bite, which I'm glad about. Maria tells me that she likes hanging out here because the waves are peaceful, and the sea breeze helps dilute the scents when there are a lot of people around.

And I get what she means as we get closer to the others.

A group of people sit around a fire. I count fifteen in total, but I can't be sure because there are games of football and beach volleyball going on.

'How do you know these people? Did you grow up with them?' I ask.

'Most of them. Some I went to school with, college . . . Some I met at my old weekend jobs. Everyone kinda knows everyone in Whitby. Small towns, y'know?'

'I've heard that before.'

She starts naming everyone in the group as we get closer, letting me know who's who, what they're like, who's related, and who in the group is dating. By the time we reach them, though, my nerves are back, and I've forgotten everything she's told me.

'There are usually a few others,' she says, briefly leaning into my side, 'but they don't seem to be here yet. Hey!' she yells, waving when a handful of people start calling to her.

Two girls run over to us to give Maria a hug, and Maria introduces me to them. 'This is Gabby. She's new in town, so be nice.'

SUCKERS

'We're *always* nice,' Ava says for her and the other girl, Willow. 'Nice tats. I have a few myself.'

'Thanks,' I say, noticing a butterfly on her neck. Her artist must be good because it's super detailed. 'You'll have to let me know where you go to get yours.'

'Defo.' She links her arm in mine and we all walk down towards the others. 'Has Maria told you who everyone is?'

'Mostly.'

'Well, the guy with bright-red hair is my boyfriend, Noah, and the jacked guy running into the water with his shirt off is Willow's boo. Those two guys there, Peter and Henry, sitting by the fire, are together and are really sweet. They're kinda like the dads of the group.'

'Maria said that, too.' They look older than the others now we're closer, but not by much. The group, as a whole, is quite mixed, which reminds me of being back in Camden.

Whitby really isn't turning out to be like anything I thought it would.

'There are a few others that hang with us but they usually come a bit later. They work late in town, so they come after they get off.'

'All right, thanks.'

She smiles and squeezes my arm. 'No problem, girl.'

I'm so relieved they're as cool as Maria had said. It's not that I didn't believe her, but still, you never know . . .

Maria steals me back from Ava when we reach the others, and we both sit down on a fallen tree trunk next to the bonfire. I do get a few curious looks, but none make me uncomfortable.

'Maria mentioned she'd be bringing a new friend,' Ben, Willow's older brother, says. 'You're from London, right?'

'Yeah, south.'

'London?' someone else says. 'What brings you all the way up here?'

'I'm spending time with my grandma,' I reply, thankful that I thought about the answers to the questions I might get asked.

'Oh, cool. How are you finding Whitby? I bet it's completely different to what you're used to.'

'Yeah, it's a lot quieter up here, but it's nice so far.'

Isla, one of Maria's friends from college, scoffs. 'You mean boring. I grew up in Birmingham until I was fourteen and my parents moved here for work. I wish I could go back. This place is dead compared to there.'

I smile sympathetically. 'City life is definitely different. Do you think you'll move back some day?'

'Nah, I plan on going travelling after I finish uni next year . . .'

Maria asks me if I want a drink from the cooler while the group start talking about their plans after they finish school.

'I'll have anything without alcohol, please.'

She nods as she gets up. 'I've got you.'

Henry asks me how old I am and if I'll be going to uni.

'I'm eighteen. And I should be starting in September.'

'What are you going to study?'

'Music, mainly.'

'Do you play an instrument?' Willow asks, genuinely interested.

'Yeah, the bass.'

She seems disappointed with my answer. 'Oh. Jason usually brings his guitar, but let's just say, his playing skills are a bit hit and miss. I thought maybe we'd have some decent music for a change.'

I chuckle. 'I can play the guitar, too.'

'Well, damn,' Ava says, smiling at Willow. 'Looks like we've lucked out with the newbie this time. Any good at volleyball?'

'Um, that's a no, sorry.'

The group laugh.

'It's cool, we'll teach you.'

Chapter Twelve

I'm awful at sports and tonight has only proved it. I sucked at volleyball and was pretty sure I lost my team the game. I decided to sit the next one out because of it and help Henry and Peter collect more driftwood for the fire instead.

I've learnt that Peter and Henry are in their mid-twenties, and they have an online business selling tarot cards, crystals and their own affirmation decks. I also understand why they got their reputation for being the dads of the group. They showed me the best places to collect wood, the bathroom if I needed it, and they even told me how to get back to town a way that isn't through the woods.

'We've taken Maria home plenty of times when she's been out of it,' Henry says, eyeing her on the sand playing volleyball.

Peter agrees while throwing another piece of wood on the fire. 'She's not been too bad recently, though. Seems like she's been finding better ways to deal with her stuff.'

'Stuff?' I ask.

'Yeah,' Henry says. 'Baggage, y'know? We've all got some.'

'Oh . . .' *Surely she hasn't told them what she is?*

Peter glares at him before returning his attention to me. 'Maria's sweet and is a good friend to everyone. Unfortunately, it just took a long time for her to find people that were good to her, that's all.'

I take that as a hint for me not to hurt her, but I don't have any intention to. 'Well, I like Maria, and I hope we stay friends.'

Maria's really taken care of me tonight, too, just like she promised. She hasn't left my side until now, and that's only because I had to practically force her to play another game of volleyball and not sit here with me.

Peter smiles, but then he looks past me and rolls his eyes. 'Ohh, here they are. We thought you guys weren't coming!'

When I turn around, I see three more guys coming down over the dunes carrying bags and shouting abuse back at Peter, who is now laughing.

One guy catches my attention straight away and makes my stomach twist, but it's not because of his sharp jawline or dark, simmering eyes.

It's because he's glaring at me like I'm an intruder.

Okay . . .

I turn back around and start playing with the ring on the can in my hands. Ava and Willow had mentioned someone who was usually a bit cold to new additions to the group earlier. Alex, I think they said his name was.

This must be him.

The volleyball game ends in a draw and everyone comes back over to the bonfire, but some go to greet the guys that have just arrived.

Maria, though, returns to our log and immediately leans close to me. 'The one with the blond hair is Jason – the guitar guy – and the one carrying the beers is Mikey. I've known him forever and he's really funny. And the tall, moody-looking one is Alok.' She speeds up her whispering then. 'He can be a prick, so be warned.'

I'm startled when a bag full of beer cans is dropped beside me, and I quickly look up.

'Hey, new girl,' Mikey says with a beaming smile. He nods at Maria. 'What's your friend's name then?'

'Gabby,' Maria says, 'and she's new to town so don't be a dick.'

He holds his hands up. 'I wouldn't dare.' He offers me his hand, so I shake it. 'Nice to meet ya, girl. I'm Mikey.'

'She knows.' Maria rolls her eyes, and he laughs.

'Why are you always so mean to me, Mar?'

She crosses her arms. 'I'm not. I'm actually really nice.'

Her response makes me smirk. *If he only knew . . .*

Mikey scoffs. 'Sure you are.'

I meet Jason next, who seems friendly enough, but when he tries to introduce me to Alok, the uncomfortable feeling returns with a vengeance.

He's wearing a white shirt and black trousers, has a typical preppy haircut, and when he looks down at me, it feels as if he is in other ways, too.

'All right?' he asks, his dark eyes cold like before. But as abrasive as he sounds, something about his voice causes all the hairs on the back of my neck to stand on end.

And then my skin begins to tingle.

What the hell?

'Hi,' I reply bluntly, my fear making me sound ruder than I intended to. I narrow my eyes at him. I don't know what the hell is happening here, but his presence has me heated in a way that fills me with confusion.

Maria laughs under her breath before mimicking my terse response, but I can't take my eyes off Alok. He's still staring at me, too, but not at my face. His attention is fixed fiercely on my tattoos.

My next inhale is an unsteady one.

He suddenly blinks before turning around to talk to Mikey, and I'm immediately able to breathe easier. My skin isn't tingling anymore either, but I'm still on edge.

'That was funny,' Maria whispers in my ear. 'Most people suck up to him.'

'I don't know why,' I mutter, but that's a lie. *It's one hundred per cent his looks*. I throw a look at his back. 'He's rude.'

'Trust me, but you're always going to get one like that in a group. And considering who his dad is . . .'

I turn to face her. 'Who's his dad?'

'Has your grandma told you about Oliver?'

I recoil. 'Are you *serious*?' *This is the son of the man who wants our kind to be hunted down? What the hell is Maria doing hanging out with him?*

Her eyes widen. 'Yeah.'

I feel even sicker now.

'I know.' She side-eyes him. 'Don't worry about him, though. He doesn't come that often.'

I scoff. 'Probably thinks this is above him.'

Her look is knowing. 'You're good at reading people, aren't you?'

'Sometimes,' I mutter, but so is she.

I stay on high alert as the night goes on, but I'm not exactly sure why. I'm still confused by my reaction to meeting Alok earlier. I can't figure out why I felt threatened.

If his dad hates vampires, surely he must too. Perhaps my soucouyant side detected the threat?

Whatever it is, there's something about him . . .

I listen to his conversation with the others once he sits beside the bonfire, but I quickly wish I hadn't.

'There were over two hundred people at the town hall on Sunday. Just a head's up – my dad's pushing for a curfew.'

Everyone begins to protest at that idea.

'He doesn't think it's safe for anyone to be out after sundown anymore. All the attacks in the past month have happened after dark.'

'I'm not sticking to any lame curfew,' Ava's boyfriend complains. 'No one even has proof that the attacks have been by vampires.'

Alok glares at him. 'What else d'you think is going around biting people, bro? That last girl saw it and said it was a woman.'

'She was off her face, wasn't she? She probably just wants the attention.'

The group starts bickering amongst themselves after Noah's offhanded comment, with each side joining in to argue their point, until Alok's voice cuts through and everyone else falls silent.

'I didn't say we had to abide by that shit, did I? I'm just telling you what I know.'

'Damn,' I mutter, watching him murder his friends with his eyes. 'Rude *and* moody.'

'Usual Alok,' Maria whispers. 'I've seen him pop off for much less—'

He snaps his head in our direction, and my heart jumps into my throat. 'What you do with what I've told you is up to you, but don't say I didn't warn you.'

Maria rolls her eyes when he turns back to the others, but I work desperately to calm myself down. My skin just tingled again, and I'm sure I can feel that flame inside me that Grandma warned me about . . .

I tell Grandma about my evening at the cove over breakfast; I leave out the part about how Maria and I almost got lost in the woods on the way home because she'd had too much to drink and couldn't remember the way. Her sense of smell saved us, though. Once she started hissing, we found the path to town again.

She sits down opposite me after making tea for us. *This cinnamon tea is my favourite.*

'Think you'll meet up with them again?'

I shrug. 'I don't see why not. The breeze at the cove kept the scents under control, and everyone seemed nice. Well, most people.'

Alok definitely has an attitude problem. He was selective over who he spoke to all night, and even when he had a drink, he didn't really loosen up. Well, at least not to Maria and me. So, after I got my reactions to him under control, we spent the last few hours whispering under our breaths and intentionally riling him up.

Childish? Maybe. But was it funny?

Hell yes.

Grandma raises an eyebrow. 'Most?'

'Well, I met the mayor's son.'

'Oh, yes. Alok is known for being a little . . . let's say, abrupt. He may not be Oliver's child by blood, but he most definitely raised him like he is.'

I put my fork down. 'He's adopted?'

'From Sri Lanka as a baby and, apparently, he had a hard time when he was younger because of his dad's obsession with vampires. For a long time, people thought Oliver was . . . unwell. It's only more recently that he's been getting supporters. So perhaps Alok has learned to be wary of people now that he's older.'

That makes sense . . . 'That's not a reason to be rude to people, though.'

'No, it isn't. But our experiences shape us, dear.' She gives me a knowing look. 'We know that better than anyone.'

I groan. I hate that she's always right.

Grandma chuckles, but she's quickly serious. 'I won't tell you to stay away from Alok, only to be careful. With more proof under his belt and his position as mayor, Oliver isn't being ignored any more. And I don't doubt for a moment that he isn't sharing that with his son.'

'I'll be careful,' I promise.

She nods and seems to let it go. 'Was Ethan there?'

I pick up my fork to finish eating. 'No, and I'm kinda glad he wasn't. I haven't figured out how to tell him I know Maria yet.' Ethan knows I'm new to town and have barely left this manor, so I can't exactly tell him I met her at a support group for bloodsuckers . . .

Grandma shrugs. 'Just tell him you met her in town, Gabrielle. The less elaborate the lie, the easier it will be to remember. You're here for a while yet, and you don't want to complicate things. Especially not with someone you see almost every day.'

She's right. 'I'll think of something.' I get up and clear away our dishes. 'I'm going to go and read for a bit. I started reading great-great-grandma Lucila's journal yesterday, and it's getting juicy.'

'Ah, you must be talking about when she met—'

I spin around from the sink. 'Don't spoil it.'

'My bad,' she says, mocking me.

I purse my lips. 'Uh-huh.'

SUCKERS

I get comfortable on the window seat with the blanket and a pillow off my bed. My great-great-grandma has just locked eyes with a guy in the grocery store, and I'm dying to find out what happens next.

May 2nd, 1924

I'd been avoiding Joyce's grocery store for a week until I had run out of several food cupboard essentials, which meant I had no choice but to visit today. I had hoped that of all the days he might visit, today would not be the day.

That was not the case.

I had been in the store no longer than five minutes when I was engulfed by the fragrance I had been running from. When I turned, he was standing at the end of the aisle.

He smiled and, so I wouldn't appear rude, I smiled back, but then I quickly picked up the rest of the items I needed before rushing to the cashier.

Apparently not one to be deterred, he followed, asking if I was having a good day and if I lived locally. I kept my answers as brief as possible while fighting to maintain my composure, but after I paid, I heard him chuckling when I was rushing out of the door.

It made me furious and, truthfully, I wanted to go back inside to give him a piece of my mind.

I hope I never see him again.

Leesha Shay

May 7th, 1924

The man, who I now know is Mister Luis Navaro, works at the bank across the street from the grocery store, which is probably how he always seems to visit when I am there. He caught me on the way out today and formally introduced himself, much to my annoyance. It seems as though he is intent on becoming familiar with me, no matter how much I very clearly try not to give him the time of day.

However, my thirst was less intense today, which came as a very welcome relief.

May 10th, 1924

Mister Navaro invited me to a show and, following careful consideration, I accepted. He delivered me home merely ten minutes ago after we enjoyed a late evening meal together in town.

He is very charming, and I was quite entertained in his presence. He talked about his love for his widowed mother and his dedication to taking care of her and his younger sister. They live in the next town.

I have not thought much of settling down with anyone these past few years, and did not even think it possible, but there is a part of me that could see me living a very lovely life with Mister Navaro, if I was not what I am.

It is a shame, but I will need to put an end to his advances soon.

SUCKERS

I turn the page, hoping she changes her mind, but my stomach leaps when I see dried tear stains all over the writing.

June 4th, 1924

I have not written in a long while, but I have been busy with Luis. We have been courting for approaching a month now. I have met his mother and sister, who both adore me, and I them. He has also met my parents, who he charmed the same way he did me.

I enjoy his company immensely and find that I miss him when we are apart, and I do believe he feels the same way. He's invited me out this weekend and said he'd like to ask me something of importance.

I think he wishes to propose.

However, I am concerned because I have not been truthful. He does not know the real me. He does not know what I become. Luis does not deserve to be trapped with someone that could hurt him. Yes, I manage my thirst for him well, but there are still moments when it becomes unbearable and I have to make my excuses.

I do not wish to lose him, but I fear he was never mine. I have lied and tricked him into loving someone who doesn't truly exist. He surely could never love me if he knew the truth. How could he?

I snap the journal shut when I see the next page's barely legible handwriting. I can't read of her breaking up with him. Not yet. My heart can't take that right now.

The sun has been burning my arm through the window for a

little while, so I decide to take a walk through the gardens. I found a little place, past Grandma's bench, with berry bushes and a wild pond yesterday, and I'm looking forward to playing my bass down there when I get it back this weekend.

I take my hoodie off when I reach the newly slabbed patio outside and, as I hang it on the back of one of the chairs, I smile as Ethan's scent becomes stronger.

'Since when do *you* hang out down at the cove?' he asks, appearing from the side of the house.

I narrow my eyes and smirk. 'How do you know I was down there?'

'I spotted you in the background of some pictures.'

'Oh . . . my friend Maria invited me. She said she knows you.'

He frowns. 'Maria, as in curly haired Maria? You know *her*?'

I cross my arms. 'Yeah, we met in town, why?'

'No reason. She's cool.'

'Yeah, she is.' Everyone keeps saying that, but I get the feeling, again, that there's something about her that people seem reluctant to talk about. Henry and Peter gave me that impression when I met them, too. And, now that I think about it, so did Grandma when I'd first mentioned her.

People don't know that she's a peuchen, so what is it?

'That's the place I was talking about,' Ethan says, kicking a stray stone at his feet. 'What did you think of it down there?'

'It was good, and everyone there made me feel welcome. The place itself isn't like anywhere I've ever been before either, so it was a nice change.'

He lifts his head and smiles. 'Yorkshire people are the best.'

'I'm seeing that. Not sure about the volleyball thing, though.'

He chuckles. 'Not a fan, then?'

'Sports haven't ever been my thing,' I say, looking away from his lips. 'Do you play?'

'I'm usually on the winning team.'

I blush. That doesn't surprise me with his height and build. I tear my gaze away from those arms. 'You'll, um, have to give me some pointers.'

His eyes light up. 'Sure thing, if you're planning to go again.'

'I can't see why I wouldn't.' *Even if Alok is there.* 'I had a good time.'

'Good to know. I'm making a cold drink for Josh and me. Want one?'

'Um, yeah, but could you leave it in the fridge? I'll have it when I get back from my walk.'

'Off to explore the grounds again?' he asks, when I walk past him down the steps.

'Yep.' *And to get some much-needed fresh air.*

Chapter Thirteen

I wipe my eyes and close Lucila's journal after reading weeks of entries without her and Luis being reunited. He'd been knocking at her door daily, begging her to open up to him, but, every time, she would hide in her bedroom until he left. Usually in tears.

It's heartbreaking to read, especially because it could be what my life ends up being like. What happens if I fall in love? What if I can't do what she did and control my thirst around someone when my feelings grow?

Am *I* destined to be alone?

Grandma hasn't talked about my grandad, but I know he died young, in his sleep, and not long after my mother was born, so part of me knows that finding love *is* possible for us. I just don't know if I'll ever be brave enough to tell someone what I am.

Or trust *anyone enough to tell them.*

SUCKERS

My thoughts turn to Kyle when I leave my room and take the hundred steps down the creaky stairs that go all the way to the ground floor. The guilt is hitting hard by the time I get to the main hall, and the cuffs of my hoodie are damp from all the times I've wiped my face on the way here.

Why am I so emotional today?

Ugh, and now Ethan's coming down the hall.

Perfect timing.

I take shorter breaths as I approach him, directing my attention to the toolbox in his hand, but he blinks when I look back up, and my stomach drops.

'Hey, you okay?' he asks softly, dropping his tools at his boots.

'Yeah, I'm fine,' I say, straightening. *Think of something. Quick!* 'How are you?' *Seriously?*

'I'm good . . . Your grandma asked me to check the electrics in one of the spare rooms.' He steps closer. 'You sure you're okay?'

'Uh-huh. Thanks for asking, but I'm fine. I'm just going through some stuff right now and—'

'You don't want to talk about it?'

I smile weakly. 'Pretty much.'

He nods like he understands. 'How about a brew to cheer you up? I make a killer cuppa. Your grandma taught me.'

I frown. 'You couldn't make tea before?'

He chuckles. 'I thought I could. The first time I made Noemie one she looked like she wanted to spit it out. Haven't made a bad one since.'

That makes me smile. 'Grandma doesn't play about her tea-making skills.'

'At all. So, tea?'

'Sure.'

'All right.' He moves his tools closer to the wall and then leads me towards the kitchen. 'Let's get you feeling better.'

I appreciate his concern as I go with him, but I also stay cautious. He smells good, as always, and it's not just his cologne. His natural scent is what triggers me the most.

He tells me to sit at the table while he boils the kettle, making small talk about him and Josh having this Saturday off. Once he places my drink in front of me and sits down opposite, his light-hearted mood seems to disappear.

'Nothing's happened here, has it?' he asks. 'In Whitby?'

'No, not at all.'

He nods knowingly. 'Something to do with the reason you're currently 400-odd miles away from home, then?'

I laugh bitterly. 'That obvious?'

'Not really, but you've said a few things since you've been here that have made me reach that conclusion. I know you said you don't want to talk about it, but I'm a good listener, and I won't judge.'

He does always listen super intensely when we talk.

You can't trust him. You can't trust anyone.

I shove the voice down and start talking. 'Before I left London, something happened, and I've sort of run away from it. It was my fault, and I know that, I just don't know how to fix it. Or even if it *can* be fixed.'

'Did it involve someone else?'

'A close friend, yeah.'

'Okay . . .' He sips his tea. 'And did you apologise?'

I shake my head. 'I wanted to but I was scared.'

He frowns. 'Why? Do you not think they'd accept your apology? I mean, if you're close, then surely they'd understand whatever happened was a mistake, right?'

I scoff. '*I* didn't even understand why I did what I did when it happened, so I doubt that. The whole thing's a mess, believe me.'

'So you've not spoken to them at all?'

I shake my head.

'Well, you clearly care about whatever it was that happened, so I think you're being too hard on yourself.'

'I'm not. I hurt them. I . . .' *I could've killed them*. 'They probably hate me, and I deserve it. I'm angry with myself more than anything.'

'We all get mad with ourselves sometimes. None of us are perfect.'

'You sound like my grandma.'

He laughs. 'She has some good advice.'

'And likes to give it,' I add.

'She does, but my mum doesn't get the chance to lecture me, so I don't mind it.' He drinks some more of his tea, but then he suddenly sits up straighter and grins. 'Wait, I have something that'll make you feel better.'

I narrow my eyes. 'I doubt that.'

He holds up a finger. 'Just trust me. Come with me.'

He's out of the door before I can stop him and curiosity gets the better of me.

We end up outside, at the back of the manor.

'OK, stand right there,' he says. 'Close your eyes and hold out your hands.'

I do as I'm told, and after something cold and heavy rests against my palms, I open my eyes.

'A sledgehammer?'

'Smashing stuff is a good way to get rid of anger and hurt, and any other pesky emotions.'

Clearly I don't appear convinced, but that doesn't deter him.

Ethan makes me change into overalls from his van and hands me safety glasses and gloves before giving me a quick lesson in swinging sledgehammers, which I find funny.

He lifts my locs to make sure my glasses are properly fixed to my face, and electricity shoots down my spine as his fingers brush my neck.

'Don't want you hurting yourself,' he says quietly, before stepping back, his eyes all over me. 'I can't decide if I like this more than those shorts you wore on Sunday.'

I laugh, but I'm blushing so hard. 'Have you hit your head today?'

He snorts in denial as we make our way back through the manor. 'Nah, not at all.' He tortures me further when he rests a brief hand on my back to guide me out to the garden. 'Remember, you need to swing it up and around your body and then let your hands slip when you bring it down.'

I struggle to keep his instructions straight in my head. *God, he smells good.* 'Um, okay . . .'

'I'll show you,' he says.

Once we're in front of a pile of paving slabs, he stands close beside me with the sledgehammer in his hands – and learning how to swing it quickly becomes the least of my problems.

My stomach begins to ache when he passes me the sledgehammer. 'The gloves should stop it, but it can hurt your hands if you don't hold it tight enough, so make sure you do.'

'Okay.' *Damn, I didn't realise using one of these was so involved.* 'Am I good to go now?' I ask, pulling my glasses down.

Please be done and move away from me . . .

Josh chuckles from where he's climbing a ladder up to a window on the first floor. 'Eager beaver, ain't ya, gal?'

'I was promised fun.' *And I need a distraction.*

SUCKERS

Ethan stacks a few more slabs on top of the others before stepping back. 'She's all yours.'

I breathe easier then, but the excitement also grips me as I bring the hammer down, just like Ethan showed me. However, I barely make a chip in the top slab, and the others only slip over themselves.

'Put your weight behind it . . . Give it all you've got.'

I close my eyes with the next swing and jump before I bring the hammer hard down in front of me, this time causing the top slab to crack clean in half.

'Ha!' I yell, accomplished.

Ethan laughs. 'That's more like it.'

And this is definitely fun.

I manage to break a handful more of the paving slabs, and my lungs begin to burn. But the deeper I breathe, the stronger I can smell Ethan; and my gums begin to throb.

I drop the sledgehammer down on the dirt beside me and whip off my safety glasses. 'That's hard work.' I take a few steps back from him, but he follows, his eyes soft with an emotion I can't quite pinpoint. 'I don't know how you do it,' I continue, rambling now. 'I need a rest already.'

It looks like he's about to say something else when we hear Grandma's car pull up, and he curses under his breath. 'I should get to that spare room. But if you ever want another go, let me know.'

'I will and thank you, Ethan. This really helped.'

He says, 'Anytime, Gabby,' before I run inside, clutching my chest. I don't stop running until I'm in my room, and then I run over to the mirror to check my mouth.

Oh god, that was so close . . .

There was no doubting the attraction between Ethan and me

after we hung out on Sunday, but I've been skirting around him in the manor since, making sure to direct our conversations away from his compliments or offers to hang out again.

But that has all gone out the window. I can still feel his hand on the small of my back, his warm breath on my neck.

I run my tongue over my fangs when they appear with the memory of his scent.

If only he knew how hard I'm struggling to resist him . . .

My desires run away with me as I walk over to my bed and, before I know what I'm doing, I've ripped the lid off the vial of blood.

I close my eyes as I inhale, and I moan while my body trembles. I imagine what Ethan's blood would taste like, if it would resemble the scent of this one; slightly sweet, coppery . . .

How would he react if I bit him?

What if he liked it?

I gasp before slipping the lid back on the vial, and then I climb into bed and slip my hand between my thighs while I see it play out in my mind.

Oh, my . . .

I watch Grandma kneel beside the unlit fireplace in the living room. She's explaining that once I have control of my shift, I'll be able to use the fire within me at will.

She reaches her hand towards the logs, and flames begin to flutter over her skin. 'And then you can' – she rests her hand down on the logs to set them alight – 'light things, like this.'

'I can't wait,' I say, genuinely excited, but the feeling doesn't stay.

She smiles as she comes to sit beside me. 'Have you begun to feel the fire inside yet?'

I nod, but I can't muster any excitement over that. I'm so

confused by what I did after seeing Ethan earlier. I know it's natural to be aroused by scents and blood, but still, the way it overtook me like it did has shaken me up.

'Everything okay, dear?'

'Mostly.' I tuck my knees up against my chest. 'Why does our desire spike more around certain people?'

She thinks about her answer. 'I suppose it's like anything we like. Some people are more attractive, some foods are more delicious, some scents are more pleasing . . . All those things can arouse emotions in the body.'

'So how do I stop it?'

'Oh, Gabrielle, you don't want to stop it.' Grandma looks at me with horror, like I'm crazy for even considering that. 'You only need to find ways to satisfy your desires in a safe way, or learn how to counter your triggers.'

I scoff. 'How? By not breathing? By never finding anyone attractive? By locking myself away forever?'

'You are a new soucouyant discovering herself,' she says, sympathetically. 'You won't always feel this way.'

I stare at the fire. 'I wish I could believe that.'

She sighs. 'Do you still have the blood I gave you?'

'Yes . . . I haven't tasted any, but I have been smelling it,' I confess, but then I think of earlier, and my confusion transforms into rage. 'I *hate* that I'm like this.'

I feel Grandma's hand on my shoulder. 'Gabrielle . . .'

'It's not fair!' I turn to face her. 'Why can't I be normal?'

Her eyes soften. 'Why would you want to be?' She sits closer, wiping my cheek when I begin to cry. 'Yes, I know at the moment things are hard, but if you try to see past that . . . Think of all the incredible things being like us entails.'

I squeeze my eyes shut, willing this all to go away. 'I don't know if I'm mentally strong enough.'

'You are, and it *will* get better, I promise you. It seems impossible now, but you *can* live a normal life. Slow and steady. I'm here to help you in any way I can for as long as it takes. You *can* do this, Gabrielle. You only have to believe you can.'

Chapter Fourteen

I rest my head against the tiles in the shower, breathing slowly as the steaming water nips at my back.
I did it again.
When I woke up, the thought of *Might as well try this again*, turned into *God, it smells so good*, and then one touch under the covers with my tingling hands led to another. The relief that came afterwards hit different this time, and there's no denying I feel much better.

However, I could do without the mixed emotions that came after the comedown.

Maybe I need to accept that 'self-love' is one of my coping mechanisms. Or maybe I'm going insane? I groan. *I really need my bass so I can shut my mind up.*

After dragging myself out of the shower, I sit on my bed to write down my thoughts from this morning, but as soon as I'm done, I bury my head in my pillow and scream at the vial of blood beneath it.

Maybe I am *going crazy.*

Seriously, what the hell is wrong with——?

I roll back over and stare at the ceiling as a realisation hits me. *My period is due.* It's got to be the reason why my emotions have been so heightened over the blood situation. It would make sense and, when I think about it, there have been moments over the past few months that I've felt like this.

I get up to get dressed. Maybe I should ask Maria about it. Surely she's been through this, too?

I unlock my phone to text her before I leave my room, but I see a message from her.

Maria: Hey, girl. You okay? Up for coming to the cove tonight? Let me know. x

It's good to know her friends haven't told her not to invite me again, but I should probably stay home considering my mood is fluctuating like the weather.

I did have a good time last time, though, and it's colder today, which probably means the beach will be a bit windier so there'll be less of a chance of scents setting me off . . .

I could talk to her in person, too.

Me: Hey, babe. I'm good, are you? I'm up for the cove. What time are you heading there? x

Maria: Around 7? Wanna meet me at the abbey again? x

SUCKERS

Me: Sure. Be there then x

Maria: Cool x

I drop my phone on the bed and walk over to my dresser, thinking about what I'm going to wear.

And I can't help but wonder if Ethan will be there tonight.

Maria's been quiet for the last five minutes I've followed her through the woods towards the cove. My gut's long told me there's something up with her, and the longer her shoulders stay hunched up, the more I want to ask what's wrong.

She smacks another branch out of her way, which I have to duck to avoid. *Is this girl for real?* She keeps muttering under her breath, too, completely oblivious to the abuse she's inflicting on me. Maybe there's something in the water, because her mood is worse than mine.

'Are you good, babe?' I ask, glaring at her back.

'Yeah.' She shrugs, but this time I hear what she mumbles after that. 'Just.'

I nearly trip when the breeze from another branch strokes my face. *That's it.* 'Nah, seriously, what's wrong?'

She hisses, I think. 'Life gets to me sometimes.' She glances back at me. 'You're new to what you are. I don't wanna . . . Forget it.'

I stop walking, but she takes a few more strides before she realises and turns around.

'What?'

'I wanna hear what you were going to say.'

She laughs bitterly. 'You really don't.'

I walk over to her, remembering who this girl can be. *I can't push her.* 'Want me to share first?'

She shrugs hopelessly. 'Sure.'

'All right . . .' I find a tree to lean my back on and then I kick the dirt at my feet. 'I bit someone back home. I didn't mean to – I didn't know what I was.' I lift my head when she stays silent. 'I ran off after he started screaming, and I burst into flames in the middle of the street. Ended up flying to my house and crashing through my bedroom window. Now I'm here.'

She blinks. 'Damn.'

Her reaction actually makes me laugh a little. 'Yeah. So, I'm here not only so my grandma can teach me how to control everything, but also because I'm running away from my problems. And to top it off, the attempts to not be triggered by things that smell good are making me do some really crazy shit.'

Her eyes narrow. 'Crazy shit, like what?'

My cheeks warm. *I can't tell her about Ethan.* 'My period is due, and when I smell the blood I'm practising with . . .' I groan. 'I've been getting myself off on it.'

She rolls her eyes. 'Girl, that's normal. No need to be shy about that. I think all of us use masturbation to take the edge off things when they get intense, which they often do. The craving for it turns us on.' She shrugs. 'And scents. They trigger the feel-good hormones.'

I immediately relax. 'Oh . . .'

She smiles. 'Bless ya. Sounds like you've been through it recently. No wonder you've been so uptight.'

'Oh, thanks.'

She crosses her arms. 'Am I lying though?'

'I guess not.'

She smiles sympathetically before coming to stand in front of me. 'About the running away thing, I would've done the same, and

I have a few times. My "gift" – as our families like to call it – have gotten me into more than a little trouble over the years . . .' She seems to hesitate for a moment. 'I might seem cool with what I am, but there are times . . . I fucking *hate* it.'

My heart aches with how she says that. 'Truthfully, so do I.'

Her eyes soften. 'It's not all the time, don't get me wrong, and there are perks to being like us. I never needed to be normal or fit in anyways, so I don't care that I'm different. It's just the thirst . . . Some days, to resist sinking my teeth into someone random, it's crippling. And I've tried *everything* . . . Every time I think I've got a hold on it, something triggers me, or my period comes around, or someone smells good, or I catch the scent of someone's wound, and it's like I've made no progress at all.' Her lip trembles. 'It's so, *so* tiring.'

My heart constricts when her eyes begin to glisten, so I wrap my arms around her as tight as I can. 'I might not have known what I am for as long as you have, but one thing I already know for certain is that it's not easy.'

She shakes her head on my shoulder. 'It's not . . . I'm sorry . . . I didn't want you to see this side of me. I wanted to give you hope.'

'You *have* given me hope,' I tell her when she steps back to look at me. 'I never would have considered going back to that group if it weren't for you, and I wouldn't be here now, hanging out with "normal" people, if you weren't.' I smile when she does. 'I already know it's not all great being what we are, but I'd rather see the raw side of it from my friend, not a lie. So keep it real with me, okay?'

She takes a deep breath and nods. 'All right, I will.'

I smile and wipe her cheeks. 'I probably can't, but is there anything I can do to help?'

'You listening to me going on has helped more than you know, so thank you.' She pauses. 'There is one other thing, though.'

'Yeah?'

'Don't try to hide it if you struggle, with *anything*. The mastering stage is hard for all of us, and the process of taming our thirst is, frankly, brutal. Like I've said, if you need help, *ask*. Loving on yourself to help relieve the tension is fine, but don't try to numb or soothe it with other stuff that's not safe.'

'Thanks.' I chuckle. 'But if I do need help, I'll ask.'

She grabs my elbow when I move to step around her. 'Promise me, Gabby.'

I blink when I see her eyes have turned a glowing green. 'I promise, I will.'

'Good,' she says, sounding relieved, and so am I when her eyes return to normal. 'Let's get out of here. I need a drink after that.'

I agree as I follow behind her again.

What the hell was that all about?

I pull my hoodie up over my head when Maria comes to sit next to me. The others playing volleyball are currently complaining about being a man down on one of the teams, and I'm really not trying to be dragged into—

'Gabby . . .?' I hear Ethan yell. 'Wanna play?'

'Nope.' I pull the strings on my hood. 'I'm good.' I've been fine being around him as I came this morning, but I don't want to push my luck.

'Oh, come on!'

I lift my head. 'Trust me, ask the others — I'm really bad!'

He rolls his eyes, I think. I've had a few cocktails tonight, which may have not been the best idea, and the sun setting over the cove is already having an effect on the shots being played by the majority of the group to my right.

If I play, they'll definitely lose.

'I thought you wanted some pointers? This is your chance!'

'Ugh, why did I say that?' I groan.

Maria giggles as she opens a can of martini and starts digging her bare feet into the sand. 'Take the hint, Ethan. She doesn't wanna play.'

'How's she gonna get better if she doesn't at least try?' Willow shouts over. 'Come on, Gabby. Just one game. It's almost dark, anyway.'

'Ugh. Fine. Don't say I didn't warn you, though.' I skulk over to my team, almost tripping when my boots sink into the sand. Bare feet would probably be better, but I'm not taking them off. I'm freezing as it is.

'That's more like it,' Jason says, on my way past him to my designated space beside Ethan.

I eye him, making everyone laugh.

Not Alok, though. He's barely cracked a smile all night. I didn't miss his inward sigh when he came down the dunes and saw me here, but I wasn't glared at, which I'm thankful for because I wasn't triggered.

Ethan quickly gives me a few techniques like he promised, while the others watch. 'Follow the ball and you'll be fine, all right?' he says in my ear.

I pray for strength as I widen my stance like he tells me to. 'If you say so . . .'

Jason blows the whistle, and I follow the ball from Ava's arms to Henry's, who lunges forward to smack it back to the other side. Willow gets it next, almost crashing into Mikey when she hits it back to Ethan. He goes back and forth with Alok and Henry after that, until Mikey fires the ball straight at me, making me close my eyes and shoot my arms up to protect my face.

'Oooh . . .'

Everyone erupts with a mixture of gasps and laughter, and when I open my eyes, I see Alok on the sand, throwing daggers from his eyes at me.

'What happened?' I ask Ethan beside me.

He smirks. 'Alok didn't even see it coming. Nice shot, Gabs. I knew you had it in ya.'

Alok dusts down his jeans when he gets up, and I shudder when his jaw clenches.

Better try not to aim in his direction for the rest of this game . . .

Not that I had been aiming at all.

'Told you I'm usually on the winning team,' Ethan says, as we make our way over to the bonfire with the others. 'Want a drink?'

'Yeah, sure.' I've warmed up now, and the win has lifted my mood.

'Well done, babe,' Maria says, when I sit back beside her and hand her a can of strawberry daquiri.

'Thanks.' I chuckle.

Her eyes light up. 'I meant for knocking Alok on his ass.'

I smirk. 'It wasn't even intentional.'

'Which made it even better.'

I catch Alok's gaze when she toasts me, and my smile slips, so I turn my attention to Jason playing 'Someone You Loved' by Lewis Capaldi on his six-string guitar. It's a little out of tune, but he's hitting most of the chords just fine, although they're quite simple so aren't exactly easy to mess up.

SUCKERS

Beside me, Maria starts to sway with her vape when Willow and Ava begin to sing, so I do the same, appreciating the moment under the moonlight.

Jason plays a mixture of songs, including some Nirvana that the girls and a few of the boys get up and dance to. It's a vibe, and it reminds me of when I used to jam with the band back in London. Drinking in the studio, coming up with new versions of our favourite songs . . . I do miss them, and I keep catching myself wondering what they've been doing in my absence. Whether they've replaced me in the band yet, and if Kyle's told them all what I did . . .

'I saw your dad yesterday,' Henry says to Alok, after he lights a cigarette. 'He asked me if I wanted to come to his anti-vamp rally in town tomorrow night. Are you going?'

Maria groans beside me. 'Here we go again.'

'Nah, I'm helping my uncle tomorrow night,' Alok says. 'You should go, though, bro. Dad's found some pretty solid evidence about where they hang out.'

Ava is visibly concerned. 'Where do they?'

Alok's jaw tenses. 'The woods, but I can't tell you which one. Don't want those dirty bloodsuckers finding out and moving locations.'

I swallow down my new level of hatred for him. *What an asshole.*

Noah holds Ava's hand. 'Where's the rally being held?'

'The town hall.'

'Not gonna lie,' Ethan says, chucking another piece of driftwood onto the fire, 'I still ain't convinced they exist. Maybe it's just a group of sickos trying to scare everyone. You know what Whitby's like. It's probably a group obsessed with Dracula.'

'Think what you want, but if you saw some of the things I have . . .' Alok stabs a stick meant for the fire into the sand beside it and twists slowly. 'There are some sick, evil things in the world, bro. You should all start carrying crosses.'

Maria snorts. 'Are you for real?'

Alok's eyes darken. 'This ain't a joke.'

'I never said it was, but crosses, really? You'll be saying garlic repels them next.'

'It does.'

Maria crosses her arms. 'And how do *you* know?'

He looks away from her in disgust. 'I just do.'

'What a dick,' I mutter.

'Forget him,' Maria insists, turning to talk to Mikey beside her. But I keep listening.

The group is definitely split on what's true and what's not. Mikey's on Alok's side, and so is Jason; Ethan, Henry and Peter think a bunch of weirdos are behind the attacks; and Ben and Willow don't believe any of it.

Jason stops playing his guitar. 'How do you explain the videos and pictures on YouTube then?'

'AI, bro.' Ben laughs. 'You can make anything look real these days.'

Alok grits his teeth. 'People have been in the hospital. Are you fucking dumb?'

Ethan glares at him after Ben recoils. 'Can you chill? Not everyone has to agree with you and your dad.'

'Was I talking to you?'

Ava and Noah start muttering amongst themselves, but I can't make out what about. Maria's trying to listen in, too, but the conversation gets more heated, and soon, Henry and Peter are trying to calm everyone down.

'This happens every time this shit gets brought up,' Henry says to me. 'You'd think they'd have learnt by now.'

Peter glares at the group like naughty children. 'Maybe one day they will.'

Willow seemingly notices my concern. 'Don't worry, we'll all be friends again by the end of the night. It's all love, really.'

Alok definitely doesn't agree. Him and Ethan just had an entire stare-off.

I force out a smile. 'It's good that you don't fall out.'

'Most of the time,' Jason mutters before swigging his drink, and then everyone laughs when he starts to strum 'Kumbaya' on his guitar.

'Let Gabby have a turn,' Willow says. 'She plays.'

Ethan immediately looks over at me and smiles. 'Oh, yeahhhh. You can play guitar, can't you?'

I hold my hand up. 'I'm good on that.' Especially after *that* conversation.

'If you lied about being able to play,' Alok snipes, 'just say so.'

Oh, so I guess it's my turn to be picked on by him now. 'I didn't lie, actually, but bass is what I play most.'

He swigs his beer. 'Sure.'

'She did say that,' Maria says, defending me. 'Leave her alone.'

'Well, if she doesn't play guitar, she shouldn't've said she could.'

Ethan throws daggers at him. 'What the f—'

You know what . . .? I hold my hand out to Jason. 'Give it here.'

'You don't have to prove anything to him,' Maria hisses in my ear once I have Jason's guitar on my lap. 'He ain't worth it.'

'I know he isn't.' I twist the pegs on the guitar to retune it. My head's foggy, so I have to concentrate, hard. The alcohol swimming through my veins is definitely going to hinder me, but when I strum the strings with my fingertips and it causes me to close my eyes, I know I'm good.

I look up to see everyone is watching me. 'Requests?'

'Can you play "Three Little Birds"?' Maria asks quietly beside me.

When I turn to look at her, I understand why and I nod, remembering our conversation in the woods earlier and feeling a little sad because of it. '"Three Little Birds", it is.' And an easy one, too.

I spit a glance at Alok when I play the first chord, but then I focus. Perhaps I shouldn't entertain his crap, but music is a part of who I am, so the hell am I going to let him try and shade me over it.

I think of my dad through the intro. He always loves me playing this. Like a lot of people I know, he's a big fan of reggae, so when I played this over and over again when I got my first guitar, it was one of the songs he never complained about. He said it cheered him up.

And now I get to do the same for Maria.

Maria gasps beside me when I begin to sing. 'The hell, girl? You sing, too?'

I chuckle when the others ask the same. 'Well, yeah,' I say between lyrics. 'I thought I told you I was in a band back home?'

'She told me,' Ethan says, and I playfully roll my eyes. 'Even better than I thought.'

'Right,' Maria gushes. '*Girl* . . . you sound amazing.'

I give her a glance and smile. She really is a sweetheart, no wonder everyone likes her. Always supportive, always encouraging others. I'm so thankful I met her.

'Dance with me, babe?' I hear Ava ask Noah, causing me to look over to them.

'Can you play "Locked Out of Heaven" after?' Willow asks, coming to sit beside Maria. 'I love that song. Do you know it?'

SUCKERS

A bit cringe, but . . . 'Sure.'

And then I catch Alok staring at my fingers, seemingly miles away.

Yeah, not got much to say now . . .

I finish the song and play Willow's request next, but I don't sing along.

'Do you not know the lyrics?' she asks, disappointed.

'Yeah, but—'

And then sirens sound from further down the cove, and we're all suddenly blinded by blue lights.

'*Ruuuunnnn!*' everyone starts to yell, rushing to pick up their things.

I stumble over to Jason to give him back his guitar, but when I spin around, I smack my face against Alok's chest.

'Watch where you're going,' he barks. 'Move!'

I gape before rubbing my throbbing nose. 'You move. You're the one going the wrong way!'

He ignores me and glances in the direction of the sirens, so I barge past him – but I trip over and hit the sand with a thud.

He curses under his breath. 'Sor—'

I yank my arm away from his grip and quickly turn onto my back, ignoring the throbbing in my ankle. 'You seriously tripped me?'

'No, I—'

'Yes, you did. Who the hell does that?'

He looks away from me briefly before offering me his hand again. 'Save it for next time. We need to get out of here.'

'Leave me alone.' I attempt to get up myself, but my right ankle throbs, so I only make it into a crouch.

'Chill out.'

I scoff and prepare to cuss him out, but Maria starts yelling behind me.

'Go,' I tell her as I finally manage to stand. 'I'll be right behind you.' The last thing I want to do is make her day worse by getting her into trouble with the police.

She turns to run into the woods, while I start hobbling up the dunes after her with Alok, annoyingly, following close behind me.

'Let me help you,' he insists, trying to wrap an arm around my back.

'No!' I hop to keep as much weight off my ankle as possible, but although I can move quite fast, I'm hindered further by the police shouting behind us.

'For fuck's sake.' Alok swoops me up over his shoulder, initially shocking the hell out of me, but then I hit his back and yell at him to let me go when he starts running.

'Just leave me!' I fight against his hold, stopping momentarily when a warmth begins to spread inside my belly. *Maybe I'll be able to shift* . . . 'Let me down, now!'

He holds me tighter. 'Just wait—'

I start screaming. If he just leaves me here, I could—

'Stop, both of you, right now!'

The heat within me cools and, with it, so does my spark of hope. There's no way we're getting away from the police.

Alok obviously comes to the same conclusion.

'This is *your* fault,' I hiss, when he lowers me to the sand.

He gives me a dismissive glance as we're told to put our hands up and lights are shone in our faces. 'Nah, this is all you.'

Chapter Fifteen

'Community service? Are you *serious*?'

The policewoman across from me remains stone-faced. 'You're lucky you're not being charged with an offence.'

'But I didn't do anything wrong!'

'Calm down,' Grandma hisses in Spanish.

I gape at her. 'I *didn't*, though.'

The policewoman thinks otherwise and starts listing my 'crimes' for the millionth time. 'Antisocial behaviour, being drunk and disorderly . . .'

I roll my eyes. *Hardly*. 'This is a joke.'

'You and Mr Shaw will report to the harbour on Monday morning where you will be met by a member of the offender management team.'

'Who's Mr Shaw?'

'Alok,' Grandma says, sympathetically.

Oh, *hell* no. 'I'm not doing community service with him.' They must be out of their minds!

'So you'd prefer the charges?'

Is this woman deaf? 'I didn't *do* anything.'

'A criminal record is for life, Miss Baudelaire. Are you sure you—'

'Gabrielle.' Grandma's stern voice cuts in before I can say anything stupid.

'Ugh. *Fine*. Can I go now?'

Her eyebrow lifts.

'Can I go now, *please*?'

'You may.' She hands me a piece of paper, and then I hear Grandma apologising to her for my rudeness as we make our way out of the interview room and down the sterile hall.

'She's visiting from London . . . She's never been in trouble before . . .'

'I understand that, but she was *seen by several officers . . .'*

Whatever.

And when I see Alok in reception with what must be his parents, the anger I felt at the cove returns with a vengeance.

None of them have seen me. It seems Alok's parents are also busy trying to fight his corner. His dad – the infamous Oliver, in the flesh – is the more animated one of the group, while the woman with long blonde hair seems to be fussing over Alok like he'd never commit a crime in his life.

Which we haven't, but still. As far as I'm concerned, and from what I've experienced in London, police don't care much about what the youth have to say. Especially when you don't 'look' English.

It seems the local mayor's status fails to get his son out of punishment, because Oliver's jaw clenches, before the policeman with them hands Alok a piece of paper.

That's when Alok turns around and sees me.

'This is your fault,' we say in unison, and then I huff before practically being dragged by Grandma out of the police station.

'You need to calm down,' she says, releasing my arm. 'You don't want to be on Oliver's radar any more than the authorities'.'

'I didn't *do* anything, though,' I insist, limping towards the car. It's dark out here so I need to be careful not to twist this ankle again. 'And community service? With *him*, of all people? If he hadn't tripped me, I wouldn't even be here!'

'It won't be for long—'

'I don't care. They were just looking for something to do. Not even the police in London are this petty. Once they'd found out I hadn't been in trouble before, they would've just sent me home.'

She eyes me before unlocking the car. 'This isn't London, Gabrielle.'

'Don't I know it.'

'What's done is done,' she says, once we're in the car. 'You've not been charged and you're safe. That's all that matters. Once you're home and get some sleep, you'll realise that, too, and hopefully be in a better mood before our visitors arrive later.'

'Ughhhhh.' I rest my head back. 'I forgot Mum and Dad are coming today.'

'Exactly. Now be grateful it's just community service they gave you.'

I sigh as she starts to drive. She's right, but I *still* didn't do anything wrong. And if Alok had just left me like I'd asked . . . I turn to face Grandma. 'One good thing did happen whilst getting caught.'

She glances my way. 'What's that?'

'I think I almost shifted when I was running from the police, but I managed to control it.'

Her eyes widen. 'Something like that happening will do it. That *is* good news.'

'Yeah, but what do I do now? How do I use it?'

She stops at the entrance to the car park to check for traffic on the road. 'You let it grow and we wait.'

The morning's long gone by the time I wake up, and although I'm excited to get my bass back in my arms today, I'm not looking forward to Mum's and Dad's reactions to my community service.

I close my eyes but open them again because it's almost one in the afternoon and I know they'll be here soon. I also need to call Maria, like I promised. She was blowing up my phone while I was at the police station, asking me if I was okay and apologising.

But I don't blame her. It's not *her* fault.

'I twisted my ankle,' I tell her while I do my eyeliner. 'So they caught me.'

'Oh my god, I'm so sorry. I never should've left you.'

I glance down at my phone on loudspeaker. 'Chill. I'm the one who told you to go. Me getting caught has nothing to do with you. If it's anyone's fault, it's Alok's. I swear he tripped me up on purpose. He was trying to help me, like it was an accident, but my gut was telling me otherwise.'

'*What?*'

'Yeah. He's such a dick, and now I have to do bullshit community service with him for, like, a month.'

'Don't lie.'

'I swear!' I rummage around in my make-up bag for my black-tinted lip gloss. 'They gave me sixty hours over the next four weeks. They said it was either that or they'd charge me for antisocial behaviour or some crap.'

I'd asked why it couldn't be condensed down into fewer days, but Alok supposedly works at his uncle's jewellery shop, so they'd had to fit it around that.

I lower my voice. 'And what makes it worse is that I was *so* close to finally shifting again, babe. Of course I was happy about being able to stop it from happening while I was around humans, but I was literally begging Alok to leave me there so I didn't have to control it.'

'Oh, girl . . .'

I sigh. 'God knows what they're gonna have us doing, but I'm already dreading it. You heard the way he was talking about us last night. I'm gonna end up killing him.'

She snorts. 'Sorry, I know it's not funny. I feel for you, I really do. Your parents are coming today, aren't they?'

'Yep, and I know for a fact they're gonna be disappointed.' I pull the tie out of my locs and slump in the nearest chair. 'How did I grow up in London without so much as a warning and then come to one of the deadest towns in the UK and get community service?'

'It's 'cause the police here ain't got anything better to do with their time, that's why. They've got more important things to deal with in the capital.' *She's right about that.* 'I know it didn't end well, babe, but I wanted to thank you for such a good night. I needed to take my mind off some things, and you did that. You were amazing on that guitar, and you really cheered me up. Why didn't you tell me you could sing?'

Well, at least last night wasn't for nothing. 'I thought I had.'

'Have you written your own songs?'

'Some. I wasn't the lead singer, though.'

'Well, I could listen to you sing all day. You remind me of Lauryn Hill with a little Ella Mai mixed in. When we find somewhere else to hang out, please play again.'

I chuckle. 'I'll play for you again, don't worry. Anyway, I have to go, but I'll text you, all right?'

'That's cool. Have a good time with your parents, and try not to worry.'

That's easier said than done. 'Thanks, babe.'

'Ethan's been looking for you,' Grandma says, when she sits down at the table with me.

I take a break from scoffing down her leftover fried fish. 'It will be about last night. He was there, too.'

'Ah, I figured it— Hello, Ethan.'

I turn around, and he nods at me, but then Grandma gets up from the table.

'Back in a moment. I need to make sure your parents' room is ready.'

'Okayyyy.' I frown at her back when she leaves, but then I blink with how fast Ethan pulls up the chair beside me.

He has bags under his eyes. 'Are you okay?'

'Yeah.' I continue eating, focusing on how good the rice tastes. 'Are *you*?'

'I'm fine. What happened last night? We waited around at the abbey for ages but you didn't show up. Did you go home another way?'

'Nope, I got caught.' I shrug, before giving him a rundown of what happened.

'The hell?' He scoots back so he can look under the table, and then my foot is on his lap and he's gently skimming his fingers over my skin. 'How is it now? Have you taken any painkillers?'

He's so . . . I watch him dote over me for a moment before I answer. 'I didn't need any. I'm still limping but it's better than it was. They put a support band, or whatever it's called, on it at the station. It's been better since.'

My soucouyant side has definitely helped speed up the healing process.

He gives it another tender caress before he carefully lowers it, and then he plants his elbow on the table, causing a wave of his scent to rush at me. 'I should've stayed with you. I never would've let you get caught.'

Ethan . . .

'Thank you, but it is what it is.' I get back to my food so I can focus on something other than the way he makes me feel. 'I have more important things to focus on right now anyway.'

Like how this juice is doing absolutely nothing *to quench my thirst.*

'You worried about what your parents are going to say?' he asks, his soft gaze making my stomach clench.

'Yeah, something like that.' Regardless of how old I am, I still care what they think of me. 'Cross your fingers that they don't give me too much of a hard time.'

He rests a hand on my arm. 'It'll be okay. They'll be happy to see you after so long.'

'I hope so.' I look at his mouth when he smiles, and my pulse begins to quicken. 'I really hope so . . . Did you get home okay?'

'Eventually, yeah.' He pulls his hand away but only to rest it on the table. 'It's a shame the police turned up. Last night was insane. I had such a good time.'

'I think everyone did.' And it was good to see Ethan outside work again. I kept seeing him looking over to Maria and me, and he made sure to offer me a drink whenever he saw me without one. 'It was a bit crazy at the end, though.'

His eyes light up. 'Just a little. You should've seen them falling over trying to get away from the police. Mikey cut his hand, too. It was messy.'

Thank God I wasn't there for that . . . 'Damn, is he okay?'

'He's fine. He can be a little clumsy sometimes. I'm just glad you're okay.' He lifts a few of my locs behind my shoulder and exhales deeply. 'I was so worried when you didn't end up with the rest of us.'

That makes my heart flutter. 'Sorry to have worried you, but I'm fine.' I get up to wash my plate, gathering myself while my back is turned. 'I appreciate you checking on me, though.'

'Of course.' I hear him get up from the table. 'I'd better get back to work before Josh starts complaining, but I'll catch up with you later. Good luck with your parents, all right?'

I turn to see him lingering in the doorway. 'Thank you.'

Chapter Sixteen

My parents weren't happy about the community service, but Ethan was right, they were happier to see me. Mum even cried. But so did I, because I finally got my bass back.

We spent last night catching up, but mostly it was them asking questions about how I'm getting on with my 'training'. Grandma sang my praises, and when the three of them said how proud of me they were, it made me realise that I'm doing better than I thought.

I just need to keep using my time with Ethan to get a better hold over my urges.

I'm hoping I'll be like my great-great-grandma Lucila and that the more time I spend around him, the easier it will be to get it under control. However, it would probably help if I knew exactly why he triggers it. Is it because I like him, or is it because of his scent and, deep down, I crave to know what he tastes like?

Ugh . . .

'How's your ankle now?' Maria asks, while I wait for her to finish vaping outside the group meeting. Grandma dropped me off a little early because I didn't want to miss the opening conversation this week.

'Better. My mum gave it a massage last night and she's always said she has healing hands. It only hurts when I walk too fast now.'

'That's a thing, y'know, the healing hands. My grandma used to say the same.' She tucks her vape into her pocket and holds the door for me to follow her inside. 'She used to cook this hot pepper soup that made me forget all my problems.' She smiles wistfully as we walk toward the hall. 'I miss that.'

'That soup sounds amazing, and so does she.'

'She was. It broke me to pieces when she passed away when I was seventeen, but now . . . I'm glad she didn't know what I was. She knew about my dad, and I got the feeling she was unsettled by it. I would've hated for her to feel the same about me.' She closes her eyes briefly and sighs. 'I would've hated for her to be disappointed in me too,' she mutters.

'Hey,' I say, holding her arm before she can open the door to the hall, but she shakes her head and opens it anyway.

'Come on, I want to hear the news this week, I heard there's been another attack.'

I follow behind her to find a seat with the others that have already gathered, my mood sombre because of what Maria's said. The more she lets things about herself slip out in conversation, the more I think she's had a really tough time since she turned eighteen.

SUCKERS

It hurts, because I want to be there for her. It's obvious she needs someone to be. She does nothing but support, encourage and help everyone else around her, yet she barely lets anyone do the same for her. *She gives herself such a hard time*. A few times now, I've wanted her to elaborate on something she's said, but when I offer a safe space for her to open up, she closes herself off instead.

I need to find a way to get those walls down.

Sanse starts by welcoming us all and asking how everyone is, but after that the discussion quickly moves on to Oliver and his rising number of vampire hunters that are due to gather in town for their rally tonight.

'As you may have heard, there was yet another attack in the town last night, and quite a brutal one at that.'

Maria's eyes widen. 'Are they dead?'

'It's touch and go.' She sighs. 'I don't want to worry any of you, but I fear this situation is something we all need to pay close attention to.'

'Do you know who might be behind it?' I ask.

Her expression tells me she at least has an idea. 'There has always been a group of vampires in town that refuse to be . . . helped. I've offered for them to come to our groups several times.'

'So they're bad?'

'I don't like to label them as that. Misguided, perhaps. Rebellious. Unfortunately, there is not much we can do about it. Their "leader" lived in this town long before any of us arrived, and promises were made to ensure she is protected.'

'It might not even be them, though,' Lorenzo says. He looks at me. 'If someone's recently changed and is struggling to tame their hunger, it could be them.'

'So a newly turned eighteen-year-old? Or do you mean someone who has been made into one of us?'

'Could be either.'

'How does someone get *made into* one of us?' I ask.

'There are only two known ways for humans to become like us,' Maria says. 'Drinking or being injected with a vampire's blood, or . . . witchcraft.'

'Oh . . .' *That's why Grandma wanted me to stay away from The Coven – that must be who they're talking about.* 'Have people been changed against their will before?'

'Yes,' Sanse says grimly, 'and it is not something we wish to be repeated, which is why we have always worked to prevent others from finding out the ways in which it can be done.'

I get that . . .

'News of a curfew within the town has been circulating,' Sanse continues, 'and I am almost certain that our mayor will get his wish. However, I will let you all know of anything else we find out at the rally. In the meantime, Larpool Woods is the current focus of the group, so those of you that like to shift into your vampiric forms there, I advise you to stay away.'

'Some were at Mulgrave, too, last weekend,' Viviana says, straightening in her chair. She's a succubus from Romania and has been a member of the group the longest, according to Maria. She's in her fifties but looks nineteen, with bright blue eyes and the most perfectly pin-straight black hair down to her hips. *No wonder people are always falling in love with her.* 'Oliver seems to be splitting his group so they can cover more ground. I assume it's why he's recruiting as hard as he is.'

Sanse agrees. 'None of you has been spotted anywhere, have you?'

Everybody shakes their head.

'We're all being careful,' Maria assures her. 'They just want a valid reason for murder. And Oliver's been desperate to get his hands on a vampire, so how do we know he isn't making up some of these attacks so that if he does get the opportunity, he has a good reason to?'

'She's right,' Lorenzo agrees. 'There does seem to be a lot of them out of nowhere, and I haven't seen much solid proof.'

'We can't be sure,' Sanse says, sounding frustrated, 'which is why we all must be careful. If you all stay away from the areas I've told you, you should have nothing to worry about.'

'They need to mind their own business,' Viviana mutters. 'If only Oliver knew how easy it would be to dismantle their little cult.'

'For real.' Maria smirks at me. 'One look in the eyes is all it would take.'

I pretend to admonish her with a shake of my head, and the majority of the group laughs. 'I believe you.'

Sanse, however, isn't impressed. 'This is serious. Not only is Oliver and his group a threat that grows stronger by the day, but new members due to join our support group here in the north have decided to join other ones in quieter areas because of it. Now, I'm not accusing any of you of heightening tensions; reports of sightings have always been rife, but we *must* lie low. We do not want any more attention to be drawn to us at this time.'

The group agrees with her, but after we're dismissed I pull Maria to the side.

'Maybe I can get some info out of Alok since I'm going to be spending so much time with him.'

'Yes! We never have details on any of the attacks,' Maria agrees. 'But you need to be careful. You saw how much he hates our kind. You can't do anything to put yourself in danger.'

'I won't.'

I don't even wanna talk to him, so I'll have to tackle that first.

After group, Mum, Dad, Grandma and I had fish and chips on Whitby Bay beach. Mum always says it tastes better in the sea air, and we all had to agree.

We checked out the town's war memorial after that and then took a wander around the shops. Dad likes fudge, so he stocked up, and Mum picked up some fridge magnets for her friends at work. I wasn't looking for anything in particular, but I did get another notebook and some more pens. I've been thinking of writing some new music and didn't want to use the same notebook I've been using for my journalling.

The rest of the day was spent hanging around the manor. Both my parents went on a proper exploration of the place, looking behind every door and around every corner. Mum said that when they found the library, Dad took as many books off the shelves as possible, one by one, convinced he was going to find a secret room.

When I left them a little while ago to come up to bed, Dad was scouring Google trying to find out the history behind the building. I told him I hadn't found anything myself, but if my dad's anything, he's determined.

I close the lid on my vial of blood before tucking it back under my pillow. I'm definitely getting better with this, which makes me happy, but I'm still no closer to consciously setting myself on fire, and it's frustrating. Obviously, I'm thankful I didn't shift when I was running from the police and expose myself in front of Alok, but it would be good to know that I have the ability to escape in future if I need to.

SUCKERS

'Gabrielle?' Mum's voice comes from the other side of the door. 'You still awake?'

'Yeah.' I straighten against the headboard. 'You can come in.'

She smiles as she appears, and so do I. It's so good having my parents here, but for some reason, I feel like our relationship has changed. I'm eighteen now, so it's not like they could ground me for getting into trouble with the police, but I still felt the way they handled the news about my community service was calmer than I'd expected. Perhaps me being away from home is making them see me in a new light.

At least, I hope it's that and not that they're scared of me.

'Everything okay, sweetheart?' Mum asks, coming to sit in bed with me.

'Yeah.' I pick up my journal between us. 'I usually get some practice in and write a little before bed. Are you okay?'

She nods while reaching for my hand, and after squeezing it gently, looks at me. 'How are things really going? With everything?'

'It's going well, like I said,' I say, hoping to reassure her, but she doesn't appear to be, and I sigh. She might not be a soucouyant herself, but I forget that she's known Grandma was. 'Some days, it's difficult. Mostly, I manage everything well, but others . . . I've had mixed emotions over a lot of things.'

She nods knowingly. 'Mum told me you've been up and down. She didn't want to invade your privacy, but she mentioned you struggled letting your old perception of the world go.'

'I did.'

'When Mum told me what she was when I turned eighteen and wasn't like her, I felt the same. My mind couldn't grasp that a lot of what I thought was made up as a child was real; that other beings existed, and I could have been one of those beings.' She bites her lip as it quivers. 'I'm so sorry we didn't tell you, sweetheart. I've thought about it every day since you've been gone. I wish I had, so you could've been prepared. Mum always told me to.'

'Mum . . .' I hug her tightly. 'I understand why you didn't . . . I know I was mad . . . But don't beat yourself up about that, okay?' I pull away from her. 'I don't want to think you're sad at home, obsessing over it. Please.'

She sighs deeply. 'I'll try. Have you spoken to anyone from the band yet?'

I shake my head, not liking that reminder. 'No, I haven't spoken to anyone back home. I'm . . . too scared.'

'I understand that, but . . . we had a visitor at the house last week.'

'Who?'

'Kyle.'

'What?' I shift around to face her more. 'When? What did he say?'

'Last Thursday' – she holds her hand up – 'and we didn't tell you only because we thought it would be better to do it in person. He asked if you were home and if he could talk to you. He seemed worried about you, sweetheart. He said they all were. Said he's been trying to call you.'

'Worried?' *I wasn't expecting that.* Angry, shocked, disgusted? Yes.

Definitely not worried . . .

She nods. 'I told him you were away but that I'd tell you he came by.'

'It's probably a trick,' I mutter, not trusting it.

Her eyes resist that idea. 'I didn't get the feeling it was. He seemed concerned. Really.'

'Oh.'

'And your dad thought so, too. Perhaps you should send him a message, see what he wants to say? You can't run from him forever. What about the band?'

'I don't know, I just assumed that they'd replace me after Kyle told them what happened.'

'Well, I think you should find out. You're supposed to be starting university next month. Do you still plan on attending Brighton?'

'I do, yeah, but I guess only the next few weeks will tell.'

'Just think about it, okay? Dad and I have talked, and we understand if you need more time. Maybe a gap year, depending on how well your time here goes. We don't want you to feel pressured. Not now that things are different.'

That's a relief. 'Thanks, Mum. I'll think about it.'

'All right.' She gives me a kiss on my forehead before getting up. 'Get some rest. Knowing your dad, we'll have a busy day exploring again tomorrow.'

That makes me chuckle. 'He said he wants to drive down to Scarborough because he's never been.'

She nods as she holds the door. 'He said the same to me. Goodnight, sweetheart. Love you.'

'Love you, too, Mum.'

I close Lucila's journal and wipe my eyes with the corner of my sheet. I'd been dreading reading more of her story for so long, but I shouldn't have been. Her story has undoubtedly been a rollercoaster of emotions, but Luis accepted her after she finally told him the truth, and they built a beautiful life together.

I get beneath the covers, smiling when I close my eyes. What a perfect way to end my day. A day spent in Scarborough with my family, and a happy ending.

But then I groan when I remember the text I received earlier.

My community service with the devil starts tomorrow at nine in the morning.

I bury my head in my pillow.

Chapter Seventeen

Grandma looks at me as I get out of her car at the harbour. 'Good luck, dear.'

'Thanks, I'm gonna need it.'

I close the car door and then carefully make my way down the steps and across the cobbles toward a tall, grey-haired man in a green high-vis jacket, standing beside the bridge with Alok and two others dressed in worn clothes.

The text message I received yesterday told me not to wear anything I didn't mind getting ruined because of the work we'd be doing, so I chose to wear the same as everyone else here: a hoodie that's seen better days, and a pair of jeans that are beyond ripped and basically revealing half my legs.

Alok studies my slight limp as I join them, and I still feel his eyes on me when I report to the community payback officer, Sam. I spot some stacked buckets, brushes and a jet wash beside him and groan.

'Nice to meet you, Gabrielle. As I've just explained to the others, today you'll be cleaning the graffiti off these walls. There are several areas in the town that need tidying up, so each block of your time will be spent doing as such.' He looks down at his clipboard. 'Are you allergic to anything?'

Yeah, that guy over there. 'Not that I know of.'

He ticks a box. 'Let's get to it then.'

We're each given a set of protective gear to use, including overalls, gloves, glasses, shoe covers and a stylish, bright-green high-vis jacket of our own. Then Sam spends the next twenty minutes telling us how to use the cleaning chemicals and warning us to wear the glasses so we don't accidentally blind ourselves.

'You and Alok can start on this wall here.' He looks to the other pair. 'You two, follow me.'

I hear Alok grumble something when Sam walks off, and I do some grumbling of my own. Removing graffiti I can deal with; it's spending time with this cheerful soul that's the real punishment. He should be doing this on his own. It's *his* fault we're even here.

Ugh. I'm already over it.

I glare at his back when he picks up a spray bottle and wets one of the scrubbing brushes we've been given, but I recoil when my thirst is suddenly triggered. Not for my usual reasons, though; at least, I don't think so. This feels different. Very, very different.

I could easily suck him dry. No, I couldn't. *He'd deserve it, though.* I blink. What the hell? *I hate him.*

Okay, I need to calm down.

Him triggering me like this is giving him way too much power. *Maybe I should try to forgive him. He did say it was an accident. Yeah, right . . . Girl, breathe . . . Think of something else . . .*

SUCKERS

I'm going to literally bake in these overalls. I wonder if they make tinted safety glasses for when it's sunny . . . Seagulls are actually quite cute, aren't they? This harbour stinks. Well, duh, it is a fishing harbour . . .

I question my sanity when I kneel to spray paint-remover on the first letter of the word. *Scratch that forgiveness part. He's definitely a part of the reason we're here.* Then I sit back on my heels and shoot a look of disgust to the slurs sprayed across the grey stone wall in bright red paint.

> **EVIL WALKS AMONGST US**
> **KILL THE BLOODSUCKERS**
> **BEWARE OF THE SUCKERS**

Why even bother with this? It's not as if it's stopped those attacks. I doubt those rebel vampires give a shit about whether this town wants them here or not either, or the woman who apparently leads them.

'People are weird,' I mutter, as I aggressively spray the 'E' again. 'Seriously.'

'You got that right.'

I roll my eyes. *Don't give him the satisfaction . . .*

But he keeps muttering under his breath, agreeing with the slurs, causing my jaw to ache with how hard I have to resist cussing him out. What makes matters worse is that this spray is hardly doing *anything*. Sam said it would basically strip the paint off and that the brush was only to clean off the remnants, but I'm scrubbing and scrubbing . . .

'This is going to take *forever*,' I complain.

'They should leave it up. People need to be warned about those vermin.'

I look up when he says that. 'Are you for real?'

He glares down at me. 'People should know about the dangers around here. You disagree?'

My arm begins to ache as I take my anger out on the wall. 'I don't believe people should be scaremongered into living their lives in fear, no. There's ten times more crime where I'm from, and you don't see things like this.' I dig the bristles of my brush harder into the 'E', switching back and forth between a circular motion and stabbing at it.

'Well, this ain't London. We care about people here, and we'll do whatever we can to warn others about the dangers. Those bloodsuckers *are* real. They lurk around at night, in the woods, hiding in the shadows, waiting to sink their dirty fangs into someone.'

'If what you're saying is true, don't you think it would've been on the news by now?'

He doesn't answer.

'Exactly, and that's because the police and the doctors treating those victims know the truth. Dracula has clearly gone to someone's head, and they're getting off on scaring and hurting people.'

He glances down at me dismissively. 'You're an outsider, what do you know?'

I inhale through my nose, trying to tame the anger spiralling inside.

Please God, let the next three hours go quickly.

'How's your ankle?' he asks, effectively giving me emotional whiplash.

Is this guy okay? 'What do you care?' I spit. 'Doing it damage is what you wanted, right?'

'It was an accident.'

'Sure.'

SUCKERS

'I tried to carry you—'

'You should've left me!' I get up to move further down the wall, away from him, when my skin begins to tingle, and it's not the chemical doing it. Forget trying to get information out of him; I can't stand him for another second. 'Just leave me alone. I don't like you. I just wanna get this shit over with. Less talking to you the better.'

He bursts out laughing after a shocked silence, and then he shakes his head. 'A right fireball, you are.'

I tear my eyes away from him before I end up shooting flames from them.

If only you knew.

'So, how did your first day of torture with Alok go?'

'He's an idiot,' I complain to Maria when I meet her at the abbey. She texted to ask me if I wanted to hang out after my community service finished, but I bet she wishes she hadn't now.

She motions for me to follow her towards the woods. 'Damn, babe—'

'He had the cheek to ask me how my ankle was, but only after he called vampires vermin and me an "outsider",' I grind out, making sure no one is around us. 'I thought learning how to tame my thirst was hard, but spending time with him . . . I don't think I can do it.'

She holds my arm briefly as she sympathises with me. 'I'm sorry to break it to ya, but you still have another fifty-seven hours to go. Maybe ask to work alone?'

'I tried that, but Sam seemed to realise it was because I don't like Alok, and he took great pleasure in telling me no.' I swear it's like he got off on inflicting further punishment.

'*You were given community service with him, so you'll complete it with him*,' he'd said before he dismissed me by turning his back.

Dick.

'Wow, what an asshole.'

'Right? I don't need all this added stress right now,' I say, clambering over the fallen tree into the woods after Maria. 'My emotions are already all over the place.'

'Yeah, and you're close to being able to shift on demand now, aren't you?'

'Yeah,' I groan.

She nods thoughtfully, but then I feel terrible.

'I'm sorry for ranting, babe. How are you?'

'I'm good, mostly.' She yanks a leaf off a tree we pass. 'Still working on my triggers. Mikey cut himself when we were running from the police.'

'Oh, shit, yeah. Ethan told me. Were you okay?'

She laughs bitterly. 'No.'

And then I have to look down, because she's shifted, and her tail is rattling like crazy.

I sidestep out of her way, but she hastily slithers ahead of me and begins coiling herself around a tree. It's then I know how stressed out she must be about this. She and Mikey always get on well when we hang out, and there have been times that I've watched the two of them and wondered if she likes him.

She hisses as she wraps herself tighter around the trunk, her scales camouflaging with the brownish greens. 'I wanted to drink that blood dripping from his hand more than anything . . . I still don't know how I didn't.'

'I get that.' I watch her loosening and tightening her body, until her hisses become less intimidating and frequent. It makes me feel bad for all the other shifters in the group who can't get out as much as they usually do because of those attacks. 'Feeling better now?'

'Yeah,' she mutters after shifting back to herself. She slumps against the tree and looks at me with tired eyes. 'I needed that. Shifting in my bedroom isn't the same.'

'I bet.' I glance at the tree behind her, making out the slight indent of her spiralled form in the bark. 'It makes me wish I had *my* shift under control.'

'So do I.' She walks back over to me, only stopping when she's a foot away. 'It's why I brought you out here. You said you almost shifted the other night, right?'

I nod.

'And after you said your period was due and you were feeling emotional . . .' She smiles. 'Wanna try?'

I'm cautious as I look around at how much height I have before the leaves above us begin.

'If you set anything on fire, I'll help you put it out,' she says, bringing my attention back to her. 'Go on, babe.'

I close my eyes and focus on the warmth deep inside me, how it feels as though it swirls and moves as its own entity. Grandma says it needs to grow, so I focus my intention on willing it to, until my skin begins to tingle.

However, that's as far as I get.

I startle when Maria rests her hand on my arm. 'Keep your eyes closed.'

I do as she says.

'The only time I ever felt a block over my shift is when, deep down, I knew I didn't want to shift. You need to want it, girl. *Really* want it. Maybe you don't feel safe enough to shift because of what happened the first time?'

That question is a slap in the face. *Maybe that's the problem.* Maybe I *am* afraid of it.

'Try to think of it as fun, because it is. Get excited thinking about all the cool shit you'll be able to do while you're on fire. How *powerful* you'll be . . . Your shift is sick, girl. I mean, you can fly!'

I smile because her excitement rubs off on me, and the tingling causes me to shudder.

'Now, think of all the feelings you've been bottling up inside. Imagine how it would feel to release all of that with fire . . .'

I inhale as the emotions rush over me, and the taste of smoke hits the back of my throat. My excitement overwhelms me. *Oh my god . . .* I can sense it's close, but as hard as I try, no heat comes.

'Gabby—'

'I can't get there.' I open my eyes to look at her — and recoil as I do, because she's cast in an amber hue.

Her own eyes widen. 'Your eyes have flames in them!' she gushes excitedly. 'Can you go any further?'

I try for a little while longer, but soon the tingles stop and my vision returns to normal.

'Don't be sad,' she says, seeing my disappointment. 'I reckon you're really close now.'

We start heading back towards the abbey. 'I'll keep trying.'

'Good, 'cause I don't think it's gonna be long. Just remember you might be tired the first few times you try. It takes a lot out of you until your body gets used to it.'

'Grandma said. She's been feeding me up because of it.'

Maria chuckles. 'She's just taking care of you. Do you feel even a little better, though?'

'A little. I'm not so angry . . . Hopefully I'll be able to *not* kill Alok again tomorrow.'

'Forget him.' She links her arm in mine when the opening to the field comes into view. 'We're going to a different cove on Friday night, if you wanna come——? Not many people know about it, but it does require a bit of a longer trek to get there.'

'Yeah, I'm up for that.'

Maybe a trek will do me good.

And if Alok is there, hopefully I'll be too tired to let him rile me up.

Chapter Eighteen

I go looking for Ethan as soon as he arrives at the manor on Tuesday morning. I have an hour before I leave for hell, and I need to spend that time on my bass.

I'm thinking rocking out for a bit before community service might calm me down, because I'm ready to try everything when it comes to not letting Alok get under my skin. I spent a lot of last night tossing and turning, questioning why he does so badly, and I grudgingly had to accept it's not just because of his better-than-everyone attitude.

Alok is hot and, unfortunately, even though he's moody, opinionated and a horrible person, my heightened hormones don't care. If anything, the more he annoys me, the more my emotions are triggered. And they're not the emotions I want to have triggered . . .

I also read some more of Helene's journal. So far, it's been more

SUCKERS

of her struggling not to chase people down into dark alleyways to suck them dry, but I have a feeling a girl who lives in her neighbourhood might be the person she ends up wanting to hurt. She's mentioned Frances a few times, and how that because her father's wealthy she thinks she's better than everyone.

That sounds familiar.

Ethan's carrying a ladder around to the back of the house when I find him. He smiles when he sees me coming, and so do I. He's had a haircut since I've last seen him, and he's gone shorter all over, making his jawline appear more defined.

'Morning.' He gives my ink an appreciative glance, but he always does when I wear a cropped top. 'Can I help you with something?'

'Yes, actually.'

His entire face lights up. 'What is it?'

'I need to know if the plug sockets in the main hall are safe to use? I want to use one.'

He rests the ladder against the wall. 'I can check for you.'

'Thanks,' I say, following him back inside. *I really love how he always offers to help me . . .* 'I only need one.'

'It's cool. It's mostly the sockets on the top floor that need replacing. The ones down here have been fine.' He pulls a rectangular device from his pocket and waves it at me when we reach the hall. 'This will tell me. Any socket in particular?'

'Um . . .' I look around, until I decide on a plug socket on the far-right wall. It's slightly curved and is on the opposite side of the stairs. 'That one?'

He kneels next to it and sticks one of the probes from his device inside, causing the machine to beep several times. But I couldn't be further from interested in what he's actually doing. He's wearing a black vest, and his arms are so damned defined . . . The way his muscles flex as he works makes me inhale sharply, which is such a bad idea, because there are visible beads of sweat across the back of his neck.

I need a drink.

I get a flashback of my fantasy of us after I smelt my vial of blood, and then my gums throb harder than my lower stomach starts to.

He suddenly stands, so I step back. 'It needs replacing. Give me a sec and I'll get one out of the van.'

I nod, and then I hold my chest while he's gone. I'd hate to screw up the friendship Ethan and I have built, so I wish my body would stop trying to complicate things. *He doesn't even think vampires and other creatures exist.* I need to stay focused.

'Got one.' Ethan smiles before getting back to the socket. 'What are your plans for this, then?'

'Uh . . .' I tear my gaze away from his fingers screwing the socket cover off. 'What do I want to do with it?'

He chuckles. 'Yeah.'

'My bass amp.' I look up at the dusty chandelier. 'This room will be perfect to play in.'

'Does this mean I'm gonna get my own personal show?'

I smile down at him. 'You can watch me play, if you want.'

'Are you kidding?' He stands up, so close that my next inhale is his scent alone. 'I've been dying to see you in your element. The guitar was good, real good, but I know the bass is gonna hit differently.'

I blush and laugh nervously. *Girl, move away before you answer that lustful look in his eyes with a kiss.* I step around him to get my bass from the bottom of the stairs. Before I turn, though, he's come to collect my amp and carries it over to plug it in for me.

SUCKERS

'Thanks.' My hands shake as I plug my bass in. *So thirsty . . . Breathe . . . or don't, because Ethan's still so close.* I need a distraction.

I think of what I have to do after this, and I can finally get my shit together enough to sit down on my amp and check that my bass is in tune.

It is, which means my parents were careful with her when they brought her up.

'Do you have a request?' I ask, as I dare to look up at Ethan.

He nods, but he's also smirking. At what, though, I'm not sure. 'I don't know many heavy metal bands, but there is one song I'd love to hear you sing, if you can play it on your bass.'

'I can pretty much play anything on her,' I say, strumming my fingers over the strings to warm up and relishing the way the notes bounce around the tall walls and ceiling. Just as I expected, she sounds incredible in here, but I only have about half an hour before I need to leave.

I wish I had longer.

'"Nothing Else Matters".'

I blink at Ethan's request. 'As in, Metallica?'

He lowers his gaze to my bass. 'That's the one.'

This guy always surprises me. I blend my practice strokes on the chords to his request, and when I tap my foot against the floorboards to replicate the drums, he does the same.

I almost miss my own intro to the lyrics from how hard I internally gush over that move.

Ethan isn't done shocking me, though. He starts humming along, singing the odd line, too, and I have to say, his voice isn't bad at all.

I was not expecting that.

But then, I guess nothing should shock me any more. It hasn't missed me that since I've been here, my passion for heavy metal hasn't been as fierce as it once was. And as I play this one, I'm filled with the same peace I was when I played Bob Marley at the beach.

I look up and catch Ethan smiling while still humming along, but his eyes say so much more than the fact I'm impressing him. The lyrics almost elude me several times because of it, so I close my eyes to finish, only to snap them back open again when he starts clapping.

'Now *that* is talent.'

The giggle that comes out of me is sickening. God, I pray he doesn't see how hard I'm blushing. 'Thanks. It was a good crowd.'

He bows while laughing, but then he looks back down at my bass. 'Are you feeling better now you have her back?'

'So much better.' I stroke my fingers over her smooth body. 'I knew she'd sound good in here.'

He looks around the room. 'Yeah, I can see why you wanted to play in here now.' He sighs softly. 'I could watch you play all day, but I should get back outside. We're working on parts of the roof this week, and I have to do most of the lifting because Josh is getting old as hell.'

I laugh as I get up. 'I need to get to town, anyway.'

'Oh, yeah . . . Will you play when you get home?'

I nod, grinning, as I put her back in her case. 'I'll make sure I leave a few windows open.'

'You better.'

Alok and I haven't said a single word to each other since we got to the harbour an hour ago, and, so far, my thirst hasn't been triggered. I definitely think between partially shifting yesterday and this morning's session on my bass, my mood is steadier.

SUCKERS

Well that and having Ethan's reaction to my playing repeating in my head.

He's so sweet.

I'd already planned to ignore Alok before I got here, so my memories from this morning came in clutch. However, it seems Alok had the same idea as me, because he hasn't so much as looked in my direction.

I spend my time watching and listening to the seagulls flying above and the distant sound of the waves lapping against the boats in the harbour. I'm also enjoying being kissed by the sun during the breaks in the clouds, because we weren't told to wear overalls today if we didn't want to, just our safety glasses.

Not sure about the incoming tan lines, though . . .

'What was your first tattoo?'

I frown before turning to Alok beside me. He's just looked away from my right sleeve, which is covered in different types of flowers, from lilies to skulled roses.

He turns back to me when I don't answer him. 'What?'

I rinse my brush in the bucket of water, debating whether I should be nice and answer his question or not. It could be a trick, though . . . *lulling me into a false sense of security so he can diss me like he always does.*

But, I suppose, *if* we got on to some degree, I could find out more about the vampire attacks and what his dad's up to. And it might pass the time quicker, which would be nice, because so far it's dragged like hell.

'A dagger on my ankle when I was sixteen. A friend did it.'

I see him nodding in my peripheral and figure that's it.

But nope.

'Did it hurt?'

LeeSha Shay

Where is he going with these questions?

'It wasn't too bad. My back piece hurt more.'

'What made you get them?'

I spray some more of the remover on the wall. 'I've always liked tattoos and piercings.' I stop talking. *I don't trust this guy.*

'I've always wanted a tattoo.'

I side-eye him. I hadn't been expecting that at all. 'So, get one.'

He hums, so I turn to face him. 'What? Will your parents not approve?'

'Not at all.' He continues to scrub his area of wall. 'Did yours?'

'My parents have always let me express myself, in whatever way . . .' I remember he's adopted. 'Do yours not let you?'

He laughs bitterly. 'Mum's cool, but my dad . . . he's always been protective.'

'So he's strict?'

He nods.

'But he can't tell you what to do forever. You're your own person, not who he wants you to be.'

He throws me a look. 'He doesn't tell me what to do.'

Right . . . *I swear he just said* . . . 'Get a tattoo then.'

He sighs. 'My tolerance for pain . . . It makes me—'

I breathe a laugh. 'You scared you might cry?'

His head snaps my way. 'No.'

'It's okay.' I smirk. 'I've seen loads of men cry while they've got their bigger ones. Just take tissues.'

'I won't cry,' he grinds out.

'Or you could use numbing cream.'

He returns his attention to the wall. 'Like you?'

I scoff. 'Never needed it.'

'Sure.'

'I haven't.'

His head rolls. 'If you say so.'

I inhale so hard through my nose, I can taste the salty air on my tongue.

He just spun that around so damn quick.

I open my mouth but quickly close it again.

He's not worth it.

'You going to the new cove Friday night?'

Whiplash, *again*. 'I planned to. Why? Are you? Thinking of tripping me up again?'

'I said it was an accident,' he yells, so suddenly that it shocks the hell out of me and I step back, as the intensity in his expression stokes the fire inside me. His eyes are so dark, I shudder. 'All right, calm down.'

'I am calm. Trust me.'

'Looks like it.' *This guy is a* psycho.

His jaw clenches, but then I swear I watch an internal struggle play out on his face. 'I'm—'

'Right,' Sam says, appearing behind us both, 'it's clear you two don't get along, but while you're carrying out your community service, you need to at least act as if you do. People are watching.'

I look around at the passers-by glancing our way and speeding up uncomfortably.

'Keep your voices down,' Sam warns, before leaving us again.

'Prick,' Alok mutters, and although I'm still shaking a little with how he just snapped at me, it does make me smile.

'I think that's the first thing you've said that I agree with.'

He shoots me a glance. 'Probably be the last thing, too.'

'Careful, that's the second.'

He huffs out a laugh and goes back to scrubbing.

I laugh at Maria's message while I wait for my food to warm up in the microwave.

Maria: He'd for sure cry like a little bitch x

Me: You know it x

Maria: Strange of him to get so mad over that, but I guess that just means he's not as unbothered by people as he tries to make out x

Me: True. Maybe I'll be the one to make him cry lol x

Maria: Hahahaha! I need to see that . . .

I look up when Ethan comes into the kitchen. 'Hey.'

He smiles on his way over to the kettle. 'You seem happier today. Shift at the harbour not so bad?'

'It was better, yeah.' I finish writing my message to Maria and press send. 'I know everyone says it's just how Alok is, but he's got a serious attitude problem.'

I still can't get over how he went off today. But on the flip side, I think that's the most emotion I've seen him show.

Ethan turns around. 'You're right about that. He's always been a hothead. He had to defend himself a lot when he was younger because of his dad's constant rants about vampires, which I get, but now I reckon he just kicks off because he gets off on it.'

I snort. 'He definitely gets mad a lot for someone who seems to have the perfect life.' Rich parents, attractive, only works because he wants to . . . 'Or maybe it's his way of rebelling against his dad? He said he's quite strict.'

Ethan's expression switches before he turns back around to the kettle. 'Oliver would make anyone want to rebel. He's evil.'

'Sounds like it.' *I really hope I don't ever meet the mayor*. 'How's the roof coming along?' I ask, changing the subject.

He groans. 'Slow. Do you want a tea?'

'No, thanks, I've got juice.' I take my food out of the microwave when the timer ends, and swallow down my feelings with several quick mouthfuls of steamed fish. 'Are you going to the new cove tomorrow night?'

He nods. 'Won't be there until late, though. We have a private job in town. We've been building an extension for a while, but the work's not regular.'

'Oh, cool, so it will be dark by the time you get there, which means I won't be dragged into playing volleyball, huh?'

He's smiling when he turns around with two mugs in his hands. 'Yeah, but there's always next time.'

I smirk. 'Let's hope the work picks up then.'

He shakes his head as he leaves. 'I'll see *you* later.'

Chapter Nineteen

Alok chucks his brush into the bucket between us as he stands up to stretch his back. 'I'm so over this shit.'

I wipe my brow. *Him and me both.*

There's, like, a million layers of paint on this wall, and it feels like it's taking just as many years to get them the hell off. This heat is also pissing me off, which is resulting in my mood being absolutely diabolical.

I throw my own brush into the bucket before resting my back against a dry area of the wall. 'I was over it when you twisted my ankle and got me arrested.'

He eyes me. 'I said it was an accident, Gabby, get over it.'

I look him up and down. 'Hard to when I still have fifty plus hours of my life being wasted on this.'

'You think I wanna be here?' His dark eyes narrow. 'I tried to help you, but noooo. You got us both caught because you were being stubborn.'

SUCKERS

'Because. *You*. Tripped. Me.'

'No. I. Didn't.' He scans the area to make sure Sam isn't watching us. 'God, you're annoying.'

I scoff as I retrieve my brush. 'And you aren't? You think you're so much better than everyone. "*If you lied about being able to play, just say that*",' I say bitterly as I glare up at him. 'You play the guitar next time then, show us all how good *you* are.'

'I was just messing around.'

'Oh, please. You were trying to call me out because you thought I was lying. You've had a problem with me since you first came down that dune and saw me minding my own damned business.'

A fragile silence falls between us for a while, until Alok picks his brush back out of the bucket. 'I don't trust people, especially not out-of-towners.'

'Good for you.' I roll my eyes. 'Just don't make it everyone else's problem. Especially when they've done nothing to you. And *I* haven't.' God, he is *such* an asshole. What a joke. 'Like everyone should suffer because you've got issues,' I mutter. 'Reality check, everyone has them.'

I scrub away at a 'K', my knuckles turning white. If only he knew how hard it was for me to even be around him without tearing his throat out. It may give me an opportunity to practise my coping mechanisms, but I hate the emotional whiplash I get from being in his presence. One minute he annoys the hell out of me, the next I'm intrigued.

Because when he isn't being so abrasive, I actually want to understand him.

'What are your issues?' he asks quietly.

I laugh, but I'm not sure if it's from shock or his audacity. 'You're the last person I'd tell. You're too judgemental. Look at how you talk about things that aren't even real.'

'Vampires *are* real,' he says, serious as ever. 'I've seen one.'

I turn my head so fast, but he's already looking dead at me. 'Don't lie.'

'My dad and I went to visit my aunt in Scarborough when I was eight and interrupted one of those suckers attacking her at the back of the house. Then, he shifted into an owl and flew away. My dad looked it up after and reckons it was a muroni – a shapeshifting vampire from Romania. It's why we've never been able to track him down.'

My stomach lurches. 'What the hell? Did she survive?'

'Barely. Dad thought he'd seen one in Larpool Woods before that instance, and once that happened, there was no doubt. Well, not for us.'

That must be why Oliver hates us so much.

'Now the town's taking vampires seriously. People are scared of being bitten, but it's the shapeshifting they should be worried about. It means you can't trust new people in this town. And even if you think you know someone, you might not. Not really.'

'Yeah . . .' I act like I brush it off, but I don't. 'Well, I can see why you're so uptight now. What other proof do you have?'

'Now Dad's the mayor, he gets access to all the evidence. People getting attacked on camera, pictures of bites, hospital reports of people losing massive amounts of blood in unexplainable ways . . . You should come to one of my dad's rallies. He's going to be telling everyone how to protect themselves from them this weekend.'

I swallow down my horror and get back to scrubbing. 'Nah, thanks, I'm good on that.'

'Suit yourself, but this place ain't the quiet, idyllic little town people think it is. Things don't just hide in the shadows, they walk amongst us, and it's not safe to be out alone at night. Not for anything that breathes.'

Hold on . . . 'Is that why you wouldn't leave me on the beach?'

He picks his spray bottle up. 'Everyone else was gone.'

Wow, so he isn't completely heartless. 'Thank you.'

He shrugs. 'I just didn't want you being snatched on my conscience.'

'Of course, it was all about you.' I roll my eyes again. 'And there was me thinking you weren't such a complete dick after all.'

He attempts to hide a smirk but fails. 'I don't care what you think of me.'

'Obviously.'

I play my bass in the hall for a while when I get home, before heading to the kitchen to get something to eat, just as Ethan comes inside to make him and Josh coffee.

We end up chatting and he tells me about his love-hate relationship with this town, and how he'd really like to have his own business one day, focusing on renovating listed buildings.

'Do you think you'll open it here as you already have a customer base?'

He shrugs. 'There are listed buildings all over the place, so I don't have to.'

'What about your mum, though?'

'She'll be moving back to Zimbabwe in a few years. She and Dad built a house there, before he passed.' He turns around to face me. 'They always planned to retire there, but I never wanted to go.' His eyes light up. 'At least not until I'm old.'

'That's a long way away to be from your mum.'

'My relationship with my parents has never been like most

people's. I love my mum, don't think I don't, but my parents raised me to be independent, and I have been from a young age.'

'I guess . . .'

'How did things go with Alok today?' he asks casually.

'I didn't feel like strangling him, so suppose it went okay. He was going on about the most recent attack. The woman's still in a critical condition, they say.'

'I heard . . . I honestly thought it was just some Dracula weirdo, but that woman lost so much blood, it's making me wonder if it is all true.'

I give him a cautious look over the rim of my glass. 'Apparently they're going to be teaching people how to protect themselves at the next rally.'

He turns around to finish making his and Josh's drinks. 'I wonder what the police will say about that.'

Grandma, Maria and I spend the entire drive to the new cove's drop-off point talking about what Alok told me on Wednesday, about the muroni.

'Sanse said there's never been one in her group,' Maria says, 'but it wouldn't matter. They can shift into anything, including other people.'

That is wild . . .

'Well, one thing's for certain,' I say as I take off my seatbelt, 'Oliver is definitely not gonna let his vendetta against vampires go, and I actually think he might get the use of weapons as self-defence approved.'

Grandma turns to Maria and me as we get out of the car. 'As long as you don't reveal yourselves, it doesn't matter if he does or not. Now, stop worrying. And stay out of trouble.'

Maria smirks as my grandma drives off, out of the woodland car park. 'Yeah, Gabrielle. Stay out of trouble.'

I roll my eyes. 'Yes, Mum.'

She laughs as we follow the path into the woods, and then she's skimming her fingers through the leaves of all the bushes we pass. 'God, I love the smell of these woods. My dad used to bring me here all the time when I first turned eighteen. I used to wrap myself around all the trunks of the pine trees when I'd shift.' She strokes the trunk of one as we pass it. 'It was so fun.'

'Did shifting come easily to you?'

She nods. 'I was *so* excited to be able to. It did get me into trouble, though.'

'Trouble?'

'Yeah . . .' She glances back at me. 'The hypnotic eyes. I'd use it to get out of homework and classes I didn't like. I accidently used it on Mum one time, too, which Dad was *not* happy about.'

'Oh, damn. What did you do?'

'She took my phone; I made her give it back. Nothing too serious, at least not with her.'

'Oh . . .'

She glances back again. 'Chill out, I haven't killed anyone or anything . . . but I have been close. Once.'

My eyes widen. 'How?'

She's quiet for at least twenty paces. 'I was upset with someone . . . I almost took their heart. That screwed me up for a while.'

I tell her about the family journals I'm reading. 'It's hard as hell controlling our emotions, especially when it comes to the more intense ones.'

'Right, there's always something to worry about. You'll be good, though, 'cause I'm going to be the friend to you that I wish I'd had.' She smiles at me when the path widens so we can walk side by side. 'And I'll make sure you don't make the same mistakes I did.' She bumps her shoulder against mine. 'I wouldn't've screwed up so badly if I'd had a friend like you at eighteen.'

I hold her arm. 'I appreciate that, but you have a friend like me *now* and I'm here for you, so no more talking bad about yourself. I think you're amazing.'

She smiles sadly. 'Thanks, girl. Any progress on your shift?'

I shake my head. 'I do think I have my thirst under control, though. The scent of that vial still arouses me, but my fangs don't come out and my heart only races a little.'

'That's amazing, girl.'

'Yeah . . .' I give her a cautious look. 'Now I wanna taste it, though.'

'What, the blood?'

I nod. 'I know there are safe ways to enjoy it . . . Do you ever?'

'Ah, Gabby . . .' She sighs. 'I tend to stay away from blood, because when I get the taste for it, I *really* get the taste for it.'

'Oh, I'm sorry. I'll ask—'

'No, don't apologise, I'm cool to talk about it. If you're sure you're good with your thirst, there are places you can go.' Her mood turns serious. 'If you want to visit one, let me know.'

'Okay,' I say, thinking about it. 'I will.'

The cove is just a smaller version of the one we used to go to, but we're keeping things more low key, so we don't draw any attention to us being here. Everyone still plays volleyball before it gets dark, but the bonfire is tiny in comparison to the ones I'd been spoilt with, which means I'm having to sit closer to feel its warmth.

Police are such killjoys.

SUCKERS

I return Alok's nod across the fire when I sit between Ethan and Maria with a can of tequila sunrise. We seem to have come to a mutual understanding at our community service now. Basically, don't bring up any sensitive topics, no personal questions, but complaining about our backs hurting from all the bending and reaching is fair game.

We've developed a strange bond over that.

'Wow, you got a nod,' Maria whispers. 'Must mean he doesn't completely hate you any more.'

I scoff. 'I wouldn't say that. That guy's mood is like a switch.'

He's scary when he's pissed off.

'Is it sad that I wish there was a guitar, or even better, a bass here?' Ethan says, leaning forward to get my attention.

I chuckle. 'No. I know I bring the vibes.'

'You should gig in Whitby,' Ava says. 'We'd come.'

'Playing for all of you is cool, but I'm on a break from gigs right now. I used to play two or three of them a week back in London. My fingers need a rest.'

'Not that they're getting one,' Ethan says. 'She plays every day at the manor. I barely put the radio on any more.'

Willow sulks. 'Lucky.'

Ethan gives me a wink and my stomach flutters. 'I am. The reverb in that place is epic.'

Jason chuckles. 'Bro is crushing hard.'

I frown. 'Huh?'

'Are you going to GothFest?' Ava asks, throwing him daggers and changing the subject. 'We got our tickets today.'

'I was supposed to ask you about that,' Maria says, turning to me. 'I can get them for us.'

My stomach clenches a little when I think about being around a massive crowd again, but I decide to be positive and remind myself that I can't hide away forever. I'm doing well with mastering my soucouyant side, and Maria will be there. 'Hell yeah, I'm up for it. What are you going to wear?'

'We can go shopping.' Her face lights up. 'We can check out those shops you've been going on about.'

'I can't wait.' I turn to Ethan. 'Are you coming?'

'I can see if I can get the day off.'

'Please, and then let me know. I could help you pick something out, too.'

He pretends to be offended. 'What're you trying to say?'

I chuckle. 'Literally what I said.'

He shakes his head and gets up, so I ask him where he's going. 'We need more firewood.'

'Take Gabby,' Maria says, chugging the rest of her beer to finish it. 'We always pair up so no one is alone. Alok made that rule,' she says, before turning back to Mikey.

'Sure, I'll come.'

He smiles, but it falters a little when he looks behind me.

I turn, only to catch a glimpse of annoyance in Alok's eyes before he looks across at Ben.

'Come with me,' Ethan says, taking my hand. 'I know a good spot.'

I haphazardly jog across the sand towards the trees, swiftly regretting my decision to go with him. It feels way too comfortable holding his hand, and my heart's beginning to race.

Not good.

He pulls me deeper into the woods, holding branches out of the way for me as we head off any visible trail. He helps me over fallen trees, over uneven ground and, using the light from the moon above in the clear sky, tramples down nettles and thorns so I don't get hurt when I follow him.

He's always so considerate.

We reach a cedar tree where several dry branches lie beneath, and we both kneel to start piling them up.

'How many are we getting?' I ask, super aware of how warm his side is against mine.

'As many as we can carry. I saw you shivering.'

'Yeah, because it's freezing.'

Before I can protest, he's shrugged off his jacket and wrapped it around my shoulders. It's like being wrapped in an Ethan blanket, and his scent engulfs me.

'Thanks,' I whisper. He's so close, and his hands are still on me.

I glance down, trying to clear my mind, but it's futile and I shudder.

'You okay?'

I exhale slowly, and my breath trembles along with my body. 'Yeah, I'm good.'

'Gabby?'

'Hm?' I finally look up at him and he shuffles impossibly closer.

'I really, *really* like you.'

My heart races while I stare into his eyes I need to get away from him, but I'm frozen at the same time. I can smell him over everything else in these woods, including the tree we're under.

'I like you, too.' God, I really do. I don't know if it's because he's always so kind to me, or how he looks at me – like he's looking at me right now – or how badly I want to kiss him and find out if he tastes as good as I imagine.

'So why does it feel like you're always pushing me away?' He blindly reaches for my hand and finds it, linking our fingers.

The feeling makes me hold my breath.

'I know you have a lot going on right now, but . . . I care about you. All day at the manor, I'm looking for excuses to take a break so I can come and find you, just to talk about nothing.' He glances down at my mouth. 'All I want to do is be around you. You're beautiful, inside and out, and smart, and you make me laugh.'

My heart aches. No one has ever said anything like this to me before. 'Ethan, I care about you, too. And I like being around you, it's just . . . I cherish what we have so much, I don't want to ruin it by complicating things.'

'You won't.' He gently strokes my cheek, but when his hand lowers, it only falls to my neck to pull me closer. 'Nothing could ever change the way I feel about you. I swear it.'

I gasp as his mouth collides with mine, and he could've set me on fire with how fiercely my skin tingles. His lips are even softer than I'd imagined, and he tastes even better than he smells . . . My senses are completely overloaded by him, and I struggle to breathe.

He groans into my mouth and my head falls back with a moan. His arms wrap around my back and my fingers are in his hair. I pull him closer, desperate to taste more of him in any way I can.

I need more. So much more.

I shudder when he skims his fingers across my lower back, all the way to my hip, and then I'm reaching beneath his T-shirt, visualising his tight muscles that he's tormented me with, all the beads of sweat that pool on his gorgeous skin when he's out in the sun, and how badly my gums have tingled when I've thought about—

I force myself out of his arms, falling onto the dirt while trembling with how close I just came to sinking my teeth into him.

He reaches for me, and I practically scramble away. 'What's wrong?'

My body jerks as I catch my breath. 'I shouldn't've done that.'

'You didn't, I did.' His gaze softens. 'I've wanted to kiss you for so long.'

'I'm sorry.' It's physically painful to look at him, because I can't stop looking at his lips, so I turn my head away. 'I am, but I just, I can't do that to you . . . We can't be more than friends . . .' I'm rambling, but I can't stop. 'You're a good person . . . My life is a mess right now . . .' I remember what I did to Kyle and picture his horrified look on Ethan's face instead, and it crushes me. 'I can't do that. It would never work . . . Someone like me would hurt you.'

He recoils from me like I've slapped him. 'What do you mean, someone like you?'

'I'm . . . I'm not—'

We hear Maria and Willow calling for us.

'We're here!' he yells before helping me up. When I thank him and apologise again, he doesn't say a word.

'What's taking you guys so long?' Willow sings out when they find us, but when they notice my expression, Maria frowns.

'What's going on?'

I shake my head as I watch Ethan brush past her.

'Ethan?'

'It's cool,' he says, snatching his jacket up from the ground.

'Babe?' Maria says, talking half the branches from me. 'Are you okay?' she whispers.

I bite my lip and force myself not to cry. 'I'm fine.'

Chapter Twenty

Ethan's just finishing making drinks for him and Josh when I find him and Grandma in the kitchen.

'Hey.' I cautiously ground myself beside the door, hoping he won't blank me again like he did on Saturday.

His shoulders tense, but he doesn't turn around. 'Hey.'

My stomach drops and, instead of the thirst I've become used to taming around him, hurt settles in its place. 'Are you okay?'

'Yep.' He stirs both coffees, and I know I need to quickly think of something else to ask him before he leaves, but I decide to just ask him straight out.

'I was wondering if—'

He turns with the mugs in his hand, and I'm slayed by the sadness in his eyes before he glances at Grandma at the table. 'I gotta get back to work.'

'Cool,' I say quietly, moving so he can pass me, but I'm so far from it.

I hate this.

I've been wracking my brain, trying to remember everything I said on Friday night to warrant him being so cold with me, but I know I didn't say anything bad, so I'm guessing that it's the rejection itself that he's not taken well.

Nice to know that's what I get for being honest.

I didn't say I didn't want to be friends any more.

I'm trying to protect him.

'Oh, dear,' Grandma says, when I join her at the table. 'You two still haven't made up, then?'

'What do you mean?'

Her eyes narrow. 'You know exactly what I mean. That boy runs out of the room as soon as he sees you coming. You used to go looking for each other, and he'd look like a lost little puppy when you weren't around. It's clear the two of you have had a falling out. I just can't figure out over what.'

Ugh . . . *I hate how observant she is.* 'I kinda rejected him.'

Her eyes widen. 'Going by how he's acting, there's no "kind of" about it.' She sighs. 'Well, that certainly explains it.'

'I didn't mean to hurt his feelings,' I insist. 'I like Ethan, a lot. He was my first friend here, and he's always been nice to me. He's been supportive and kind when I really needed it, and he's cute, obviously . . . but we can't be more than friends.'

She frowns. 'Why not?'

'The obvious? We live in completely different worlds, and I don't want to hurt him.' My heart aches with just the thought. 'Ethan's good, whereas I am, well, I can be dangerous.'

'So you're swearing off relationships forever? Ending our bloodline?'

I laugh with shock. 'That's a bit dramatic, don't you think?'

She remains straight-faced. 'No, not really. Gabrielle, how do you think you got here?'

'As in . . .?'

She tsks. 'Well, you weren't the product of an immaculate conception, were you?'

'Obviously.'

'Exactly, so the women in your family have found love, even being what they were, and as far as I'm aware, none of them had soucouyants as their partners, or any other type of vampires for that matter.'

I look towards the window. 'Yeah, well, they're different. I don't trust myself not to hurt someone. Not again.'

She pulls my attention back to her by holding my hand. 'You're speaking from a place of fear, do you not see that? Has reading your ancestors' journals not taught you anything? Yes, at the moment, you are learning how to control your urges and make peace with what you are, but you're letting it determine your future. Ruin it, even.'

I shrug. 'Maybe I might change my mind in the future, but right now, I'm not ready.'

'But how do you know what you're ready for if you don't try? Everyone gets scared sometimes, especially when it comes to matters of the heart. Giving your grandfather a chance was terrifying for me. I'd met a few men I felt fondly for before him, and I'll admit, I always ran in the complete opposite direction. But, eventually, I had to stop running, because I wanted a family of my own, and regardless of what I am, I deserved it. I deserved to be loved, and so do you.'

She's brought up Grandad, finally. 'How did you meet Grandad?'

'At my friend's wedding. I was the singleton of my friend group for many years. What do they say? "Always the bridesmaid, never the bride"? I'm not sure if it was because I'd just watched my friend marry that I was vulnerable to the idea of falling in love, or if your grandfather simply arrived in my life at the perfect time, but something about him was different.'

'What were you most scared of? Him finding out?'

'Telling him the truth about me, yes, but when my feelings for him deepened, I *had* to take that chance. I was prepared to run if he wasn't accepting, to disappear if I had to, but thankfully, by the time I told him' – she smiles wistfully – 'he was absolutely smitten and would have accepted me no matter what.'

I gush internally. 'That is so sweet.'

'And *he* was. He was the most wonderful husband. I only regret that I didn't push him to visit the doctor sooner. Your mother missed out, and so have you. He would have loved you. He always encouraged me to be myself. When he passed away, it broke my heart. He knew me better than I knew myself, and I still miss him terribly, every single day.'

I squeeze her hand to comfort her. 'I'm sorry.'

'Don't be. I would still take the years we had together over none at all, and that is what I am trying to say to you. You must *live*, Gabrielle, take chances. You mustn't let your fears stop you from having the life you deserve.'

'I just . . . I don't think I can right now.'

'It is always your decision, but I don't want you to close yourself off from love, dear. It truly is one of the most beautiful experiences of life.' She pats my hand. 'And yours is just beginning. Once you master who you are, learn to trust yourself, which you will, you will realise that.'

'I hope so.'

Alok and I are being made to repaint a wall in the town centre for our community service today, and I'm not going to lie and say I'm comfortable being put on display in such a public place. The looks of disgust by passers-by have been relentless, too, as Sam's job title is plastered in white block letters across the back of his high-vis vest.

Alok's been glaring back at several of the nosy busybodies, like he's here for some serious crime against humanity or something; which, if I'm honest, has been funny and actually cheered me up a little.

'Did you want to help?' he growls at an old man when Sam's occupied with the other offenders.

I snigger when the man's greying eyebrows touch his hairline, and he quickly diverts his attention elsewhere.

'Didn't think so.'

'God knows what he must be thinking.' I chuckle.

Alok abuses the roller in his hand, his jaw tense. 'He should mind his own damned business.'

I roll my eyes. 'I meant as in, what we've been given community service for.'

He crouches down to reload his paint-roller. 'Murder, hopefully.'

'I don't think they give community service for that.' I kneel to start cutting in the bottom of the wall. *They said this is grey paint, but it looks more blue.* 'Y'know, I'm surprised you have a job. I can't imagine you give very good customer service with your attitude.'

'My uncle owns the place.'

'Ohhhh, so he *can't* sack you then.'

He scoffs. 'He wouldn't. I'm the hardest worker he's got. We get on well, too. He likes having me around.'

'Don't fly off the handle with him then?'

He narrows his eyes when I glance up at him. 'I like him, too.'

'Lucky him.'

He smirks, I think. 'The people who know the real me usually are.'

'Well, maybe you should let more people get to know you. Maybe lose the temper, too.'

'I don't – *shit!*'

'What?' I ask, then I hear something clatter on the ground beside me.

It's Alok's extension pole. It's snapped, and there's paint on his hair and forehead.

I bite my lip and pick the broken roller off the ground so I can hide my silent laughter. 'It'll wash out – it's not the end of the world.'

'I can hear you laughing, Gabby,' he says, right before something wet and thick splatters against the back of my head.

I brush my fingers across my locs and then glare at him when I see paint on my hand. 'You did *not* just do that.'

He smirks. 'It'll wash out, it's not the—'

'Not as easily as it will yours, you asshole!' I throw the broken roller back at his feet. 'Do you know how hard it is to maintain locs? I don't even know if there's anywhere in Whitby I can get them taken care of!'

The smile slips from his face and he suddenly looks remorseful. 'I'm sorry, I was just trying—'

'What is going on?' Sam hisses as he appears beside Alok.

I bite my tongue. 'Nothing.'

Sam looks at Alok's hair, then mine, and his jaw tenses. 'Keep the paint on the wall,' he says to Alok before he storms off.

He's definitely sick of us.

I look down at the paint on my hands and then Alok – blue paint in his hair and dripping down his face. The situation is so ridiculous, I start laughing.

'What's so funny?' Alok asks, eyeing me like I've lost my mind.

'Blue is *so* not your colour,' I say.

He's smiling then, and I notice he has a slight dimple. Even with paint dripping across his face, he's still annoyingly attractive.

He shakes his head and goes back to the wall.

Chapter Twenty-One

Thankfully, when I moaned to Maria about Alok getting paint in my locs yesterday, she told me her friend could give me an apple cider vinegar wash, treatment and a redress, so we're on our way to her house now.

'How are things with Ethan?' she asks, struggling up the hill the same way I am. This area of Whitby might have beautiful views of the sea and cliffs in the distance, but damn, it's a killer to your thighs. *This is basically a hike.*

'Still bad. He started working on a different part of the roof when I went out to sit with Grandma in the garden today. I'm trying not to take it personally, but it's stressing me out.'

'It would me, too.' She stops walking to rest her hand on her knees and catch her breath. 'It's sad, 'cause if he knew the truth, he might've reacted differently. Instead, he probably thinks you were messing him around.'

I start walking again when she does. 'I get he might think that . . . Telling someone you like them back, letting them kiss you, and then rejecting them doesn't exactly make sense, but if he only knew how close I was to biting him . . . I don't want to hurt him like I did Kyle. I mean, shit, I'd only just started to control my thirst around him.'

I stop hearing Maria's boots scraping the path, so I turn, and I see her gaping at me.

'Girl, you never told me that. Since when have you been feeling that way around Ethan?'

'Since I got here. It got worse the more time I spent with him.'

She comes to link her arm in mine. 'I guess it's been good practice, but . . . damn. That doesn't sound like fun at all.'

'I know.' I sigh. 'I knew I'd have a lot to deal with coming here, but I in no way anticipated anything like this.'

'Don't beat yourself up about it. Sometimes there isn't even an obvious reason why we want to sink our teeth into someone. I can't tell you how many times I've been walking down the street minding my business and I've been triggered.'

'I hate that it can be so random.' I'd have more of an idea why Alok triggers me sometimes if it wasn't.

'Me, too,' she says, leaning closer in support. 'I wish I could give you some better advice, but actual relationships have always been tricky for me, too.'

I sigh hopelessly. 'I just hate that I've hurt him. I feel so bad, especially because I do care about him.'

'Ethan is the sweetest. Always has been. And you two would make a cute couple . . .'

I roll my eyes. 'Not helping, Maria.'

'Ugh, fine. So you're going to stay single forever? Be, what do they call it, abstinent?'

I laugh. 'Why do you have to say it like that? Are *you* seeing someone?'

'No, but I do – nothing serious – and why shouldn't I? Everyone has needs, and I can still enjoy hookups without blood.' She smirks. 'Although . . . being with another bloodsucker is *hot*, I won't lie. Bloody *and* hot.'

I laugh when she does, but deep down I hope I do end up finding someone like me. It would be so much easier, and sure, it's not that I feel like I need to able to bite the person I love, but I don't want to have to forever live without that either . . .

I notice we're walking at a snail's pace now, and we're definitely late. 'Have you ever been in love?'

She's thoughtful. 'There was someone . . .' She pulls me down a short path to a red door with the number ninety-seven on it. 'I guess I was like you,' she says, when she faces me. 'When you care about someone, you don't want to hurt them, even if it means staying away from them and hurting yourself instead.'

My chest tightens in response to her answer. 'Girl, that was *deep*.'

She smiles, but the pain beneath it is unmissable. 'You wanted real,' she says, before the door opens. 'Hey, Vina, girl. This is Gabrielle.'

'Found somewhere to get your hair done, then?'

I glance at Alok beside me. We're back at the harbour scrubbing more vampire slurs off the stones. 'Yeah, lucky for you I did.'

'Lucky for me?'

I smirk as I feel him staring at me, but I focus on the crack in the wall I'm trying to jam the bristles of my brush into. 'That's what I said.'

My locs have been cleaned and redressed, and they smell like sweet coconut oil. I know Vina really scrubbed my scalp, too, because each time the breeze passes, it's like my head's being sprayed with peppermint.

He starts scrubbing again. 'It looks good.'

I choke on my next breath. 'Well, damn. Thanks.'

'Just being honest. Glad to see you're feeling better.'

I frown. 'What does that mean?'

'You've barely said anything the past couple of days.'

'Well, *excuse* me for not realising our mutual hate of each other had levelled up to mood watching. I didn't think we talked like that.'

His gaze burns the side of my face. 'We talk.'

I scoff. 'We *bicker*.'

He shrugs. 'That's still talking. So, was it getting your hair done that's put a smile on your face, or something else?'

I return my attention to the wall. 'You're quite chatty today, aren't you?'

He clenches his jaw. 'It helps pass the time.'

I roll my eyes. *Of course.* 'It's my hair. I'd been worrying about finding someone to do it since I got here.'

'Hmm . . . so it's not because Ethan's stopped being a baby?'

I spin around, my brush accidently spraying his boots with water. 'What? How do you know about that?'

He shrugs, his expression even. 'Mikey mentioned he was sulking about you turning him down.'

'Oh . . .' Boys act like they don't gossip, but I reckon they do the most. 'He's not happy with me, that's true.' I stop talking then, because we are *not* friends like that.

'Pathetic,' he mutters, and I glare at him. 'What? He is.'

'Why? Because he doesn't worship the ground you walk on?'

SUCKERS

He huffs. 'We just haven't got much in common.' He picks up the bucket of cloudy water between us. 'I'm gonna go change this. Could you spray over my bit of the wall again while I'm gone?'

'Uh, yeah, sure.'

'Thanks.'

I frown at his back while he walks over to the van.

Maybe he is just trying to pass the time. Or maybe he's finally starting to trust me a little?

I text Mum and Dad to check up on them when I get home, and then I spend some time on my bed effectively meditating in an attempt to shift.

Fire . . . Flames . . . Transform . . .

I sigh when I open my eyes, and the tingling across my skin ebbs away. I feel like it's right there . . . I know I'm strong enough for it, but I just can't get further than flames dancing in my eyes.

I keep thinking back to the night I was with Kyle, trying to remember what happened just before I shifted then. *I was scared, out of breath, literally running for my life* . . . But Grandma says I shouldn't need fear to shift.

But at least I have my thirst under control, which means I can ask Maria about that place again . . .

I pick my phone up from beside me, but it's Kyle that's heavy on my mind when I open my messages. I keep writing texts to him that I never send. I've started them with a mixture of apologies, casual 'Heys', and asking what he came by the house for, but before I press send, I get scared and delete them.

I do want to message him, though, especially because Mum said he seemed worried about me. Maybe he thinks I was going through something mentally. I mean, they'd all noticed I hadn't been myself the last few months, so maybe he put the bite down to that.

Or maybe that's wishful thinking . . .

My thoughts spiral, so I play some Arch Enemy on my bass on the window seat to relax. Maria said to get excited, and Grandma keeps saying to stop overthinking it. Watching Grandma shifting was so cool. And who wouldn't want the ability to fly? Like Grandma said, it's the most efficient way to travel.

I put my bass down beside me and close my eyes again.

Chapter Twenty-Two

'He keeps looking over here. Maybe he feels bad now.'

I lean into Maria's side, keeping my attention on the fire spitting in front of us. It's freezing, and there's spittle coming from the sky, like it's trying really hard to rain. 'That's his problem.'

Ethan's ignored and avoided me all week, so I've had no choice but to get over the whole thing. If he doesn't want my friendship without wanting something more, then I have to accept that we can't be friends at all.

'I've just never seen him like this.'

I snort and kick the sand at my feet. 'Don't worry about him. I'm not.'

Mostly.

It's not been too awkward at the gathering tonight, but I'm not really feeling it. Between Ethan watching me like a hawk and the skies repeatedly threatening a downpour, I'd rather be in bed with my bass.

Maria shivers beside me, too, but then Mikey comes to sit beside her and offers her his hoodie. *I wonder if he's the someone she talked about . . .*

'Don't let him put you on a downer,' Alok says, when he comes to sit beside me. He offers me a can of tequila sunrise. 'Here, drink that.'

I take it from him, but I'm confused. 'Why are you sitting here and not out there with everyone else playing volley?' Although I don't think they're actually playing any more. At least not to win, because there's barely any moonlight with all the clouds above us.

'I'm tired.' He swigs from his bottle of beer. 'Between that bullshit community service and work . . .' He eyes me as he lowers his drink. 'You look tired, too.'

I narrow my eyes. 'Oh, so you've come to insult me? Why am I not surprised?'

He laughs, actually laughs, and I feel like I've jumped universes again. The dimple in his right cheek is back, and his eyes lighten to a coppery hazel.

I frown down at my drink when I crack it open, the fluttering in my stomach catching me off guard. 'You must be drunk.'

'I'm far from—'

'How's the community service going then, Alok?' Maria asks, leaning forward to see him.

He groans, and Maria chuckles.

'Gabby's said it's been fun. How many hours have you got left now?'

'Too many,' Alok mutters. 'But it's bearable . . . Can't say much about the company, though.'

SUCKERS

I roll my eyes when he smirks. 'The feeling is mutual, believe me.'

'They still got you painting the town?' Mikey asks, inserting himself into the conversation. 'I saw you down there the other day.'

I shake my head. 'We've finished that now. We're back to scrubbing that suckers graffiti off the wall at the harbour – it gets resprayed literally every night.'

Maria rolls her eyes. 'Sad pricks.'

'For real.'

'I reckon Gabby's asked to go back there,' Alok says. 'She was too worried about getting paint in her precious hair.'

'Oh, please,' I scoff, looking at Mikey. 'Alok got it in his hair first and almost cried.'

'But who actually did?' he fires back. 'My locs' – he pretends to cry – 'do you know how hard it is to wash locs?'

We all laugh at his impression of me, but I'm the most shocked.

'I do *not* sound like that.' I flick my locs over my shoulder. 'And they *are* hard to wash.'

'Well, don't you all look cosy,' Ethan mutters when he comes to get himself a drink from the cooler.

Mikey tells him he's wasted, but Maria and I give each other a look.

'Is he jealous?' she hisses.

'Over what?' I say, keeping my lips even. 'He's the one not talking to me.'

'Right.' She turns to Mikey. 'Come on, let's see what the others are doing.'

'All right,' he says, before following her across the sand.

I wait for Alok to leave so I can ask Ethan, who is still standing beside the cooler and staring at us, what the hell his problem is.

But Alok clearly doesn't get the hint.

'I'd sit somewhere else,' Ethan tells Alok, after gulping down half a can of beer. 'She might make you think she likes you, but really, it's all an act.'

The comment stings. 'You *must* be wasted.'

'I'm far from,' Ethan insists, before turning his attention back to Alok. 'Don't waste your time. She can't stand you either—'

Before I can say anything, Alok rolls his eyes. 'I told you he was pathetic.'

Now Ethan looks hurt. 'Oh, so that's what you two have been talking about?'

I look at him. 'No. I'd never—'

'*I* called you that,' Alok says, getting to his feet. ''Cause you are. Look at you, acting like a little—'

In a rush, Ethan skirts around the fire and shoves Alok before he can finish his sentence.

'Ethan, what the hell?' Panic overwhelms me then, and Maria rushes over.

'I'm going home,' I tell her. 'I'm over it.'

She glares at Ethan. 'You're a real prick. You wanna be an asshole just because she wouldn't go on a date with you? Grow the hell up!'

He blinks. 'Gabby, I didn't mean—'

'I don't want to hear it,' I snap.

'I'll walk back with you,' Maria says. 'Let me just—'

'I'll walk you back,' Alok says from behind me. 'I have work early in the morning anyway.'

Ethan glares at him. '*I*'ll walk her home.'

Maria turns around and starts cussing him. 'You're the reason she's leaving!'

I grow even more uncomfortable when the others stop throwing the ball and start watching them argue, so I grab hold of Maria's hand and tell her it's fine. 'I'll walk with Alok.'

I hate the look on Ethan's face when I say that, but if he comes with us, either we'll be arguing the entire way home, or he and Alok will end up physically fighting.

Ethan throws his bottle into the fire before disappearing down the beach, and I feel sick.

'Don't worry about him,' Maria says, hugging me goodbye. 'Text me when you're home.'

'I will.'

I silently walk towards the woods with my head down, listening to Alok following close behind me. If I'm honest, I really wanted Maria to walk with me, but I didn't want to take her away from Mikey.

'Gabrielle, wait.' Alok runs ahead of me before I duck through the entrance to the woods, then he turns his phone light on and goes inside first.

It's even darker in here with dense trees above us, and I already miss Maria and her epic senses.

'Thanks,' I mutter as Alok lights the way, but I keep my mouth shut after that.

This is going to be the longest thirty minutes of my life.

The trees become even more tightly packed, so I turn my phone light on too; and I pull my jacket closed when a shiver runs up my back. Maybe I should send Alok back and see if I can shift? It's creepy enough in here that I could definitely scare myself enough to, and it would mean I would get home quicker.

'Do you know the way?' I ask Alok, when he hesitates as to which trail to take at a small clearing.

'Yeah, don't worry, we're good.' His reply is terse, but I also sense he's not liking being in here either.

And no one would blame him. It's so quiet, the silence is hurting my ears. There's no breeze, barely any moonlight breaking through, and every time something rustles, the hairs on the back of my neck and arms prick up.

I don't know what it is, but something in my gut feels off.

Stop. I take a deep breath as I step over a pile of snapped branches after Alok. *It's fine. It's just your mind playing tricks on you.* There are two of—

I shriek when I almost trip over, and I hold my chest as my heart races.

Alok turns and blinds me with his phone light. 'You okay?'

I squint, and he lowers his phone. 'Yeah. I just tripped. I'm fine.'

'All right.' We start walking again, but soon enough he sighs. 'This is taking too long.'

I agree. I might be one of the people he's scared about meeting in these woods, but I can still feel fear, and it's becoming all-consuming.

'We need to pick up the pace. It's not safe out here.'

'I'm walking as fast as you—'

'Shush,' he hisses, rushing back towards me, and then he turns the light off on his phone. 'Turn yours off, too. Quick!'

'What?' I whisper as I do as he's asked, but when I look back up, I notice lights flickering through the woods.

He pulls me to his side. 'Someone's coming.'

'Do you think it's the police?'

'I don't know. Maybe. Shit, the curfew was meant to be approved today.'

'What?' I hiss. 'You never told us!'

'I forgot.'

We slow our breathing as we listen and watch as the lights

brighten. There are a lot of voices, but I can't make out what they're saying.

'It's my dad,' Alok hisses. 'Fuck.'

'*What?*'

He grabs my hand and starts dragging me in the opposite direction. 'He'll kill me if he finds me out here.'

We force our way through the trees, making new tracks through the bushes, but the rustling behind us suddenly picks up, and survival mode kicks in.

'We know you're in here! Give yourselves up now, and we won't hurt you!'

Alok takes off then, running so fast I'm yanked along until I meet his pace. Branches slap my face, my boots get caught in low-lying vines, and it becomes a fight to stay upright.

'Slow down,' I plead. 'I can't keep up.'

'Do you want them to catch us?'

'No, but . . .' I struggle to catch my breath. My heart is pounding so—

No, no, no.

Not now.

My skin begins to heat, and with my next sharp inhale the flame inside explodes. Panic rushes me as I look down at my hand in Alok's, glowing bright orange and about to burst into flames.

Please don't . . .

But no amount of silent begging stops the glow from spreading, and I begin to stumble behind him, desperate for him to let me go.

I don't want to burn him.

'Alok—'

'I'm not leaving you.' He's panting himself. 'Don't stop!'

'I . . .' Everything around me becomes crystal clear. The path forward, the veins on the leaves on all the trees surrounding us.

I can't stop it now.

Alok's going to see. *Feel.* He's going to know that I'm one of those creatures he despises.

I lift my head and open my mouth to warn him, but I yelp in absolute shock. Alok is no longer Alok. The hand gripping mine is triple the size now, and when my eyes follow along his arm, I see that Alok is taller, his muscles bulging out of his shirt. There's smoke surrounding him and whirling past me.

Is it coming from him?

'Alok?' I choke out.

He grunts, and I gasp, dragging the most intense scent of sweet, coppery blood into my lungs with it, and flames flood my eyes.

I stumble as my hand is ripped from his when he begins to run faster, and as Oliver and his men's yelling becomes louder, the real possibility that I might be about to lose my life halts my shift in its tracks.

Breathe. Breathe.

I feel the fire simmering just beneath the surface as I steady my footing to run again, but now a new fear settles within me. I've lost sight of Alok, and I can't leave him here.

I have to find him.

The edge of the woodland comes into view, but although I'm relieved to see it, I'm no less afraid. I can hear Alok's heavy breathing, telling me he's still close.

I see a trail of smoke through a path of shredded bushes to my right as I slow to attempt to calm my burning lungs. Then, as I cautiously follow it into the clearing, my heart leaps into my throat.

'Alok?' I whisper before he turns, and I come face to face with the giant. 'What the . . .' I stare at the towering form that holds all Alok's features, but with illuminated, piercing, bloodied eyes and palest skin.

Smoke rises from his body, and I cover my mouth.

It *was* coming from him.

How is he . . .?

'Alok?' I say again cautiously, trembling as I approach him. His eyes are fixed to mine, and his scent is stronger than ever. It triggers my fangs to appear, so I stay back. 'Don't come any closer,' I warn as he begins to walk towards me.

But he doesn't listen and only stops when he's right in front of me. He looks down at his hands before meeting my gaze. Something about the way he looks at me tells me he's just as confused as I am.

When I blink again, he's shifted back to himself.

'You . . .' I blink, again and again, questioning everything I've just witnessed. 'You were just . . . Alok, you were . . .'

'I—' He steps closer cautiously, like he's expecting me to bolt. 'Are you hurt?'

I shake my head, but it's more to rid my senses of the lingering sweetness in the air. I don't feel in control of myself at all right now. I'm beyond triggered in so many ways, and my mind is clouded with Alok and his scent and the fact that he's *one of us*.

He starts to walk backwards, mistaking the understanding in my eyes.

'Alok—'

He holds out a hand. 'You need to stay away from me, Gabby. I can't control it and I-I don't want to hurt you.'

'Alok, look at me,' I insist, rushing forward to grab his arm when he closes his eyes and shakes his head. '*Look* at me.'

He finally does, and the raw vulnerability I witness is crushing.

It's strange seeing him like this, and along with the overwhelming urge I feel to hold him, I think of how I can reassure him in some way.

I call on the fire inside me, still simmering beneath the surface, using his remembered scent to fuel it. *Just a little* . . .

After he becomes cast in an amber hue, he glances down at my mouth — just as my fangs nick at my lower lip.

He gasps and his expression shifts into something painful. 'Y-You're . . . Gabrielle?'

I nod. 'I'll explain everything, OK? But right now, we need to go.'

He suddenly pulls me into his arms and releases a relieved sigh. His heart is *thumping*. He's as terrified as I am.

I hold him back tightly, welcoming the comfort his embrace brings, but when he releases me and I think we're finally about to get out of here, he pulls me right back to him. He holds me close around my waist, and after a scan of my face and a searching look into my eyes with his dark ones, he kisses me.

I'm caught off guard, but that fades away when I taste the sweetness of him mixed with a heavy dose of smoke. I'm not the only one who whimpers either, and when my fangs reappear with how quickly heated the kiss becomes, I'm almost positive that mine aren't the only ones I feel.

His blissfully scape across my lips when I gasp, and I clench *everywhere*.

More tingles come when my shift threatens, but before I can step away to calm it, we hear more voices and pull apart from each other, breathless.

Alok seems to come back to his senses and quickly grabs my hand again. 'Let's get out of here.'

Chapter Twenty-Three

I swipe the call from Maria off my phone again before switching it to vibrate. I can't talk to her right now. What would I even say? I can't believe what just happened myself.

If only reading minds was one of my gifts, because I could really use it right now. Alok is so quiet as we walk in silence through the field, the cool night air soothing our anxiety, but there's no way his mind isn't racing like mine.

I have so many questions for him but I can't bring myself to ask him them yet, so I keep my mouth shut, too. However, I can't stop repeating one to myself: *Why wasn't he burnt by me?*

I know he must have felt my warmth: I was so close to shifting again . . .

My phone vibrates with a text, so I quickly check it.

Maria: Are you home yet? We heard voices in the woods and dipped. Call me! x

Me: I can't talk right now, but I'm almost home x

'You can go now,' I say to Alok after we cut through a hedge and Grandma's manor comes into view up ahead. 'I can make it from here.'

'I'm not leaving you until you're inside,' he replies tersely.

I roll my eyes. 'It's literally right there.'

He doesn't respond, just keeps walking.

For God's sake.

'Fine. Then we need to talk about what happened, Alok.'

The clouds have cleared so the moonlight is illuminating his face quite well, but I can't unsee those blood-red eyes. I don't think I'll *ever* be able to unsee those.

He guiltily diverts his gaze elsewhere. 'There's nothing to talk about.'

'Alok—'

His jaw clenches. 'Goodnight, Gabby.'

'Fine,' I say, hiding the hurt when he turns to walk away from me. 'I'll see you on Monday.'

He doesn't reply, but he won't be able to escape me at community service, and we both know it.

It's seven in the morning, and I'm mentally and physically exhausted. Sleep came but wouldn't stay, and even when it did, it was flooded by images of last night. In my waking moments, in the dark of night, I feared the shadows in my own room. Each scuttle, creak and thud I heard from above me or outside my window had me on edge.

And the nightmares . . .

SUCKERS

After all the talking bad on vampires, all the defending his dad and supporting his hate for them, the hunting, the rallies; and all the while, Alok's not human either.

And now he knows my secret.

That didn't even cross my mind last night. I know I should be worried, because I don't trust him not to sell me out to save himself, but all I can remember is the expression on his face when he backed away from me in the forest — like he was terrified of himself.

And so was I. He was *huge*. I wonder what he even is.

The memory of him kissing me also returns, making me shudder. The warmth of his mouth on mine, the taste of smoke on his tongue, and the way he held me all make my stomach flutter before I'm hit with a wall of guilt.

Ethan.

I shake the thoughts from my head and decide to focus on something more helpful. I open Google. Probably not the best idea, but it might at least give me a hint.

Creature that looks like a demon and has red eyes

The pictures that come up don't resemble what Alok looked like, nor do the images after a handful of other searches.

Think, think . . .

Giant with blood eyes Sri Lanka mythology

A mythological creature called Riri Yaka comes up, and my stomach drops when I see the pictures.

That has to be him.

Riri Yaka is a vampire in Sri Lankan mythology . . .
Snatched from his mother, he became a blood demon . . .

What the hell?
I need to talk to Grandma.
I get out of bed, but I have to drag myself down the hall. I wasn't even this tired after the first time I shifted. And I'd planned to go to the group today. *I might not make that . . .*
But I might not anyway after Grandma finds out about last night. I've potentially put her and the others in danger with Alok finding out about me.

'A riri yaka, yes, Gabrielle believes so, too . . .'
I check the clock on the kitchen wall again, growing more anxious the closer it gets to Josh and Ethan turning up for work. I'm *so* not ready to talk to Ethan about last night. All I want to do is go to sleep now that Grandma's made me eat something.
My head hurts so bad.
'Yes, she is okay . . .'
Grandma wasn't mad at me when I told her what happened, thankfully. With everything going on in the town, she's worried more than anything, and now this has happened, so am I.
She hangs up the phone after saying goodbye to Sanse. 'She said not to worry but to keep a low profile. In regard to Alok, if he is a riri yaka, you need to be careful, because they are known to have explosive tempers if not in control of them.' Her expression turns serious when she sits down. 'Do not push him, Gabrielle. If he knows what he is, he's been hiding it and does not want it to be known. But if he didn't know . . .'
I've asked myself that a few times: whether he knew. He's

nineteen, so I'm leaning more towards yes, but I won't know for sure until I speak to him.

Grandma exhales deeply. 'Of all the things you could have discovered during your time here, I do believe that this is the most shocking.'

I yawn, but I have to hold my head because it throbs. 'I'm so sorry for putting everyone in danger.'

'You haven't. He only knows about you, not anyone else, and that is how it shall remain. You, my dear, need to get some rest.'

'I wanted to go to the group—'

She shakes her head. 'Not this week. You need . . .' She looks behind me to the hallway when we hear someone coming.

I check the time and brace myself, but only Josh appears.

'Morning, ladies,' he says, cheerfully.

'Morning,' we both reply.

'Are you making the coffee this morning?' Grandma asks him.

'Only for myself. Young Ethan's picked up a tummy bug, apparently, so it's just me here today.' He flicks the kettle on. 'I reckon he was spoilt having last Saturday off, if you ask me.' He shakes his head. 'These young 'uns.'

Grandma gives me a look. 'Hopefully he feels better soon.'

'I'm sure he'll be fine . . .'

So he's chosen to avoid me completely now?

'Gabrielle?'

I look up at Grandma. 'Yeah?'

'Go and get some rest.'

I sleep all day and then get cussed out by Maria on the phone when I finally get the chance to call her at seven.

In the end, I find that I can't bring myself to tell her the truth.

It feels *wrong* to share Alok's secret, especially when I know very little. I want to talk to him properly first.

'He basically walked me home in silence. I think he realised I wasn't in the mood,' I lie, chewing my bottom lip.

She tells me about the voices she'd heard in the woods. It seems like Oliver and his little crew lost track of me and Alok and ended up following the noises coming from the cove. They all made it out fine, thankfully.

I find the vial of blood under my pillow and begin to roll it between my fingers. 'I was so frustrated that I almost shifted on the way home.' It's only half a lie.

'Thank God you didn't around Alok,' she says, sounding relieved. 'I give it a few more days, if you practice.'

'Yeah, but Grandma's told me I'm not allowed to try again for a while, because of how exhausted I am.'

'It gets better, I promise. Have you eaten?'

'Yeah, a few minutes ago. I'm back in bed now. How was the group?'

'It's not good, Gabby.' She sighs. 'They don't think that woman is going to make it, and tensions are running high . . . Oliver had the curfew approved, and there's talk of people carrying wooden stakes as a precaution.'

I gasp. 'What the hell?'

'I know. Sanse is scared – we all kinda are. She said she'll be contacting the other vampire beings in town.'

'Oh god . . . this is getting so out of hand. Maybe we should be trying to find out what's going on?'

'You need to rest, and right now, we need to lie low.'

If only she knew how badly I'd screwed up.

Chapter Twenty-Four

I spent most of the weekend in bed, and although I'm no longer exhausted, I'm still tired, so the absolute last thing I want to do is spend three hours scrubbing the harbour walls.

Grandma rests a plate of liver and eggs in front of me. 'I'll have nice fresh sheets on the bed for when you get home, all right?'

'Thanks, Grandma.' I sigh as I pick up my fork and briefly close my eyes. 'I think I made it worse by trying to shift again last night,' I confess.

'Gabby, I told you—'

'—not to. I know. Trust me, I'm suffering for it now.' I want to get my shifting under control in case I need to make any sudden getaways. Friday spooked me in more ways than one, so I want to be prepared for *anything*.

She shakes her head while I start eating. 'No more practising for a few days. I mean it.'

'I won't. But . . .' I smile. 'I did manage to set my hand alight, like you did.' I remember the amber flames dancing across my skin. I felt like such a badass.

She purses her lips to try and cover a smile. 'I did say you were close to summoning your shift at will.'

'You did, and you were right.' I eat a few more mouthfuls of liver and suddenly feel so grateful for her. 'I do appreciate everything you're doing for me, y'know, Grandma. For the time you've put aside for me, for helping me with all that you have. I'm just sorry for getting into so much trouble. I'm not trying to complicate your life.' I know how much she enjoys her peace.

'Aht.' She waves her hand to brush me off. 'Complications can sometimes follow people like us, especially when we're newbies. Those journals should have taught you that.'

'Yeah, but you could be making my life so much harder.' She hasn't even told me to tell Mum and Dad what happened. She said it was my choice, and I decided not to.

She frowns. 'Why would I? It's hard enough.'

'True, but still.'

She studies me intently while drinking her tea, and when I finish eating, her expression turns serious. 'I meant what I said about Alok. Don't push him.'

'I won't, I promise.' Grandma told me a little more about Sanse and her vampire type over the weekend, so I'm fully aware how dangerous demon vampires can be. I've also been down Alok's rabbit hole, so I know I need to be careful. Granted, Google didn't have as much information on him as it does other vampire types, but what I read was enough on top of what I've seen.

I definitely can't push him.

I'm dying to know if Oliver knows. On one hand, I think

surely he can't, because he wouldn't be so hellbent on hunting our kind. But on the other, what if he does know and is hiding it for Alok?

Both Grandma and I turn to the door when footsteps approach, but it's only Josh again.

'Still sick?' Grandma asks, concerned.

'Yep,' Josh says. 'Looks like it wasn't just a twenty-four-hour thing. The boy sounded like death warmed up on the phone when he called me this morning.'

'Oh dear . . .'

Maybe he got sick in the woods. He was drunk, and it was a cold night. I should text him . . .

'Are you ready to go?' Grandma asks, getting up.

'Yeah.' *No.*

I'm nervous walking down to the harbour. Alok is here, not that I doubted that he would be, but after everything I've read and found out about him, I'm nervous to see him again.

What's he going to say?

He keeps his eyes on the water when I report to Sam beside him, which annoys me. He had his tongue in my mouth a few days ago, and now he can't even look at me?

'It seems as though the vandalisers had better things to do last night, so there isn't much to do here today,' Sam says, attempting a joke. 'Once you're finished here, we'll be moving up to the abbey. The council would like us to tidy the graves up there.'

RIP to my knees, but at least it will give my back a rest.

We're told to get our things, and then as I follow Alok over to the wall, he abruptly turns to face me, startling me.

'I shouldn't have kissed you. It was a mistake.'

I ignore the surprise hurt his words cause — even though I'd been thinking the exact same thing — and notice the dark circles under his eyes. 'Um, okay.'

He nods before continuing to the wall, and then he gets his things ready like nothing else happened.

'Is that it, then?' I ask, standing with a spray bottle in my hand. 'Is that all you're going to say?'

He shrugs. 'There's nothing else.'

'Don't play dumb with me, Alok. I want to know what the hell you turned into.'

He eyes me while he sprays the wall. 'I don't know what you're talking about.'

I scoff. So I guess he's decided to go with denial. I shouldn't be surprised, seeing as though he avoids almost everything. 'You can't be serious.'

He stays silent, and my frustration grows.

'Alok—'

'Just leave it alone!' His eyes darken like the last time he got angry with me, but this time, they're blacker than the night.

I know I promised Grandma I wouldn't push it but I can't help it. 'Was Friday your first time?'

The glimpse of despair in his eyes tells me that it wasn't, but he doesn't answer.

My heart aches for him then. 'How am I supposed to help you if—'

He turns on me, his dark hair wild and his expression like thunder. 'I didn't ask for your help, or your pity, Gabrielle.'

'Alok—'

'Get to work, Gabrielle!' Sam shouts over to me. 'Those walls aren't going to clean themselves.'

I smile and nod back at him as I grab my brush.

I'm not letting this go, Alok.

'What the actual fu—'

'I know.' I lie down on my bed to talk to Maria, because I'm still tired. 'I still can't believe it myself.'

'I don't think I've ever been so shocked in my life. You're not pranking me, are you?'

'I swear, babe.'

I finally decided to tell her about Alok, mostly because I don't know what else to do.

'I wanted to tell you the other day but . . . I wanted to talk to him first. Properly. That didn't work out, though.' I sigh my torment down the phone. 'He told me to leave it alone and then ignored me for the whole three hours.'

'Damn . . . He's doing the most.'

'He is, but it's because he's in denial. I'm telling you, Maria, it's like he doesn't want to believe that he's one of us.'

'But he must've known something's been up with him. Everyone's vampiric side kicks in at eighteen and he's just turned nineteen. What's he been doing to control his thirst? The cravings? How's he managed to suppress his shift?'

'Not everyone gives into the cravings, though, do they?'

'No, but come on. That's the hardest part to get under control.'

I get off my bed to sit by the window. 'I get that, but he's closed off with almost everyone. And what if that's the reason why? Maybe he's scared of what might happen. Ethan said he's been more angry recently.'

'I mean, it would make sense, but . . .'

'What?'

'What if he's hiding something? What if the attacks in town have been him quenching his thirst?'

My stomach drops harder than I do when I sit back down. 'Shit.'

'Right. Either way, he's dangerous, babe. You really need to be careful, especially because you seem to trigger him. You say he gets mad around you a lot.'

'Yeah . . .' I get a flashback of him kissing me, and how concerned for me he was before he did.

I didn't tell Maria about the kiss — like Alok said, it meant nothing. So better we pretend it never happened.

Still . . . 'As much of a moody prick as he is, he must feel so alone.'

We have to help him.

'You can't force help on him, though, girl,' she says, as if hearing my thoughts.

She's right, and I know she is, but I can't seem to let it go.

'What about Ethan? Has he texted back yet?'

I pull my phone away from my ear to check. 'Nope. Nothing.'

'Forget him, too, then. Rest, play bass, and practise your shift when you're allowed.'

She makes it sound so easy.

'I will.'

Chapter Twenty-Five

Sanse calls an emergency meeting on Thursday night in the same place the group meets on Saturdays. I'm not sure what it's about, but it must be serious, because even Grandma and Maria's dad, Matias, is here.

She's not the only older head here either; there are at least a dozen, and there are two women sitting next to Sanse at the very front of the packed hall that are giving off serious head-honcho vibes.

'Who are they?' I whisper to Maria.

'I don't know who the red-haired one is on the right, but the insanely beautiful one with the head scarf is Kesa. She's an abere: someone who craves blood *and* flesh. I've only ever seen her once before, and that was after a child was bitten and almost drained in the town. Supposedly the work of The Coven.'

'Oh . . .' *Eats flesh? My god . . .*

'Yeah. Whatever the reason for them being here, though, it's bad news.'

'Thank you all for coming,' Sanse says when she stands. 'It's lovely to see so many old faces. However, the reason for us being here is not.' Her smile falls. 'Unfortunately, the woman who was attacked died this morning, and, as a result, tensions in the town have escalated.'

Maria and I look at each other while everyone starts muttering their horror. It's obvious what she's thinking, because I'm thinking the exact same.

Was it Alok?

'I know, I know,' Sanse soothes. 'I was equally as upset when I heard the news. Since our group was established, I, and many others, have actively worked to keep Whitby safe, taking in and nurturing young and seasoned vampire beings alike that need our help. However, it seems our town is welcoming a growing number of creatures that risk threatening all our safety, so we must be very careful . . .

'Now,' she continues, clasping her hands together, 'we are not entirely sure which types of vampires have been responsible for these attacks, but we have managed to look at some of the evidence Oliver has. We believe one of the attackers to be male, due to their stature and height, and he did not leave any marks on the victim, which narrows our suspect pool down dramatically.'

Maria shifts in her seat and sighs, but before I can ask her what's wrong, Sanse introduces the two women beside her.

'Please welcome Kesa and Lani, who are the heads of our region for those of you who have not met them before. Between us, we'd like to answer any questions you may have . . .'

Maria snorts under her breath. 'They say that, but they won't be fully honest, trust me,' she whispers to me. 'They always keep the most worrying information to themselves so that the anxious ones don't start to panic.'

'Can't blame them for that,' I mutter, already anxious myself.

'Could the attacks be by a new group of vampires?' Viviana asks at the front. 'Perhaps they only need some guidance or access to blood if they are struggling with their thirst?'

'It's a possibility, as are many others,' Sanse answers her. 'Which is why we would like to find those responsible before Oliver does. Not only to put an end to the attacks but to help others like us, if they should so need it.'

'Do you think they'll get the use of those stakes approved?' Lorenzo asks, visibly concerned over that matter, like most of us here.

Sanse sighs heavily. 'We can't be certain, but it is looking likely.'

There are mutters of horror around the room, and I give Grandma a look.

She pats my hand before briefly leaning into my side. 'It will be okay, Gabrielle.'

'We won't be able to leave our homes at all at this rate!' a woman angrily yells from behind us. 'I'm already isolated having to stay away from the woods.'

Many agree with her and the room quickly unsettles, but I sympathise with most of the arguments I hear. Some people think that more needs to be done to disband the witches at The Coven in case they *are* the ones behind the attacks, whereas others believe that we should form our own group to hunt down the culprits.

Kesa stands, and the room swiftly falls silent. 'We understand your concerns,' she says softly, 'really, we do. However, our priority, as always, is to keep us all safe, which means right now, we all need to do everything we can to stay out of Oliver's way.'

There's a chorus of sighs after Kesa says that, but as frustrated as people clearly are, they don't protest.

She looks around at everyone in here, her gaze sympathetic but firm. 'Thank you. Please trust that, as always, we have all your best interests at heart. You can also leave here knowing that myself, Sanse and Lani — amongst others — are using every resource at our disposal to put an end to all the unrest in our lovely town.'

Sanse stands again then. 'Before you leave, we would like to speak to a handful of you regarding these incidents. Many of you will know who you are, so please stay behind. The rest of you are free to leave or mingle. Thank you.'

Maria's shoulders slump. 'I'm one of those people,' she says, getting up. 'I'll call you when I'm done.'

I frown up at her. 'Huh? Why?'

Grandma rests a hand on her arm as she passes. 'It will all be fine, Maria.'

She smiles. 'Thanks.' And then I watch her go to the front to sit with her dad.

'Come,' Grandma says. 'We can go.'

But why can't Maria?

'What's going on?' I ask Grandma once we're in the car. 'Why do they want to see Maria? I thought they said they thought it was a male?'

'It is extremely difficult to visibly see a mark left by a peuchen, and they'll be questioning anyone else who can do the same.'

'But how could they even think Maria would do something like that?'

Grandma checks her rearview mirror before she pulls out of the parking space. 'It's just how they do things. She'll be fine.'

But I don't trust it, and nor do I like it.

SUCKERS

I pull out my phone to text Maria so I can offer her some support, but I see another message waiting for me.

Ethan: I'm fine. I'll be back in work tomorrow. Thanks for checking up on me.

'Ethan messaged back. Said he's feeling better.'

'Oh good. He must have been feeling terrible if it's taken him this long to reply, though. I'll make some soup for when he's in tomorrow.' She glances my way. 'And hopefully you two can get back to normal.'

'Yeah . . .' But I'm more concerned about Maria now. 'Could Alok be responsible for the attacks?'

'At this moment in time, Gabby, anything is possible.'

I lean more towards it being him as I write a message to Maria.

Me: Hey girl, hope you're okay. Grandma just told me they talk to everyone with your skill but I think it's bullshit. Everyone knows you'd never do anything like that, so don't worry xxx

I hit send and cross my arms.

Sanse said it's not just one person behind the attacks, so even if Alok is involved, he's not the only one. Could he have somehow ended up in The Coven? What if they found out what he was first and pressured him into hurting people for them?

I feel sick.

Maria doesn't call me back until almost nine o'clock.

'It's all good. Like we heard, they think a guy killed that woman.

From how they described him to Dad and me, I don't think it's Alok either. The guy was stockier.'

'Oh, okay . . .' I put my bass back in her case and sit on the edge of my bed, and then I tell her about my theory. 'What if the bad vampires got hold of him?'

'It's possible. Sanse did say there's a handful of different attackers. Not just men. But we'll all be kept updated. The heads will be keeping a close eye on us for a while, too. I don't think things have ever been this bad. The thought of stakes in the hands of vampire haters is seriously terrifying. I really hope they don't get approved.'

'Same. I just want to know the people behind this mess so it can all stop.'

Maria sighs. 'Trust me, girl. Hopefully you'll be able to find out something from Alok tomorrow.'

I don't hold much hope of that. *If* he talks to me. I might as well not exist to him now.'

'That was before this happened, though. He might have thought of vampires as vermin before, but at least one person knows he's one of us now, whether he likes it or not. And his dad's followers wouldn't think twice about sinking one of their stakes into him.'

I shudder. 'I'll let you know what he says. I'm guessing there's not going to be any meet up this week?'

'No, the group decided not to. Not that I can blame them.'

'All right, well, if you're free Sunday, maybe you could come over and have drinks?'

'Isn't that place haunted?'

I laugh. 'No. It's old, but it's not haunted.'

'Oh, okay, then sure. We need to plan our shopping trip for GothFest, too. Willow and Ava have pretty much dragged everyone into going.'

'Hopefully it's not cancelled.'

Maria groans. 'Don't say that. I need something to look forward to.'

That makes me sit up. 'Why? What's wrong? Are you okay?'

'Nothing, I'm good.'

'All right, I'll text you tomorrow, then?'

'Okay, babe.'

I give Alok the side-eye while we clean the graves at the abbey. In my opinion, finding out he's a blood demon and the timing of all these attacks happening is too much of a coincidence, and now *I* don't trust *him*. To be honest, with everything that's been going on recently, I'm finding it hard to trust anyone.

'What?'

I yank a bunch of weeds out from beside a headstone.

'Gabby?'

I look across to where Alok's working. 'What?'

'Why do you keep looking at me like that?'

I return my attention to my grave. There are flowers engraved into this one. The last one I worked on had two young boys' faces on, so I worked extra hard on making sure it looked nice and tidy. This gravestone is a man's who was born in the seventeen hundreds.

Alok sighs. 'Is this about that woman dying?'

I sit back on my heels to give my arms a rest. 'Why would I think that? It's not like you could be involved, could you? Being normal and all.'

He clenches his jaw. 'Everyone's angry about what happened. My dad's planning a protest on Sunday.'

'I heard they might be given stakes. Did you help make them? Should I add "traitor" to the list of your shitty behaviour?'

His jaw clenches. 'Why are you being like this?'

I scoff. 'Uh, maybe because you haven't said a word to me all week. You haven't wanted to talk, that's cool, but now, neither do I.'

'It's not like that.'

I get back to my weeds, but he keeps trying to talk to me, and it gets me vexed. 'You know I want to talk to you about what happened, so until you're ready for that, I'm not interested. Shit, you know my secret, yet you're acting like you don't have one.'

'I don't—'

'I know what I saw. Stop trying to gaslight me.'

'I'm not.' He checks where Sam is before moving to the grave closest to mine. 'I was going to say, I don't want to have any secrets from you.' He appears tormented then.

My anger immediately turns to sympathy. 'You can't run away from it, Alok. Have you at least found out what you are?'

He shakes his head while brushing down the sides of the headstone in front of him. 'I just know I'm evil.'

I gasp with horror. 'No, you're not. Look, Alok—'

'Less chat, more work, Gabrielle,' Sam says, sounding fed up. 'I don't know how many times I need to remind you why you're here.'

I look up at him and smile. 'I was just resting my arms for a second.'

'Hmmm. If you think this is hard, imagine what prison is like.'

My smile slips. 'I'd rather not.'

He eyes my bucket of weeds. 'Get back to it then. Keep up the good work, Alok.'

'*Keep up the good work, Alok,*' I mimic after he's out of earshot. 'Dick.'

'Isn't it time for our break?' Alok calls after Sam, getting to his feet, and I notice that even without the height of his shifted self, Alok is pretty tall and intimidating. 'Surely there are laws against such abuse of human rights – even for us criminals.'

Sam grimaces. 'Fine. Five minutes,' he says, before stalking off.

I stand and stretch, grateful, but then Alok stalks off.

Maybe he'll talk now?

I follow him to a quieter part of the abbey, to the pond beside it, shaded by the ruins. You can see the sea from here, but when Alok sits down and sighs, all my attention falls on him.

He closes his eyes and I join him, basking in the shade after working out in the sun. When I open them again, he's looking at me.

I break the silence first. 'I'm a soucouyant,' I say, hoping me opening up to him might build some kind of trust between us. 'It's a bloodsucking creature but from, like, Caribbean folklore. My Grandma has the gene, but it skipped my mum, so . . . my parents never told me about it. I turned eighteen and it's like I felt *different* all of a sudden. Things were louder and brighter, and smells were stronger. I started hiding away a lot.'

He scans my face before plucking a blade of grass from beside him and tearing it to tiny pieces, so I continue to talk – even if he just listens.

'I ended up here because . . . there was this guy, Kyle, who I was close with back in London. He kissed me and I should've stopped it, but I didn't and . . .' I wince, remembering the look of horror and disgust on Kyle's face. 'There was blood everywhere. I almost killed him.'

Alok is watching me from the corner of his eye now, his expression unreadable. 'But you didn't.'

'No, he's alive, but that doesn't change how I felt. How I *still* feel.' I tuck my knees up against my chest. 'I just . . . I want you to know that I get how weird this shit is. How scary things can be. I want you to know you can trust me, Alok.'

He swallows, his Adam's apple bobbing, and closes his eyes. 'It's only happened a couple of times before, okay? And never in public. So, I . . . I guess I just pretended it didn't.' He pauses. 'I was scared that my dad would find out and that I had put you in danger, again, and . . . it just happened. But then you looked at me like . . . like I was still me.'

A fist tightens around my heart. 'Alok, you are still you.' I lean closer to him. 'Even when we shift, we're still us.'

'D-do you turn into the same . . . thing . . . as me?' he asks quietly, his gaze holding mine.

I shake my head. 'I burst into flames.'

His eyes fly open, and he looks at me like he can't tell whether I'm joking or not. 'This is all so fucking crazy.'

I breathe a laugh. 'Tell me about it. I can fly, too. So imagine hurling through the air, on fire, not knowing what the hell is happening to you.'

He raises his eyebrows. 'You didn't?'

'I did.'

His lips twitch after a moment of silence, and then we're laughing, a weight having lifted from both our shoulders.

It feels good to laugh.

His eyes soften when we both fall silent again. 'Gabby—'

'Five minutes are up, get back to it!' Sam yells.

I groan when the moment is spoilt, but when Alok gets to his feet and offers me a hand to help me up, I let the disappointment go.

'Thanks,' he says quietly on our walk back over to the graves.

I smile to myself, and then at him.

It's a start.

Chapter Twenty-Six

I eat breakfast early and then sit on the steps at the front of the manor. I've been missing out, because I realised this morning that the sun rises in this direction. I didn't catch this morning's sunrise when I came out here, but I did catch the stunning streaks of amber merging into a red glow over the sky above me a little after.

The half-hour of quiet has done me well. I've thought about a lot out here, trying to clear my head. Or at least, I've tried to. Maria hasn't replied to my message from last night, and I'm worried that maybe I've been putting too much of my shit on her.

I've thought about our conversation in the woods a lot recently, wondering if I've been selfish by overusing her support and not offering enough back in return. She's got her own life and her own struggles, and although she never makes me feel like she hasn't got time for me, I don't want her to start thinking our friendship is one-sided.

I'd hate it if she felt that way, because I really do consider her to be a good friend, if not my best friend. It's why I texted her earlier asking if she was okay and if she needed anything. Not that she's replied to that text either.

Everything in my life seems to be going so wrong . . .

I hear the van coming up the gravel drive, bringing a twinge of anxiety with it. It's been a week since I've seen Ethan, and he was upset with me the last time I did.

He jumps out of Josh's van and smiles when he sees me, but then as if a distasteful memory returns to him, he quickly looks away.

I slowly get up from the step when Ethan and Josh come toward me carrying their tools.

'Morning, love,' Josh says, cheerfully. 'Looks like I'll be having some help today, or at least be having my coffee made for me.'

'Lucky you.' I chuckle. 'Hey,' I say to Ethan, noticing his skin looks paler than usual. It makes my stomach drop, because he must have been really ill.

He looks me up and down with tired eyes. 'Hey.'

Josh heads inside, but Ethan hangs back.

'Are you sure you're well enough to be here?' I ask, resting a hand on his arm. 'You look tired.'

He frees himself from my touch to readjust the handle of his toolkit. 'I'm good,' he says, but it's followed by a heavy sigh. 'I'm sorry, Gabby. For ignoring you all last week, and for the cove. Maria was right, I've been acting like a prick.'

'Because I said we couldn't be more than friends after we kissed?'

He nods, and I see the guilt in his eyes. 'I was hurt, and you weren't talking to me—'

'Because *you*'d been ignoring me. You're the one who went cold after that kiss. Just because I said I couldn't take things further, didn't mean I didn't want to stay friends.'

'I know. I'm sorry, I was wrong. If I could take it all back, I would. It's just . . . you're a beautiful girl, Gabby. You're crazy talented, and you're funny, and those things are only scratching the surface of why I care so much about you.'

Those words soften me. 'I wasn't lying when I said I liked you too, but my life is complicated right now. I don't know how long I'm going to be here, and there are things back home I'm dealing with that you don't know about. It would be selfish for me to drag you into my mess.'

'I get that, but—'

I shake my head. 'You *don't* get it, and I'm glad you don't. I don't want to hurt you . . .' I stop talking then, not wanting to slip up. 'I cherish your friendship, Ethan. Since I arrived, all you've been is kind and caring, but I really can't give you anything other than my friendship in return.'

He closes his eyes briefly and sighs, and then my heart aches with the look he gives me after. 'I don't want to lose your friendship either. I've missed you, Gabby.'

'I've missed you, too.' And that's the truth. 'It's really boring around here without you.'

He chuckles. 'Nice to know.'

'You still don't look well, though. Grandma's making soup for you.' I step toward him, but he steps around me to the door.

'I'd better get to it. I've missed enough work as it is, and I don't want a headache from Josh.' He laughs, but it feels fake.

I turn to watch him disappear, happy we're back on speaking terms.

But a bad feeling settles in my stomach.

After I'm home from group, I spend some time in my room writing music, and then I practise my shift. Not only because Grandma's now given me permission to, but because it's the only other thing I feel like I have control over.

However, I still can't shift fully, no matter how hard I try, and I feel as though all the things I have to worry about are preventing it.

I'm starting to think Maria feels a way about being called in to talk to them over the attacks, and I don't blame her. I hated that she was made to stay behind to talk to them, so I can only imagine how she felt. There's no way she'd do something like that, and I haven't even known her long.

'Poor Ethan still looks sick, do you not think?' Grandma asks when I pass her room on my way downstairs. 'I might suggest he go home.'

I nod as I linger in her doorway. 'That's probably a good idea. He wouldn't listen to me when I suggested it earlier.'

She hums to herself, but then she asks me how I am.

'Frustrated,' I answer, to sum everything up. I go to sit on the edge of her bed. 'I'm glad Ethan and I are talking again, but with the attacks . . . And I still can't fully shift. It's right there, but . . .' I shrug. 'I don't have much time left before I go home.'

'Everything will settle down soon.' She comes over to me and gently holds my arms. 'And you're doing just fine. You have your thirst under control, which is the most important thing, and I don't doubt you'll shift any day now. By the time you go back to London, all these worries will be gone.'

'I hope so.' Yet I doubt it. 'I just don't want to run from my messes again.'

'You won't. A lot of what you're worrying yourself over doesn't even concern you.'

'It doesn't feel like it.' I check my phone when it vibrates, but it's Mum checking in, not Maria, and it eats me up.

I'm going to have to go over there if she doesn't reply soon. I *know* something's wrong.

'Grandma, I'm worried about Maria. She's not replying to my messages. I think maybe I've leant on her too much.'

'It's not that,' she says, sounding guilty.

I lift my head to look at her. 'Huh? Do you know why she's not replying to me?'

Her expression turns grave. 'Gabrielle . . .'

Chapter Twenty-Seven

I run to Maria's front door, taking a deep breath before I knock. Grandma thought I should leave her be until she texts me back, but maybe people leaving her alone when she needs them most is partly to blame for why she didn't tell me. She's not used to people being there for her like she is for everyone else, but I'm not those people.

Hurt consumes me while I wait for someone to answer the door. *I can't believe she thought I might not be friends with her after I found out.* She must be crazy. After all she's done for me since we met? After how understanding and compassionate she's been through all I've told her?

An older woman, almost a spitting image of Maria, opens the door. She has long hair too, and the same, but visibly confused, friendly eyes. 'Hello?'

'Hello, I was wondering if Maria was home—?'

'She is but she's sleeping at the moment.' She regards me closely, and the bunch of roses in my hand. 'And your name is . . .?'

'Oh, sorry, I'm Gabrielle.' I hand over the flowers. 'Could you give those to her?'

'Hello, Gabby. Of course I can.'

'How is she?'

'Better than she was,' she says grimly.

'I'm glad to hear that,' I say, but inside, I'm gutted because I can't see her.

'Did Noemie tell you what happened?' she asks curiously.

I nod, barely holding myself together now. 'When she wakes up, could you tell her it doesn't change anything? That I don't feel any differently. I still think she's amazing—'

'Mum,' I hear her shout, 'you can send her up.'

'Are you sure?' her mum asks, looking up the stairs.

'Yeah.'

'All right.' She opens the door wider and hands me back the flowers when I go inside. 'Her bedroom's at the end of the hall.'

'Okay, thanks.' I'm relieved I'm getting the chance to see her, but I'm nervous, too. Matias told Grandma that she could tell me what happened to Maria, but I don't know if she was meant to tell me everything that's happened to lead up to this, and I don't want Maria to be mad that I know.

The door to Maria's bedroom is open, so I follow the grey carpet around to my left until I see her sitting up in bed. I don't know what I was expecting, but she looks okay, apart from the heavy bags around her eyes.

'Hey, babe,' I say, hovering at the foot of her bed.

'Hey,' she says quietly. 'I'm surprised to see you here.'

I walk around to the side of the bed so I can hand her the roses.

'And I can't believe you thought I wouldn't want to be your friend after I found out.'

'Most people don't. Or they act different.' She closes her eyes as she smells the flowers. 'These are so cute, thank you.'

'Well, I'm not going to.' I sit down on the edge of her bed when she says I can, and then I slowly reach for her hand, relieved when she lets me hold it. 'I'm so sorry.'

'*You're* sorry, why?'

'Because you've been making sure I'm okay, but I didn't do the same for you. I knew there was something going on . . . I hate that you felt like you couldn't tell me.'

'It's not that I didn't want to. I nearly did.'

'That day in the woods, when you made me promise I'd ask for help with my thirst if I needed it?'

She nods. 'I just didn't want you to know how bad things could get . . . You were already going through it yourself. I didn't want to put my burdens on you.'

'But we're friends. You're my *best* friend. How else am I supposed to be there for you if you can't talk about your struggles, too? You've heard mine, over and over.'

She looks towards the window. 'I didn't want to plant ideas in your head.'

'You wouldn't have.'

'Maybe . . .' She sighs as she looks back at me. 'Did your grandma tell you everything?'

I nod, remembering what Maria told me in the woods about her almost taking someone's heart out and how remorseful she looked. 'She told me about the excessive blood consumption starting after what happened after you turned eighteen, and you still needing extra sometimes to keep the thirst at bay.'

Tears well in her eyes. 'I never meant to hurt that man.'

'Hey,' I say, holding her hand tighter, 'have you forgotten why I'm here? I hurt someone, too. You should've known then that I wouldn't've judged you.'

'You didn't know what you were when you did that. *I* did. I gave in to it, and it felt good – at least until I realised what I was doing and stopped. The guilt ate me up after, though, which is why I told Dad. He convinced me to tell Sanse so she could help, which is when I started drinking the donor blood every few months. But then I stopped because no one else I knew needed it like I did. I wanted to be strong.'

I refute that. 'You are strong. And just because you don't know about others that need help with the thirst doesn't mean they don't exist. The thirst is such a huge part of what we are.'

'Yeah. That I hate sometimes.'

'And you're *allowed* to. I hate it sometimes, too, and I bet if you ask at group, others will say the same. It was ruining my life in London long before I knew what it was. You're too hard on yourself, babe.'

'How can I not be when I can't stop being triggered?' She closes her eyes, and I can feel her torment. 'I was doing so well until Mikey cut his hand, and then the obsessive thoughts about blood all came rushing back.'

'Oh, babe.'

'That's the real reason I had to stay behind with Sanse. When I was in deep, the people around me were, too. We were mixing the blood with other things . . .' She grimaces. 'Stronger things that I had no business messing around with. Then later, we found out the guy who'd been supplying me had really hurt some people in the town, and because I was associated with them . . .'

'But you're being punished for a mistake you made ages ago. Will it always be like this?'

'I don't know. It's why I have to attend the group regularly, so they can keep an eye on me. The recent attacks have been so triggering . . . As soon as I heard, I knew they'd be looking to see if I was involved.'

'Well, I know you weren't, and I'm going to find out who it is.'

She widens her eyes. 'Gabby—'

'You can't stop me, so don't try. You just focus on feeling better, all right? Let the people who love you take care of you. And if you need regular blood to keep those thoughts and cravings at bay, then I think you should make peace with that. No one but Sanse has to know if you don't want them to, and it doesn't make you a bad person or weak for needing it. It means you're taking responsibility.'

She gives me a look and smirks. 'Your grandma said that, didn't she?'

I roll my eyes. 'She's rubbing off on me, okay? And she's usually right.'

She smiles. 'Unfortunately, older heads usually are.'

'How was she?' Grandma asks when I get back in the car.

'She's okay but she's beating herself up.'

'Poor soul. She's really been through it.'

'Yeah, and I hate it.' I plug my seatbelt in so we can head home. 'I did give her some of your advice, though, so I'm hoping she listens to it. I just wish she could see herself how I see her, because I think she's amazing.'

'She is. What she's been through could have happened to any of us.'

'Exactly. I told her the same. I don't think she's had many good friends in her life, though. I know she's close with her parents, but I think she's dealt with a lot on her own.'

'Sanse said the same, but maybe things will change now that she has you.'

'I hope so, but even that worries me. I'm not going to be here for much longer, and I don't want to leave her, especially not while she's like this.'

I'm praying she decides to take blood regularly, like I suggested, because that would not only be good for her, but it would put my mind at ease.

'You can stay in contact, and you can always come and visit her. And I hope you do, often. I'll miss you when you're gone.'

I turn to face her, and she glances at me.

'I haven't stressed you out that much then?'

'Oh, stop it.'

I smile. 'I'll definitely come and visit you. Even though things are messy right now, I've really enjoyed spending time with you.' If I'm honest, I'm starting to dread leaving.

'So have I.' She reaches over to pat my knee. 'Are you feeling better now?'

I relax back into my seat. 'Much. Thank you for taking me over there, and for stopping to let me get those flowers. She loved them. I asked her mum for a vase before I left so I could put them beside her bed.'

'They'll make her feel better.'

'I hope so,' I muse, but then I'm quiet for the rest of the journey home.

I want to find out who's behind these attacks, but I don't know this town well enough to do it on my own.

I wonder if Alok will help me.

* * *

I follow close behind Alok to our section of graves on Monday morning, ready to ask my question as soon as we're far enough away from Sam. I don't know if he's going to do it, but he is in as much danger as the rest of us, so I hope he does.

Alok kneels at the grave beside mine but, as usual, he's quiet. This is our last week of community service, which, although I've hated most of the time, I'm also going to miss, in a way. Alok and I had been getting on quite well before the shifting incident, and as much as he likes to act like he's an ass, I can almost confidently say he's not. At least not under all of that hard exterior and front he puts on.

He's quite the caring soul, only he doesn't make it known. Comments from Maria about his rule of no one being on their own, and the way he acted the night in the woods when he thought his dad might catch us, have proved that. I just wish he would let someone care about him, because there's no doubt in my mind that he needs help coming to terms with who he is.

I watch him work for a bit while also working on cleaning my first grave, but once I've checked that Sam's occupied with the newest criminal, I figure it's now or never, because like it or not, my time here is running out.

'Alok—'

'I can't talk about it any more, Gabby. Please.'

'It's not about that.'

He looks up, seemingly surprised.

I start pulling weeds so Sam doesn't catch me slacking. 'I need your help.'

'*My* help? What with?'

'Finding out who's responsible for the attacks in town,' I say, paying close attention to his reaction.

He continues to brush down the headstone in front of him. 'And how am I supposed to help you with that?'

No weirdness. Okay . . . 'You know this place better than I do, and . . . I'm going back to London soon and I don't want to leave knowing the people I've grown to care about will still have it hanging over them.'

He's quiet for a long moment. Then: 'Okay, fine. Do you have any idea how to track them down? The attacks have been random so far.'

I stare back at him. *He's actually going to help me.*

Maybe this will help him come to terms with what he is, too?

'Why are you staring at me like that?'

I blink. 'No reason, sorry. Um, not really. I think the first thing I should do is go to one of your dad's rallies. I need to know what they're planning.'

He glares at me. 'You wanna risk that? Have you forgotten about those stakes? What happens if you . . . y'know?'

'I won't.'

'Gabby . . . I don't think that's a good idea.'

'Please, Alok. I really need to see what's going on myself.'

He remains silent, but when we move to a new section of the graveyard and see a freshly dug grave, he sighs. 'You think this is for that woman?'

Sadness grips me, along with how much more serious this has all become. 'I don't know.'

'There's someone else buried here that was murdered by a vampire. Quick, I'll show you, before Sam comes.'

He leads me over to a black marble headstone placed only eight months ago. The young guy was only nineteen.

'Alok? I'm not trying to push you, but I have to ask. Do you have anything to do with any of these attacks?'

His eyes tell me he's wounded, but instead of getting angry like I expected, he shakes his head and leads me back over to the graves we're working on. 'I swear, I'm not involved with any of it.'

I kneel and get back to work, sighing in relief.

And pray he doesn't make me regret trusting him.

He stays quiet for a while as we work, but then I feel him look at me. 'The next one is tomorrow night in front of the town hall. You can come with me.'

'Thank you.'

'But you stay beside me the entire time, and wear something with a hood, just in case.'

'I will.'

He nods before looking past me. 'Better get to work. Sam's coming this way.'

Ugh, of course he is.

Chapter Twenty-Eight

Alok pulls me closer to his side as we make our way through the heaving crowds of people outside the town hall, and I welcome it, even though he smells better than I think he ever has and is triggering me a little.

I met him at the harbour and was surprised when I saw him waiting for me in a full suit. He said he hadn't had time to go home and change after work, but I don't know if I fully believe that.

He's not said much to me during the walk up here, but he has told me off multiple times. He's already lost me once, and I only found him because he's taller than a lot of other people here. 'Pay attention to where you're going,' he hisses, but without a doubt, he's scared too.

Everyone here is so angry.

I grip his coat sleeve tighter. 'I am.'

I've been nervous about coming as it is, knowing I'd be

surrounded by people who hate me, but also because I knew it would be a test for managing my thirst. This isn't like a gig where I'll have my bass to distract me from the scents I might pick up. But thankfully, so far, apart from the odd one that draws my attention, I'm managing okay.

It's boosting my confidence, no doubt. I start uni in two weeks, so I really need to put the work in to get a grip on situations like this especially. I don't want to miss out on parties and gatherings in Brighton, and when I was playing my bass earlier today I missed gigging for the first time in ages, so I do intend to get back to it.

I doubt it will be with Kyle and the others, because I still haven't contacted him, but I do want to play in front of an audience again. Maybe with a new band, or maybe solo with an electric guitar instead. Maria thinks I could do it, and I have a growing collection of my own songs now . . .

I grasp Alok's arm tighter as a group of three men suddenly barge in front of me, all carrying sharp, pointed stakes the size of their forearms and yelling chants to excite the crowds.

'*Kill them, kill them* . . .'

My next breath catches. They're carrying homemade petrol bombs. 'Alok . . .'

He follows my gaze before pulling me back and taking me a different way towards his father at the front. 'They tried to set fire to The Coven today. They were having shutters put over the windows when I left work.'

'What the *hell*?'

Alok shudders. 'I've never seen it like this before . . . These people want blood.'

'How many people are usually at these things?'

'Maybe twenty?' He holds my hand tightly and begins to physically move people in front of him. 'Excuse me . . . thanks . . . Maybe thirty, max.'

I swallow uncomfortably. 'But there are hundreds here. If not more.'

He looks down at me, his expression grave. 'People told themselves the videos and pictures were AI, but now that someone's died . . .'

We get closer to the front, finally, even passing some women with their children, until we reach the town hall steps, where Oliver is standing behind a podium. There's a microphone set up on it and a large screen behind with an amp underneath, and there's a pile of flyers detailing their next meeting.

This is so much more serious than I thought, and I wish I never came.

'Son.' Oliver smiles, but he isn't as welcoming to me. Perhaps he blames me for his son having community service. 'Gabrielle, right?'

'Yes. Hello.' I want to throw up now that I'm face to face with him. He's wearing a black suit, shirt and tie, like he's about to attend a funeral, and somehow, he appears older than he did when I first saw him. His forehead is heavily wrinkled, and he has deep, dark circles under his piercing blue eyes that are unmistakably suspicious of me.

When I saw him at the police station, he was defending his son, so it was easy to hope that he wasn't the judgemental, hate-spewing man that he was rumoured to be. Now, though, as his gaze lingers to the point of being uncomfortable, my inner fire feels threatened, and so do I.

I must have been crazy to think this was a good idea . . .

'Hmmm.' He assesses me a moment longer before giving me a half smile. 'Nice to have your support.'

'Uh, thanks?'

He gives Alok's shoulder a warm shake. 'Why don't you and your friend stand back there? We're about to start.'

'Thanks, Dad.' Alok motions for me to follow him to a small area between two middle-aged men. Once there, we wait for Oliver to address the still-growing crowd.

People are shouting angrily and repeatedly shunting their stakes in the air.

'Thank you all for coming,' he says, but it takes a while for him to quieten everyone. 'I understand your anger and, believe me, I feel the same. Let me begin by showing you the victims . . .' He turns to the screen where a picture of the woman who was murdered is shown, before several other pictures of other victims of vampire attacks.

The crowd becomes even more enraged.

'Now, these are the images we have of potential suspects . . .' The screen shows multiple hooded men and woman, their faces barely visible.

There are then several gasps and angry shouts from the crowd when stills of attacks caught on camera are shown on screen, which Oliver allows for a moment before he settles the crowd again.

I can't even lie, I'm just as stunned as they are. The glimpse of the image of the young male victim staring terrified at a hooded man in front of him gives me chills.

'I have been assured that our local police are working their hardest to apprehend them,' Oliver says, 'but we all must stay vigilant and look out for one another. No visiting the woods on your own, abide by the curfew unless in public places, and do not go out in groups of less than four.'

Most of the crowd cheers then, but many aren't satisfied.

'The police have barely done anything! None of us can sleep at night! What happens when those shapeshifting suckers start breaking into our houses?'

'You will all leave here with a stake, and you have permission to use them in self-defence. Keep one beside your front doors, beside your beds . . .' Oliver beckons Alok to him then, and I can only gape when he lifts a wooden stake from his podium.

I instinctively step forward, barely able to breathe when Oliver holds Alok by the arm.

'Thrust deeply into the chest, over the heart.' Oliver lifts his hand, lowering it swiftly before stopping at Alok's chest. 'That will end them nice and quickly.'

The protesters go wild.

But while they cheer, the forced calm on Alok's face breaks me. When his eyes meet mine on his way back over to stand with me, he looks as desperate as I feel.

'However,' Oliver continues casually, 'if you manage to catch one, there will be a reward for doing so.'

What the hell?

'Now, as our biggest event in Whitby is approaching, we wish to ask for your help. We expect this year's attendance for the GothFest to be the highest it's ever been, which means the chance of attacks and these vermin coming into town will be higher. There will be a risk, and we understand you must think of your families first, but if you can join one of the groups policing the festival over the weekend . . .'

I reach my hand out to Alok's beside me, attempting to offer him comfort when I sense him becoming more and more closed off, but he pulls it away as soon as I touch his skin.

My thoughts turn to how they're going to seek the attackers out, and the fact that there will be deadly stakes in the hands of intoxicated people out for blood and revenge . . .

We have to find those responsible before they do. If the attackers are hurting people intentionally, that's one thing and they deserve to be punished. But if they're new to this life like I am and need help to control their gifts, they at least deserve the chance to be caught without being harmed.

I'm lucky that I've had support, but I know not everyone like us will have that.

Oliver answers a few more questions before telling the assembled crowd about the many anti-sucker groups online that they can join to keep updated about the situation, and then he gives them the date of the next meeting and town protest, before asking for anyone wanting to help to stay behind.

I feel sick when most people do, including some of the mothers. This is *bad*.

Alok is completely silent as he walks me home, and he has been since he practically dragged me away from the town hall.

I watch him out of the corner of my eye. He's deep in thought, but his expression is still blank. I know he's dealing with some internal conflict — seeing one of his dad's rallies from an entirely different perspective — so I decide to take Grandma's advice this time and not push it.

'Thanks for walking me home,' I say quietly when we reach the doorway to the manor.

He nods before he turns, and then I watch him walk away. He heads back down the driveway until I can't see him any more, and I go inside.

Grandma's bedroom door is open when I go upstairs, so I sit on her bed with her and tell her what I found out.

She's horrified. 'We need to be very, very careful.'

'I know. It was so bad. There were so many angry people there. So many more than I thought there'd be.'

'And you can't blame them. We need to hide anything that links us to being soucouyants.' She gets up from the bed only to kneel and pull up three of her floorboards, and then she starts grabbing books from her shelves. 'Go and get your necklace.'

I run to my room to get it, and she quickly gathers it in with the others, before lowering them beneath the floorboards.

'I didn't see Sanse there, but do you think she was? Do you think she knows how bad it's getting?'

'She'll know, but she won't want to worry everyone, not when some of them are worried enough. Don't—'

'I won't tell anyone at the next group meet. Hell, I wish *I* didn't know.'

She puts two more boxes inside the floor before replacing the boards and warning me to be careful with my journal. 'What did Alok think about it?'

'I think he feels the same as us. Maybe even worse now. Oliver used him to show the crowd how to stake a vampire.'

She gasps with disgust. 'He did *what?*'

I nod, grimly. 'His own son. I know Oliver doesn't know he's one of us, but . . . it was awful, and Alok barely said a word after.'

'That poor boy, I'm not surprised.'

'I hate that he's alone in all this, Grandma. I just wish he'd ask for help.'

She holds my hand firmly. 'You're right to realise that it is *he* that needs to ask for help – if he needs it. But you're also doing the right thing not telling him about the other vampires in Whitby or the group, at least for now. I know it's a difficult balance.'

'It is.' I sigh as I get up to leave. 'I'm going to practise my shift.'

'I think that's a good idea.'

I'm half asleep when I hear a clattering in my room. I switch my lamp on and see Alok, half hanging through the window.

'Alok?' I hiss. 'What the *hell* are you doing?'

'G-Gabby,' he slurs as I scramble out of bed. 'Sorry, couldn't find the front door. This place is huge.' He lands on the floor in a heap, just before I reach him, and I immediately smell alcohol mixed with his sweet scent. He's still wearing his suit, too.

'I'm, like, three floors up, how did you even—?'

'Magic,' he chuckles.

I shake my head as I attempt to help him up, but then I gulp down a rush of nerves when he looks up at me with dark, hooded eyes.

'I could smell you. I always can.'

'Alok, you're drunk,' I mutter, directing my gaze to his feet until he's stable. Then I help him over to the end of my bed so he can sit down. 'You need water.'

'That guy – what's his name? I couldn't remember. Kevin, Kris—'

'Kyle?' I ask, returning to sit beside him with the bottle of water from my dresser.

'Yeah, Kyle,' he spits. 'He's an idiot. I was drinking and thinking . . .' His sharp gaze goes to my mouth. 'A kiss of death from you doesn't sound so bad.'

'You don't mean that. The alcohol—'

'I looked up what I am,' he whispers, cutting me off. 'Riri yaka – a blood demon. I'm a *demon*, Gabby. I told you I'm evil.'

'No, you're not.' When he scoffs, I grab his chin so I can look him in the eyes. 'You're *not* evil.'

His eyes search mine — for what exactly, I'm not sure, but it's suddenly hard to breathe.

'You can't believe everything you read, Alok — especially about vampires. I'm supposed to be an old hag that goes around obsessing over grains of rice.'

He grins and my heart clenches. 'I read that when I looked you up.'

'Do you think everything else fits?' I ask, offering him the water. 'What you read about riri yaka?'

He nods but ignores the bottle. 'I always thought my mother died when I was born, but now I'm not so sure.'

I'm relieved when he finally takes the water and drinks some, but he doesn't give it back to me after. He rests it on the bed and then when I rest a hand on his arm to comfort him, he holds it tight and closes his eyes.

'Mum and Dad could never have their own children, so when they got the chance to adopt me, Mum said their dreams came true. Watching my dad at those rallies, and the way he talks . . .' His eyes open, full of torment. 'He can't ever find out. *Ever.*'

'You don't know, he might—'

'No, I *do* know. It's why I've spent the last year pretending that I'm not what I am. He can't find out, Gabby, he can't. You saw what he did, with that stake . . . He'd— He'd kill me.'

He's breathing really hard now, and I can see his hand trembling.

'Hey, hey,' I soothe. 'He won't find out. I'll help you learn to control it, okay? I promise.'

He begins to relax then, and I think back to what I've learned so far and what he might be able to use to control himself.

'Our other form is highly tied to our emotions, so you have to try to control them, okay?' I say. 'From what I've seen, you're pretty good at that.'

He laughs at my sarcasm as I get up to retrieve his phone, which is vibrating by the window. 'Being around you has taught me more than I've learnt in a year. You're so damn frustrating.'

'*Me?*' I scoff as I turn around, but my footsteps back over to him falter.

There's no trace of the humour visible mere seconds ago. Instead, his gaze is trailing my body in the very thin nightdress I have on.

'Someone's calling you,' I say quietly when I hand him his phone, but he completely ignores it and gets up. He grabs my waist, lowering his face to mine with a look so dark and dangerous, my entire being feels on fire.

'You feel warm,' he says, scanning my face.

I realise my skin is tingling, fiercely. 'I— Does it not hurt?'

He frowns. 'What?' he asks, his breath caressing my mouth. 'Does what hurt?'

'Me.'

He blinks and looks down, quickly snapping his head back up when he sees the glow to my skin. 'Am I causing that? Are you . . . are you going to shift?'

I nod, knowing that I should push him away, but his gaze holds mine, and I can't.

'Do it,' he dares, when my eyes begin to flame. 'It won't hurt.'

'How can you be so sure?'

His eyes soften, but his hand on my waist tightens. 'Just trust me.'

I gasp when his lips capture mine, trembling when the smoky, sweet taste of him hits my tongue.

I quickly pull back, though, because as he moans against my lips, I burst into flames.

His eyes are blood-red when I look at him, but it's the darkness inside them that silences me. 'I told you.'

He kisses me again, more fervently this time, and I feel like I'm melting into his arms. His embrace is tight, his breaths hurried like mine, laced with the alcohol . . .

'Alok, stop.' I push a hand against his chest, surprising myself with just how little force I need to put some space between us. 'We can't do this, you're drunk. *Shit.*'

We stare back at one another as we catch our breath, but his eyes lower again. And then widen with surprise.

'You weren't joking,' he says, following the flames rippling over my skin.

I roll my eyes. 'No, I wasn't.' As happy as I am that I've finally managed to shift again, this entire situation is far from good.

He smiles. 'You look *incredible*.'

That makes me smile, but then I'm filled with guilt. What would Ethan think if he knew I kissed Alok. *Again?*

The flames disappear with that thought, and only the amber hue remains in my eyes.

His eyes return to normal as if he can hear my thoughts. 'I'll go.'

'Alok, I didn't—'

'It's cool, I should get home,' he says, picking his phone up from my bed. He's back to his closed-off self. 'See you in the morning?'

'At least let me see you out the front—'

He shakes his head as he climbs out of the window. 'I'm good. Night, Gabby.'

I sigh as he disappears. 'Goodnight, Alok.'

Chapter Twenty-Nine

I stand in front of the mirror, excitedly gushing as the flames ripple around me. I figured, after last night, I should try to shift again, especially as I wasn't tired when I woke up.

And I did it!

However, I haven't quite figured out how to shapeshift into different fireforms, so I might need some pointers from Grandma for that.

'I'll go and make breakfa—' She beams a smile at me as she comes into my room. 'Look at you,' she sings happily, and I realise this is the first time she's seeing me like this.

She trails a hand down the length of my arm when she reaches me. 'Wow . . . it's been a long, long time since I saw someone else like this.' She must be talking about her mother, because she's mentioned watching her shift as a young girl and how magical she thought it was. 'How do you feel?'

SUCKERS

'Good. I did it last night as well and I wasn't tired when I woke up. Does this mean I'm keeping that flame topped up?'

She chuckles. 'I should think so.'

'I can only get this form, though,' I say, when she stands in front of me. 'I don't know how to do the rest.'

'All right.' She goes to lock my bedroom door and close my curtains before returning to me. 'So, all you need to do now you've got this far, is envision yourself as the form you desire.'

I frown. 'That's it?'

She smiles. 'That's it. You can close your eyes if you need to for now, or however you think will work best, but if you can see yourself as it, you can be it.'

Okay . . .

I close my eyes and imagine myself as an orb, burning fierce like the sun, glowing brightly like Grandma did . . .

'And there you go.'

I open my eyes, hastily looking for my limbs but finding none. 'I did it!'

'You did,' Grandma says, proudly. 'Give me a twirl.'

I concentrate to spin around, and I'm beyond excited when I accomplish it.

'Now come and rest in my hands.'

I float over to her palms, still amazed that we can't burn each other like this. *Or Alok.* 'Uh, what now?'

'Just like before. Imagine yourself slipping through my fingers, or becoming particles, or dust – whatever works for you, dear.'

It takes me a little more time to manage that, but with some gentle pushing and encouragement from Grandma, I begin to slip through her fingers. 'Oh my god, I'm doing it!'

'You are.'

'It feels so weird. Like I'm in a million places at once.'

She chuckles as she watches me remould myself into a ball. 'I know exactly what you mean.'

I become conscious of the time so I shift back to my human form, and once no longer on fire, I hug Grandma tightly. 'Thank you.' But I also think of Maria.

I can't wait to show her.

'You are more than welcome.' Grandma rubs my back. 'Fun, isn't it?'

'*So* fun.' My heart is on cloud nine right now. 'I can't wait to try it again later.'

She releases me and chuckles. 'You'll have plenty of time for that, but for now, you should eat, or you'll be late.'

I follow her downstairs, but instead of going into the kitchen with her, I head out to the front of the house and find Ethan looking for something in his van.

'What you looking for?' I ask, scaring him.

'Shit, Gabby.' He holds his chest as he turns to me. 'Was that payback?'

I chuckle. I notice the colour is back in his face, and he's looking better than ever.

'I just wanted to make sure you were feeling okay.'

'I'm great,' he says, turning back to his task. 'What have you been up to?'

I begin rambling about nonsense but am distracted by his T-shirt riding up his back and how good he smells. My thirst hasn't been triggered around him for a while, but now that he's feeling better, it seems that's stronger, too. And then I remember Alok and the feeling of his mouth on mine and how it had triggered my shift, and I'm filled with guilt.

I clear my throat and tell him about the anti-vampire rally; how I had been hoping to hear more about the attacks.

His eyes widen in alarm. 'Why the fuck did you risk going there when——?'

I shriek my surprise at his outburst before taking a few steps back. 'Ethan, what the hell is wrong with you?'

He tries to compose himself, but even when he apologises, his jaw is still tense. 'I just don't think you should've gone, Gabby. Those protests aren't safe. There are other ways to find out info without putting yourself at the centre of those psychos.'

I cross my arms. 'It's not like they're after me; I wasn't in any danger,' I lie. 'And I wasn't alone. I went with Alok, so it's not like—'

'*He* went with you? Are you fucking serious right now?'

'Yes, because— Actually, you know what? I don't need to explain myself to you.' I huff. 'I get that you've not been well, but I don't deserve to be spoken to like shit.'

'I wasn't— I didn't mean—'

'I need to go,' I snap before I storm away from him.

How dare he?

'All good?' Alok asks when I arrive at the abbey, and I get the feeling he's testing the waters after last night.

'I'm good.' I decide to keep the mood light, especially after my argument with Ethan. 'How's the hangover?'

He chuckles as we collect our buckets. 'I don't get hangovers. Those stopped about a year ago.'

I roll my eyes as I follow him to the graves, but I'm glad to know he's okay – or at least acting like he is. Even though our kiss kept playing on my mind as I lay in bed long after he'd left, what he'd said about finding out what he was had also kept me awake.

He's opening up more and more . . .

Alok doesn't bring up our kiss or what he said in my bedroom while we clean the graves, but he does bring up the attacks. We spend a lot of time trying to see if there's been any pattern to them.

There isn't.

I groan. 'This is so annoying. We need to find a way to draw them all out.'

'But how?'

'I don't know.'

He eyes me. 'So figure out how, because we're not accomplishing anything right now.'

'Yes, we are, we're doing what we do best. Arguing.'

He throws me a quick glance, but I see his smirk.

'I saw that.'

He shrugs. 'You're funny. Sometimes.'

'A lot of the time, thank you. Even when you used to hate me, I used to see you trying not to let a smile slip.'

He fully laughs. 'Someone's been keeping a close eye on me.'

'Yeah, so I could figure out why you were such a prick.'

His eyes soften. 'I had to be careful who I was around, that's all. Anyway,' he says, turning his attention back to his headstone, 'I heard my dad mention trying to lure them out at GothFest, but he's worried about putting any more locals in danger.'

'How would he do that, though?'

'I don't know, but you've already got a ticket, right?'

'Yeah . . .'

'All right,' he says, but I still feel his gaze on me for a while longer. 'I've got one, too. The whole group is excited for it.'

Willow added me to the group chat, so I already know. 'What are you going to wear? Want some suggestions?'

He scoffs. 'I don't need any.'

I smirk. 'Oh, I'm so sorry.'

'What are you going to wear?'

'You want to ruin the surprise?' I ask him playfully.

He chuckles. 'Nah, I wouldn't want to do that.'

I was beyond excited when I finally saw a message from Maria after community service, asking if I wanted to meet her in town for coffee. I'd messaged her this morning, asking how she was, so when she'd replied and said she was feeling better, I literally ran to Sherlock's Coffee Shop.

It's a cute, little blue terraced building in the town centre, all wooden décor and tables, with orange stringed flowers hanging in the windows. It's giving Halloween vibes in the middle of summer, and it's also busy, so I'm not sure where we're going to sit . . .

'You look *so* good.' I hug Maria when I find her inside near the queue, waiting for me. She's had her hair braided, and she's glowing. 'I love that jacket, too.' It's green and has chains hanging from the sleeves. Definitely something I would wear.

'Thanks, girl. Dad got it for me yesterday from that second-hand shop near the memorial. Said I deserved it and that he was proud of me.'

'Aww, I love that. Sounds like something my dad would say. So are we celebrating something, or . . .?'

She nods excitedly when we join the queue. 'I took his advice and yours. Decided I didn't need to prove how strong I was to anyone.'

My stomach knots with excitement. 'So does that mean . . .?'

'Yep. Once a month for now, but if I don't need it, I don't have to go. I already feel so much better.'

'Oh, babe . . .' I hug her again, tighter this time. 'I'm so happy you've thought of yourself first, and I'm proud of you, too. You seem happy with your decision——?'

She breathes a sigh of relief. 'I am. I'm *so* over denying myself, and it's like you said: no one has to know if I don't tell them, right?'

'Right. It's none of anyone's business.' I grin at her. 'How have you been apart from that?'

'Bored as hell. I've missed you, and the daily updates of Gabby's life.'

I laugh as we move up closer to the counter. 'I didn't want to stress you out while you were resting.'

She's visibly upset by that. 'You wouldn't have. I know you've got gossip. Let me get these and you can fill me in.' She looks around. 'We can go sit on the beach. This place is the best for coffee, but not for sitting in.'

'That's cool, but I'm getting these.'

I ask her what she wants when we reach the barista, and after getting us both macchiato lattes, we walk down to the beach. Maria chooses a spot close to the water, but far enough away from anyone else so we can't be heard.

'So, fill me in,' she says, after taking her trainers off so she can dig her toes into the sand. 'I know you have some tea.'

'Maybe, but first I wanted to tell you some good news.'

'You and Ethan are together?'

I wedge my coffee cup into the sand. 'Huh? No. What the hell?'

She giggles. 'Oh, my bad, go on.'

I shake my head and hide my grimace when I remember this morning. 'I can shift now. Like, on demand.'

'*What?*'

'Yep. I can't wait to show you. And . . .' I look around to make sure no one's looking, and then I make my eyes flame. 'Sick, right?'

'Girl, that is literally fire. I can't wait to see the full thing. You are gonna show me, right? I still feel salty that Alok almost saw it before me.'

'That wasn't intentional, believe me.' *Neither was last night . . .*

'Maybe not,' she says, oblivious to my emotional torment, 'but it's still not fair.' She shakes her hair back in mock annoyance. 'And how is community service with the devil going? Is he still in denial?'

I shake my head, and she widens her eyes.

'He's admitted it?'

'Yep, we've talked about it.' I fill her in with everything that's happened, omitting a few things, but Maria's not dumb and I have a feeling she can tell.

'So how did you get him to talk about it?'

I sip my coffee. 'Talking about myself. He seems more comfortable opening up when I do.'

'Makes sense.'

'Yeah . . . He's also been helping me.'

Her eyes narrow. 'Do what?'

I'm reluctant to tell her, so I tell her about the rally first.

'That doesn't sound good,' she says, quietly.

'It isn't,' I admit. 'But now we know what we're dealing with.'

'Yeah,' she muses. 'So do you know exactly what they're planning for GothFest?'

'A few things . . . I don't want to trigger you.'

'Why? Because there's blood involved?' she says, lightly.

'I don't know if there will be, but their plan is to lure vampires out with something.'

'Well, even if they do, it doesn't work like that, babe. And now that I can have it when I want, I'm good to be around it, really.'

I still hesitate to tell her what I saw at the rally, though, especially after Grandma said not to tell anyone.

She crosses her arms across her knees. 'I thought you weren't going to treat me any differently?'

'You're right, I'm sorry. Well . . .' I tell her about the rally and what Oliver did to Alok.

She gapes at me. 'You are *not* serious?'

I nod, grimly. 'He was so shaken, and so was I. I knew Oliver was evil, but even I was shocked when he pulled that move.'

'And his own dad? That's horrible,' she says quietly. 'I can't believe I actually feel sorry for Alok.' She shakes her head. 'Those things are scary. I still can't believe the police have allowed people to carry stakes for self-defence.'

'I know. Do you think Sanse knows about all this? Do you think she'll warn us off going to the festival at the group meet on Saturday?'

'The group isn't on. Sanse and a few of the others are already planning to go to the festival.' She shakes her head. 'I can't believe you went to that rally with all those wannabe killers.'

'I had to. I had a feeling Sanse wasn't telling us everything, and she wasn't.'

'Don't take it personally. Honestly, Sanse's main priority is to keep us all safe and as stress-free as possible. She probably already knows what Oliver's plan is; she just doesn't want to worry us.'

'I get that, but I want to help find who it is doing the attacks, and I don't want to go back to London knowing this is still going on.'

SUCKERS

There's no denying that she's upset about that, but if I'm honest, so am I. Every day that passes, I feel less happy about leaving here.

'So you've decided to still go to uni then?'

'Yeah, mostly . . . I figure now I'm getting my triggers under control, I haven't really got an excuse not to, and if it does get hard, I'll think of something else.'

She reaches over to squeeze my hand. 'Good for you. What about Kyle? Have you texted him yet?'

I hate the way my stomach reacts when he's mentioned. 'No . . . I've been close a few times, because I do want to know what he wanted when he called around to my parents, but I'm still scared of what he's going to say.'

'Maybe just leave it, babe,' she says with a shrug. 'I mean, will you see any of your band mates at uni?'

I shake my head.

'Then let them find a new bass player. I'm sure you can find a new band to play in when you start uni. Or solo it, like I said.'

'That's all well and good, but I feel like I owe him an explanation.'

'I guess. You've still got time to think about it then, but don't feel pressured. You've got the chance to start over now. There haven't been any police at your parents' door, and you didn't send him to the hospital, so if you need to put it behind you, do it. If he was that desperate to find you, he'd have been at your house every day.'

'That's true . . .' I drink some more of my coffee and think about what Maria's said. It would be easy to just walk away from London and start fresh in Brighton, but I don't want it hanging over me. What happens when I go home to visit my parents and I bump into him or someone else from the band? I don't like the thought of that.

'So, we're still going to GothFest then,' Maria says, before suddenly clapping her hands excitedly. 'When are we going shopping?'

'Now?'

'Hell, yeah. Mind if I invite some of the girls?'

'Of course not. We can all help each other find outfits.'

'They're going to be so excited,' she says, pulling out her phone, but then she looks at me and gasps. 'It can be your leaving do! The others will love that. They've been asking if I was going to plan something before you left. Willow's already planning to come and visit you in Brighton, by the way. I told her you might be solo gigging, and she can't wait for it.'

I laugh. 'She's so sweet.'

She starts texting on her phone. 'Where should we get them to meet us?'

'Tell them to come here. Oh, and before I forget . . .' I hold Maria's arm so she meets my gaze. 'Make sure you don't let on to Alok that you're one of us. I don't care that he knows about me, but not you.'

Chapter Thirty

I spend the next afternoon after community service message-deep in outfit discussions in the GothFest group chat, and I also run the boots I promised Maria over to her house.

She's going to wear a black leather skirt and latex body suit that will match with a jacket I've already seen her wear, and I'm going to semi-match with a checkered leather skirt, a white, ripped, cropped top and my denim jacket. And of course I'll wear my favourite boots.

I loved how excited everyone was yesterday, and how they're all embracing the dark theme of the event. However, I have been a little sad, too, because Willow and Ava keep mentioning it being my goodbye party in the group chat, and it's starting to make me think I've made the wrong decision not to take a gap year.

There'll be no more fresh air — well, not until I get to Brighton; no more wild parties on the beach, being forced to play volleyball;

no more long, tiring walks home through spooky woods; playing bass in the most epic hall I've ever played in; leftovers or wise advice from Grandma . . .

No more Ethan or Alok . . .

It's going to be lectures, study, and making new friends again.

I'm not even excited about uni any more . . .

It's funny how things work out. I may have come here emotionally broken because of the craziest of reasons, but I'm so thankful that I did. Yes, the others in the group don't know my biggest secret, but they accepted me when I felt lost and knew no one, and frankly, they've made my summer. If it wasn't for them, I don't know what or where I'd be right now.

Ava: The weather says it's going to be hot on Saturday now. Should I wear shorts instead?

Maria: Stop changing your mind.

Willow: Wear a skirt like me, babe.

I smile as I read the messages. *I really hope they don't kick me out of the chat after the festival.*

'I found the pictures,' Grandma sings when she joins me on the patio, carrying a thick black photo album that's worn along the spine. 'Ready to see?'

'Definitely.' I move my glass of water out the way and shuffle my chair closer to hers. 'I've been waiting for this.'

'Well, wait no more.' She opens the album up, and my eyes immediately widen. There's a black and white picture of her as a young girl on a trike, and she has the curliest hair.

'That was my favourite toy.' She smiles lovingly at the photo. 'I rode it until the wheels fell off.'

'You didn't?'

'I did. My father fixed it repeatedly until he couldn't any more. I bought your mother one similar when she was that age. She loved hers just as much.'

'She looks a lot like you there,' I say, when she points to a picture of her a little older.

'Wait until you see the teenage ones. Your grandfather used to say she was my double.'

'Does she have his personality?'

She thinks about that question. 'She does, yes.' She flicks through the next few pages quickly, showing me more pictures of her childhood, but then the transition from black and white to colour happens, and the exciting photographs start coming.

'I'd wear that,' I say, when I spot her dressed in fishnet tights and an oversized biker jacket. 'That too . . . wow . . . You had style, Grandma.'

She chuckles. 'I know I did. Fashion was the thing to do back then.' She shows me some pictures of her in corsets next, and I wish she had kept them.

'They'd be vintage now, y'know? Worth thousands probably.'

'If I had them now, they'd be of no use. I made sure I got my money's worth.'

'So, you wore them until the seams fell apart?'

'You could say that . . . Let me see . . .' She turns to the back of the album, and that's when she shares her pictures of Grandad with me. 'This was on our wedding day.'

'That dress is stunning . . . and you look so happy. You both do.'

She smiles wistfully. 'We were so very happy . . .' She turns the page quickly. 'This was when your mother was born . . .' She only shows me a few more pictures after that, and then she closes the album.

Poor Grandma . . .

I hold her hand when she strokes the front of the album. 'Thank you for sharing these with me.'

She nods. 'It was my pleasure to. I'm going to come and visit you a lot more than I used to,' she says, suddenly tearful. 'I'll very much miss you when you leave.'

'I'm going to miss you, too, so much. I don't think I would have gotten through these past six weeks if it wasn't for you.'

'Well, I'm happy to hear that, but if you ever need me again, you know I'm only a phone call away. Or a text,' she adds, rolling her eyes.

That's definitely a reference to how much Maria and I message each other.

'Do you know how to send them back?'

'You know I do, young lady.'

I laugh. 'I was just joking.'

Grandma tells me about the group being cancelled this weekend and Sanse's plans to attend the festival with Kesa and Lani, but I tell her I already knew. She doesn't tell me to reconsider going, but she does caution me about staying far away from Oliver and any of his followers . . .

I do like how Sanse seems to genuinely care about other vampires, whether they're seemingly good or bad. Now Maria's told me more about the way she's helped her with her gift and cravings, I'm hoping they find a way to find all the rogue vampires, because it means Sanse will help them, and not try to kill them like Oliver will.

SUCKERS

It makes me hate that Alok still doesn't know about her or the group, because I think it could help him in so many ways if he did. Leaving him to carry this burden on his own has been eating me up inside. I couldn't think of anything worse than being alone with what I am.

That really makes me want to take a gap year . . .

I'm going to miss him. Our relationship may not have started off great by any means, but during our community service, playing detectives and the moments we've shared alone, I've seen a side of him that I don't think many people have. But they should, because although hard on the outside, he has such a kind heart.

I go to lie on the grass in the gardens to kill time before lunch, but then I get sad because this will be one of the last times I get to do this. *I'm going to miss this place so much.* I definitely want to come back to visit. It's gone so quickly.

'Ah, this is the life.'

I turn my head to see Ethan, who's just lain down on the grass beside me, but I don't smile at his attempt at a joke. 'It was.'

He turns his head to face me, and I see regret in his eyes. 'I'm sorry for how I spoke to you, Gabby. I was way out of line. Just, when you told me you'd gone to that rally, I was so worried about you.'

I sigh as I look back up at the sky. 'You could've just said that.'

'I know. I just can't seem to stop myself from feeling protective over you. This town is . . . it's not safe.'

I turn my head back to face him. 'I know it's not, but I'm a big girl, Ethan. I can make decisions for myself.'

He sighs. 'I know.'

I do understand his concern, especially because I know how

much he cares for me. Hell, Alok even took some convincing before he agreed to take me.

'I forgive you, but only if you come to the festival on Saturday after work.'

His eyes do that twinkly thing when he smiles. 'I promise I will try my hardest to come.'

I hope he does.

'You gonna miss it here?' he asks.

I nod and close my eyes, overcome with that melancholy feeling again. 'Amongst all the drama, this has been one of the best summers of my life.'

He slips his hand in mine, so I open my eyes. 'Bet you didn't expect that when you got here, huh?'

'Nope, not at all.' I look back up at the sky and let the warmth of the sun caress my face. 'Depending on how long you take to get this place straight, I might come back to stay with my grandma again next summer.'

'We should be finished by then, unfortunately.' He's quiet for a while. 'You'll have to invite us down to visit you at uni.'

'I will.' Him, especially. *When I think about not seeing him almost every day* . . .

'I hope so.' He squeezes my hand gently before letting go, but when I turn to face him again expecting him to leave, he doesn't. He just looks at me in silence, and I follow his eyes scanning my face, then my ink . . .

'What are you doing?'

He slowly shakes his head, but then he sighs when Josh calls him. 'I'll be glad when the roof is finished.'

I sit up when he stands, annoyed that he has to leave so soon. 'Same time tomorrow?'

His eyes light up. 'Can you make it lunchtime?'
'Definitely.'

'What's got you so quiet?' Alok asks as we start packing our things away at the abbey for the last time. 'You've been miles away the entire morning.'

I sigh as I rinse off my brush in the bucket of water. 'I'm scared about Saturday. I don't want anyone getting hurt.' I turn to look at him when I feel his eyes on me. 'I don't want *you* getting hurt.'

The excitement in the group chat has been great for taking my mind off the attacks, but the closer the festival gets, the more frightened I become about what Oliver is planning to do to lure us out, because no one seems to know. Not even Alok.

'I won't get hurt, and no one else will either. I won't let that happen.'

'I don't mean just physically.' I check my phone, gripped by sadness when I see our time together is done. 'What if you're triggered? What if you shift by accident?'

'I won't. Stop worrying about me.'

'I can't . . .' I busy myself with my things again, desperately trying not to break down and cry. *If anything happened to him because of me . . .*

He holds my arm, his eyes soft when I look up at him. 'Hey, as long as we stick together, we have nothing to worry about, right?'

I nod.

'Then it will be okay. We'll watch each other's backs.'

I exhale deeply. 'We will.'

'So *stop* worrying, all right?'

'All right . . .' I'm still worried, but I force a smile. 'As mad as things have been here, I'm really going to miss it,' I say, changing the subject. 'It's funny, too, because when I found out I'd be coming here, I thought it would be the deadest, whitest place on Earth.'

He's smiling when I look up at him. 'That's funny.'

'Right. Considering none of my favourite people here are white.'

He smirks. 'Better not say that around Willow. She'll cry.'

'You'd better not tell her then.'

He chuckles as we walk over to Sam's van. 'She won't hear it from me.'

'Well, damn . . . Didn't have you doing me favours on my bingo card, but if I'm honest, there's a lot about you that I got wrong when we first met.' I look up at him after putting my bucket down for the last time. 'You're a good guy.'

'Wow!' Sam butts in dramatically — damn, I hadn't seen him round the other side of the van. 'So not only have you paid back your community in four weeks, but you've buried a grudge.'

'It's shocking, really,' Alok says, 'considering we weren't allowed to talk much.'

That makes me laugh.

Sam eyes me. 'I never stopped you two from talking, I merely had to remind Gabrielle to work and talk at the same time.'

I gape at him. 'I worked hard *all* of the time. I had the cut-up hands and sore fingers to prove it.'

'Ah, well, let's hope it's enough to stop you from finding your way back here, then.'

Alok and I groan, but Sam just laughs.

He shakes both our hands. 'It was a pleasure to meet you both, but please don't come back.'

'We won't.'

Chapter Thirty-One

I do a happy dance in the mirror after ripping another couple of holes in my fishnets. It's been a while since I dressed up like this, and although it's taken a few hours, I'm feeling good as hell.

My ink's on show – I decided to skip the jacket because of how warm it already is – and I'm praying my make-up will hold out. I've gone extra dark on that, too, which also means more chance of it melting off me.

I even bought some skull charms for my locs, and when I spin around to make my skirt flare out, they clink against each other. I may have missed Metal Fest, but I'm hoping today's going to make up for that.

'I'm ready,' I say to Grandma when I find her seated at the table in the kitchen. 'What do you think? Think teenage Grandma would approve?'

She turns from the stove and gapes at me. 'She'd be losing her mind.' Her eyes light up when she sees the charms. 'I love those.'

'So do I. It's been way too long since I dressed up like this. I've missed it.'

'You're going to be in your element.'

'I know, but as much as I'm excited . . . I'm so nervous, Grandma.'

She nods knowingly as she gets up to go to the kitchen drawer. 'Understandable, but you're prepared, and you know what to do if it gets too much.' She turns with a stake in her hand, and my stomach lurches. 'You need to take this. Everyone in the town is carrying one, and if you're seen without . . . well, you'll fit in with the others if you have this.'

I take it from her, despising how sinister it feels in my hand. 'Just holding it makes me feel sick.'

'I felt the same, but it's more important than ever that today, you fit in. Sanse thinks so, too.'

Sanse's warned everyone about Oliver's presence at the festival today and his intentions to lure the vampires out. Although we haven't had confirmation of them using blood to do it, we've all been warned to take breathers at the harbour, in case it gets too much. Which is fine with me, but I'm still worried about Alok and Maria.

Alok seemed to listen when I talked to him about how to stay in control, and I know Maria's drinking blood to control her thirst, but that won't stop any of us being lured by its scent.

Grandma pulls me out of my trance by taking my arms. 'It will be okay,' she soothes. 'Stay alert, yes, but Sanse and the others will be there, so try to have a good time. The vampires responsible may not even show up. It's been quiet for a few days now. Maybe the threat of those *things*' — she frowns at the stake — 'scared them off.'

'I hope so.' I tuck the stake into my crossbody bag. She's right, they might not show up, but I still haven't told her what my ulterior motives are for going to the festival.

I wasn't sure how she'd react if she found out I was hoping to do some vampire-hunting of my own.

'Are you leaving now?' she asks, when she lets me go.

I nod and say goodbye. I'm meeting the others at the memorial, which is only a twenty-minute walk from here. *The love of walking's begun to rub off on me.* First, though, I go to find Ethan. I'm dying to know what he'll think of me in full goth glam.

Josh whistles when I find them around the side of the house, which makes me laugh. 'Looking good, gal.'

'Thank you,' I reply. And when I look to Ethan beside him, my stomach flutters like crazy.

His eyes travel the length of me, escalating my pulse further; but as he smiles, his jaw suddenly tenses. 'You look incredible,' he says, but then he quickly looks away and abruptly picks up a plank of wood at his feet.

He may have given me a compliment, but it seems to have pained him to.

I won't lie and say it doesn't hurt. Maybe he's upset about Alok being able to come with us and not him.

'Do some moshing for me,' he says, passing the wood to Josh up the ladder.

'I will . . .' I linger, not wanting to go without him. 'I wish you could come with me now.'

He smiles, but it's forced. I can read him like one of my ancestor's journals. I want to ask him if he's okay, but when I open my mouth to, he tells me to have a good time.

I'm deep in my feelings during the walk to town. Ethan's been so hot and cold recently, and it's messing with my head, because I'm noticing that although his eyes and facial expressions tell me one thing, his body language and some of his behaviour say the complete opposite.

I've wondered if he's finally getting sick of *my* hot and cold behaviour. Us kissing, me spending time with Alok, me hating Alok, then me getting on with Alok, me telling Ethan I don't want a relationship, and then me still seeking him out around the manor . . .

I need to talk to him because I know something still isn't right between us, but I'll have to wait till Monday now. Maybe if I can find out what's really going on with him, we can get back to how things were, because I miss the way we used to get on, and the time I have left to spend with him is quickly running out.

I see the others excitedly running over to me when I reach the path to the memorial, and I'm blown away by all the fits. Everyone looks incredible, and my heart is hugged from the inside. The group chat already told me how much effort they were putting in to today, but seeing them all with their faces painted and their elaborate outfits tributed to the gothic culture has me happier than I've ever been.

And to think I worried about what to wear when I was getting ready to meet them for the first time.

'You all so look amazing.' Willow and her boyfriend are dressed as Wednesday Addams' parents; Ben is wearing a black wig and is giving Eric Draven vibes in *The Crow*; and Mikey *must* have a sister – who is most likely going to be really upset when she finds half her make-up missing.

'Have fun?' I ask after I compliment his dark eyeliner and blood-red lips.

He smirks. 'A bit too much. Props to Maria, though, she helped get me together.'

'Ohh . . .' I compliment her look the most when she gives me a hug. 'You look *so* hot. Props for your work on Mikey, too. He looks epic.'

She smiles when she steps back. 'He looks all right.'

I shake my head. Now I know why he's always complaining about her giving him a hard time. 'You all excited?'

'Hell, yeah,' Jason says. He's wearing a dark green suit and is holding a plastic axe. 'Just waiting on one more now.'

Peter groans. 'The one who's always late.'

'Who——?' I look past Henry and see Alok strolling towards us, like he's got all the time in the world. He's wearing a full black suit, hands shoved deep in his pockets and, to my surprise, is rocking a whole load of fake piercings, including a septum and fake tunnels in his ears.

He looks good.

Way too good.

'Looks like everyone went all out,' I say, only half present. *Damn, why am I only just fully appreciating that chiselled jawline now?*

'He looks good,' Maria says, leaning closer to me.

'I know, right . . .' I watch him as he greets the boys, the rest of the group, and then finally ends with a smile at me.

That's after he checks me out, but I do the same to him. If I ever tried to deny the attraction between us, I can't now. I don't know if it's the fact he's a vampire and invulnerable to me, but there's something . . .

'Looking good.' He reaches to softly flick one of the sculls dangling from my locs. 'I was expecting some kind of spray, or paint.'

I roll my eyes. He just can't help himself.

He smirks before turning back to the others. 'Drinks first? The marketplace has a load of tents up there.'

Live music, too, unless my ears deceive me. 'Do you dance?' I ask Maria, when we start the trek up there.

She smiles mischievously. 'Girl, I'll dance to anything.'

'And that's just another reason to love you,' I say, linking my arm in hers.

Our first stop is to a pop-up bar tent to get drinks, but Maria, Alok and I stay alcohol free for now. I haven't smelt any blood around or seen anyone wielding a stake, and I also haven't managed to get Alok alone to find out what his dad finally decided.

Maria also keeps showing me the messages between her and Sanse. 'Nothing to worry about yet,' she mutters. She glances behind me. 'What's Alok said?'

'He hasn't yet.'

Willow's waving everyone over to her near the stage where an indie rock band is playing, so I take my chance to grab Alok and find somewhere private for us to talk.

He leads me down one of the many alleyways leading off the marketplace and then leans over me so other people can pass.

'What's going on?' I ask, really wishing the wall would move back. *And there I was worrying about being triggered by blood . . .*

He looks over his shoulder at another wave of people coming and then bites his lip. 'Wait a second.'

'Okay.' But I don't know if I can. Him *looking* this good was torture enough, but smelling him . . . I imagine his fangs digging into his lips, and mine . . . I can't handle it.

Can demons seduce people without knowing?

He finally looks back down at me when the alleyway empties, and I don't miss the glance he sends to my lips. 'There's been a surveillance room set up at the lightboat station. Some of my dad's guys are watching the festival from there. Dad's been hush-hush about everything else.'

My stomach knots. 'Okay.'

'If they use, y'know, are you going to be okay? I don't want you being caught on camera shifting, Gabby.'

'Obviously it's going to bother me, but I've done enough work on my thirst to manage it. How do you feel about it?'

'I'll be good.' He adjusts his hand beside me on the wall, but he stays close. His eyes lower to my ink, and my heart starts racing. 'I'll try to get us into one of the surveillance rooms, okay?'

'Yeah . . .'

He inhales deeply but then steps away when another rush of people comes along, and although I'm relieved, my body's left frustrated. 'Let's get back to the others.'

ASAP.

'What did he say?' Maria asks when I get back and start dancing beside her. *Who doesn't love Led Zeppelin?*

I shake my head, not wanting Alok to know I've told her. 'Nothing that can help us so far.'

The disappointment in her eyes is clear. 'Shit.'

Chapter Thirty-Two

It's nine in the evening, and most of our group are well and truly under the influence. I'm hating a little, because although we're having an amazing time, the three of us non-drinkers can't risk even one.

I smile at the couples dancing around us, heads banging and bodies swaying. An indie band called Nitemares is currently rocking out on stage, hyping everyone up for the last band's performance that is next, which is causing the marketplace to fill up fast.

Some traders have already left, but there are plenty of tents around, providing face-painting, trinkets, food, drinks and clothing, amongst other things. We just had a street artist, who has set up beside the stage, draw a picture of us, too, which Jason said he'd copy and send to us all.

I'm not sure if it's going to make it out of his pocket, though, because he's the drunkest of the group. He's currently slurring his words while attempting to get a red-haired girl's number.

'There's no way he's getting those digits,' Maria says, watching him with me. 'She's about to walk away in three, two— Told you.'

I shake my head while giving her a look. 'You really need to find a way to make money from your intuition, babe.'

'I do, don't I? Although it's not helping us find these attackers.' She sighs. 'Not that I haven't had a good time, but I was expecting a little dark action tonight.'

'You and me both.'

I'm gutted that none of the attackers have made an appearance tonight, and that's been heavy on my heart for the last few hours. I was hoping that I could spend my last week here with Maria knowing they'd been captured and all this terror was over, but I guess not.

Alok's disappointed, too. We've snuck away a few times to discuss the situation, but whatever his dad's planned, he's keeping it close to his chest.

'Gabby . . .?'

I turn to Maria, who's staring behind me, so I follow her gaze to someone spraying **SUCKERS BEWARE** on the side of a building. I chuckle. 'Thank God that's not my problem any more.'

Maria glances at me. 'Yes, it is. *Look.*' She points out someone else spraying another wall a few shops down. 'That's not paint.'

I notice how deeply coloured the red graffiti is right before the coppery scent of blood awakens my senses. 'Don't look at it,' I tell her, holding her arm to start dancing again. 'There are cameras watching everyone.'

'Shit, yeah.' She smiles tightly at Alok when he looks at us, and I pray to God he hasn't clocked on to her.

'I'll be right back,' I whisper in her ear, after ten minutes of discreetly watching more graffiti pop up. I keep noticing Alok's shoulders tense up.

Alok follows me over to the drink tents, and I ask him if he's okay.

He quickly looks behind me while we're in the queue. 'It's the graffiti, isn't it?'

I nod.

'I thought so.' His jaw clenches. 'It's . . .'

'I know,' I say, sympathetically, 'but you have to breathe through it.'

He widens his eyes at me. 'Breathing is the last thing I wanna do.' He clenches his fists before looking back over to the group and smirking. 'People will think we're fighting.'

I snort. 'Since when have you cared about that? I'm sure they're used to it by now.'

He rolls his eyes, but then they soften. 'I'm going to miss your annoying ass.'

'That doesn't mean much, coming from you.' I laugh when he acts offended. 'Just playing. The feeling's mutual.'

That surprises him. 'So you don't hate me any more?'

'Oh, please, you know we're friends.'

His eyes darken. 'Friends?'

And I can immediately tell what he's thinking.

Friends don't know the taste of each other's lips . . .

I swallow and change the subject as we make our way up the line. 'I know you've dealt with everything on your own for a while, but I just want you to know, if you ever need help, I'm here for you.'

He stares down at me for what feels like forever. 'Thank you.'

SUCKERS

'There are others, too,' I tell him, feeling like now is the right time to. 'They're here tonight.' I glance around at the people around us. 'But they can help with all sorts – not that I'm saying you need it, but just in case you ever feel alone with things . . .'

His lips twitch as he pulls out his vibrating phone. 'Thanks, but things will be a lot easier for me when you go back home. No offence.'

I huff. 'Oh, thanks.'

He glances up from his screen. 'It's not for the reason you think, Gabby. I just mean, well . . . I won't be triggered.'

My stomach twists when I remember what he said in my bedroom the other night. 'You were serious about—'

'Even when you're not around, I can smell your scent. I have since I walked down that dune.'

I gape at him while he looks back down at his phone. '*That's* why you were so mean to me.'

He gives me an apologetic smile. 'I— *Shit.*'

'What?'

'A text from Dad. People are fainting near the indoor market.'

I gulp. 'They've probably just had too much to drink.'

He shakes his head. 'Sam in the surveillance room has seen something strange on the feeds. Something about clouds. Dad wants me to go up there, so I'm safe.'

'What about the others? We can't leave them.'

I look over to Maria who is watching me and senses something is wrong.

'They'll come, too,' Alok says, tapping my arm for me to leave the queue with him. 'Let's go.'

'What are we going to tell them?' I ask.

He gives me a look. 'The truth.'

'What were you two talking about?' Ben asks when we reach them.

'We're going up to the lightboat station,' Alok says casually. 'Someone's seen something on one of the cameras. Do you guys wanna come?'

'Hell, yeah,' Jason says. 'I wanna see.'

Willow complains about the cold and starts encouraging everyone else to go, so we begin to make our way there.

Maria and I fall back a little, so I can fill her in on what's going on.

'Clouds?' Maria asks.

'Seems so.' I keep my voice low.

She frowns. 'And they definitely fainted?'

'Yeah, apparently a few people. Do you know of any types of vampires that can do that?'

'One,' she says, visibly disturbed. 'It's rare as fuck, though, and it involves magic.' She pulls out her phone and sees a text from Sanse. 'Shit.'

'What?'

She starts typing like crazy while I lead her by her arm so we can keep up with the others. 'Sanse says Kesa's seen a lugat jumping through the shadows. They've been following him for the past twenty minutes.'

I gape at her. 'What the hell's a lugat?'

She shakes her head after she tucks her phone away, and then we walk faster. 'They have to stay in dark places so they only come out at night. It's how they're able to escape so easily. Humans can't see in the dark, can they?'

'But not all the attacks have been in the night or in the dark, and people have been bitten . . .'

Maria swallows. 'Which means there must be a gang of them.'

My concern for the others reaches unbearable heights as I text Alok what I've just found out. 'Let's hurry.'

The room being used for surveillance barely fits us with all the screens across the desks showing the feeds. The cameras are looking over various parts of the marketplace, and only Sam is here, so when Alok offers our help, he eagerly accepts.

The others sit against the wall opposite to where we are, on the floor, and I can already hear talk of getting something to eat and cabs home, so I'm not sure how long we're going to be able to keep them here. *In safety*.

'You watch those ones,' Alok says, putting a chair in front of the screens on the left-hand side. 'I'll take the middle.'

'I want to help,' Maria says.

'You can help me,' I tell her, dragging a spare chair closer to the desk, and then we all keep our eyes glued to the screens.

'It could be anyone,' I whisper to Maria beside me. 'There are too many people.' I can't see anything in the shadows, but I have seen Sanse a few times. Oliver, too, and multiple groups, openly carrying stakes.

'Listen to your gut,' Maria hisses. 'You saw the stills at the rally, didn't you?'

'Yeah, but everyone's in either a mask, wearing fancy dress, or has some other kind of disguise.' My eyes hurt from flickering between all the lone people on the screens. 'Unless they . . .' My heart leaps. 'Ethan's here.'

'Aww, he made it,' Maria says, spotting him walking with the crowd in front of an arcade not far from here. 'Let's go and get him.'

'I'll come with you,' Alok says, getting up with us.

'We leaving?' Willow asks, looking up hopefully.

'No, we're just going to get Ethan and then we're coming back,' Maria tells her, before we leave. 'Text him to tell him not to go anywhere,' she says to me. 'We'll lose him otherwise.'

I send a quick message for him to stay put, but when we get there, he's nowhere to be found. The three of us are suddenly pushed out of the way when paramedics rush past us, and my gut turns.

'Come on,' I say, pulling Maria's and Alok's arms. 'Let's follow them.'

A woman's lying on the ground moaning when we catch up with the paramedics. Her skin is pale, but there's no blood.

'She looks like a corpse,' Alok mutters.

'I thought the same.'

'Hey, guys.'

We turn around to see Ethan, and I'm relieved.

'Thank God,' I say, hugging him. 'I told you to stay put.'

'Sorry, I only just saw your message and was heading back there.' He holds me tightly before I let him go. 'What's going on?'

'Something's going down.' Alok practically spits. 'We're hanging out at the lightboat station.'

'All right, cool.'

We head back to the surveillance room, but there's no news on the latest attack. Ethan joins us in watching the feeds, but I can't seem to concentrate.

Something doesn't feel right, but I don't know what . . .

Ben yawns, and then so does Willow. 'How much longer is this going to take?'

'Someone's ready for bed,' Henry says, chuckling in the corner.

'She's not the only one,' Ava moans.

'I want food first . . .'

I lean forward when I see movement in the doorway of a coffee shop the next street over, and then I recoil when I glimpse a set of amber eyes peeking out. 'Look at camera six,' I whisper to Alok, knowing Maria will hear.

He leans towards me to see, so I mouth '*Is that the lugat?*' to Maria. She nods.

Alok gives me a look, and then my phone. 'You gonna . . .?'

'Yeah . . .' But before I can send a text to Maria to ask her to let Sanse know, her phone rings.

'Gabby, can I talk to you?' Ethan asks, appearing beside me. He looks tired all of a sudden, and I get the feeling he's going to tell me he's leaving already.

'I'll be back in a sec,' I whisper to Maria before I leave with him, but I catch Alok's sharp gaze when I close the door.

'*Hurry up,*' he mouths.

I nod before following Ethan along the corridor to a staff room. 'Is everything okay? Are you feeling sick again?'

He sighs as he paces beside the window, but then he suddenly turns to look at me. 'I know you're a soucouyant, Gabby.'

I stare back at him in shock. '*What?*'

'I know,' he repeats, walking over to stand in front of me. 'I've known for weeks. It wasn't intentional, but when we were working on the roof, I heard you talking to Noemie.'

'I-I don't know—'

'It's okay,' he reassures me, gently holding my arm. 'You don't have to deny it. It doesn't change a thing between us.'

My mind races as I think about him knowing all this time and not telling me. 'Why didn't you say anything?'

Hurt appears in his eyes. 'I was hoping you'd tell me. I kept giving you chances. I told you that nothing would change how I felt about you.' He lifts my locs over my shoulders and glances down at my ink. 'I love you regardless.'

I blink up at him in realisation. 'That's why you got so angry about me going to that rally.'

He nods. 'It's also the reason why you said we couldn't be more than friends, isn't it?'

'I didn't want to hurt you,' I say quietly. 'I care about you too much.'

'I know . . .' He leans down to rest a tender kiss on my lips, but when the fire inside me is suddenly stoked, I pull away.

'Ethan—'

We both turn towards the door when we hear heavy footsteps in the hall and the others talking loudly.

'Gabby, wait—'

'I can't,' I say, as I rush towards the door. 'I need to know what's going on out there.'

I find Alok and Maria outside the surveillance room, and they both seem relieved to see me. 'What's going on?'

Alok glances behind me, his jaw tense. 'We need to go.'

I follow Maria down the steps, closely followed by Alok. 'What's happened?' I hiss. 'Did they catch the lugat?'

She glances at me when we hit the bottom step. 'I think Lani's dealing with him.'

'Where did the others go?'

'Home. Safe.'

My gut twists, and then I can barely breathe with how hard my heart starts racing. If they found that lugat, good, but why is she still so tense?

Sanse is waiting across the cobbled street with Kesa. Maria holds my arm and makes an excuse about needing to use a cash machine down the bottom of the road, so we start heading down there.

And they follow.

Alok keeps looking at me, but I shrug in response. I don't know what he expects me to say. Unless Maria told him who she was when I left that room.

She wouldn't, would she?

Maria uses the cash machine and draws Ethan into a conversation with her so I can quickly speak to Alok. 'What's going on?' I hiss.

'Ethan—'

'Get away from him, son!' Oliver's shout makes me jump. He's marching towards us with an army of his followers, all armed with stakes, and those homemade bombs . . . 'Ethan, stay where you are.'

My heart leaps into my throat. 'What's going on?'

Maria suddenly grabs my arm as Ethan knocks into her when he sets off running. 'Gabby, he's the one draining people,' she says, frantically holding on to my arm. 'Sanse was calling me when you left the surveillance room. Ethan's a jiangshi!'

'No . . .' I shake my head and try to back away from her, but she won't let my arm go. Instead, she pulls me against the wall because another mass of people wielding stakes starts running down the hill.

I follow their angry gazes to Ethan, still trying to escape from the street.

It can't be . . .

'Don't try to run,' Oliver warns him, snatching a stake from one of the men with him. 'There's nowhere to go . . .'

I look up at Alok when everyone begins to shout. 'You need to go—'

'No.' He keeps his attention forward, watching everyone begin to corner us. 'What should we do?'

I see Lani appear beside Sanse and Kesa as they attempt to approach Ethan as he desperately looks for a way out of the street, but there is nowhere, and we have literal seconds before we're all ambushed. 'I don't—'

Oliver suddenly clutches his chest, and so do a handful of others with him, and I shriek in horror.

'Ethan, don't!' I run to grab his arm. 'Stop.'

He turns to look down at me, and I'm relieved when Oliver and his group stop, gasping for breath.

Ethan shakes his head. 'I . . .' He looks around at everyone yelling threats at him. 'I'm sorry.'

My heart really does break then, and I burst into tears. 'I don't understand.'

'I was going to tell you.' He grabs my face, wiping my tears away with his thumbs. 'I had them change me so I could be with you, Gabby.'

I sob with hurt and regret. 'Why the hell would you *do* that?'

He looks hurt and recoils from me. 'Gabby—'

'Go home,' Sanse says to me as she approaches with Kesa and Lani. 'We'll take him.'

Ethan steps back. 'Take me where?'

'We can help you,' Lani says, approaching more cautiously now. 'We know you didn't mean to hurt anyone.'

Ethan keeps backing away, and from the corner of my eye, I see one of the men with Oliver throw something at us.

I duck, but a wave of blood crashes into Ethan side, covering my face when it splashes off him.

'No, no, no . . .' I look down at the red liquid covering my arms and struggle to keep my shift under control when I taste the copper on my lips.

Ethan's loud groans force my attention to him, but no relief of a distraction comes. His face has turned ash white, and his eyes are pools of black. Fangs protrude from his top lip, at least twice the size of mine, and a thick, heavy scent of death combines with the sour metallic one.

I step away when I see Lani and Kesa creeping up on him from behind, but the blood draws me back, and I tremble in place while I fight the fire within that's desperate to ignite.

I don't want to hurt anyone . . .

'There's the proof,' Oliver yells. 'Now get him!'

Maria screams when Oliver and his group charge at us, but it turns into a hiss as she shifts, and within a split second, she's towering over them all. 'Stay back,' she warns, while rattling her tail.

I turn to Alok, praying he's been missed, but he's suffered the same fate as Ethan and he begins to shift, towering above us all. Amongst the chaos, he stares blankly at the blood at our feet, smoke rising from his body and his chest heaving rapidly . . .

I cautiously step closer to him. 'Alok . . .'

But another group of angry followers suddenly crashes into us, and we're all separated.

'I can't hold them all,' Maria yells. 'Do something!'

Gaps begin to form around me, and I catch glimpses of Lani and Kesa with their hands out as they try to hold them back, but then I'm struck with a searing pain in my left arm and cry out in pain.

I spin around, barely escaping a stake coming at me from above before I snatch it from the woman's hand, and then the man beside her is grabbed by Alok's huge hand and dragged back.

My eyes burn, and the woman who stabbed me falls as she stumbles. I set the stake alight, and then grab another from the next man I see, but there are too many . . .

I wave the burning sticks out in front of Alok and me so we can force our way through to one of the others, but I'm struck again in my shoulder.

This time, when my fire begs for release, I unleash it.

The force of my shift causes a mass of Oliver's followers to fly through the air before hitting the cobbles, and I'm finally able to see Maria and Sanse. They're holding back their own clusters of the group, but I can't see—

'Ethan!'

He makes an attempt to get to me now that there's space to, but more hunters arrive, and I quickly lose sight of him again.

'We have to get to him,' I plead to Alok. 'We can't let your dad's followers reach him first.'

'I see him,' Alok says, stepping ahead of me, and as I follow him more people are tossed away from us.

The deafening yelling and screaming seems to be lessening, but as we all defend ourselves, painful moaning and groaning begin to echo against the cobbles instead.

But it's still taking too long.

I cascade myself into particles and slip through arms and bodies towards Ethan, causing screams from those I've burnt to yell out. I hate that I'm hurting them, but if I don't . . .

Ethan.

I surge higher instead, thrusting myself in his direction when I spot him amongst the crowd. I shift as soon as I land, but when I cautiously reach my trembling arms out, flames continue to ripple across my skin. 'Ethan, please.'

SUCKERS

He steps back and closes his eyes. 'Get back, Gabby,' he warns. 'I don't want to hurt you.'

'Then go with Sanse, please,' I beg. 'She'll help you.'

He opens his eyes, and I die inside when I see his anguish. 'They'll lock me away.'

'They won't,' I plead as I panic. 'They can—'

Lani and Kesa rush to his side to grab his arms, but he struggles in their grip before managing to set himself free; and then I watch in horror as everyone else in his path falls to their knees, including me.

I clutch my chest as I struggle to breathe, relieved when, a few moments later, I'm able to draw a smoky breath into my lungs. As I struggle to my feet, Ethan is nowhere to be found.

There's no sign of Lani either, only Sanse and Kesa, also struggling to rise.

Sanse looks over to Maria as she rests a hand against the wall. 'Hypnotise them. They can't remember this.'

'Alok!' Oliver is crying out. 'Alok. Son?'

'What do I do?' Maria asks Sanse.

'Leave Oliver for now. Make the others go.'

Maria disperses the uninjured first, and then she slithers through the wounded on the cobbles, hissing as she looks into their eyes . . .

Once back to herself, she runs to check my arm and shoulder. 'Are you okay?'

I nod. It hurts, but not as badly as my heart.

'Son, talk to me . . .'

I turn to see Alok staring at his dad, eyes blood-red but emotionless. Oliver is obviously traumatised, repeating his name, over and over again, but Alok doesn't answer.

'Alok?' I say softly, walking over to him. He's taller than I remember, and when I rest my hand on his thick, warm arm, I have to reach above my chest. 'Hey?'

He drags his gaze away from his dad to me, panting so hard his chest heaves. 'The blood,' he says, his voice hoarse.

'I know. I want it too.'

He closes his eyes, and I see the internal battle reflected on his face. 'Help me.'

'I wish I could, but I don't know how.' I'm covered in it, too, so I step away from him, but he reaches down to grab my hand.

'Stay.'

I ignore my own internal struggle to remember what Grandma's taught me, praying that something will work for him.

I move my hand up to his chest. 'You have to calm this. Breathe steadily, slowly . . .' I do the same. 'I know how much you want it, but you have to resist. Think of how angry you'd be if you gave in. It's not worth it, trust me. It will just get worse.'

'She's right,' Sanse says, coming to offer him comfort, too. 'Slow and steady . . .'

He glances at her when she whispers in a language I don't recognise, and finally, his chest stops heaving and human Alok returns.

He lowers his head, so I hold him tightly. 'I know how hard that was, but I'm so proud of you,' I say quietly.

His arms tremble around my back, but he lifts his head when Oliver calls his name from behind me again.

Oliver's distraught. 'Son? Since when . . .?'

Alok doesn't answer, he only stares back at him in silence, and I know it's because he's scared of being rejected by him now that he knows what he is.

SUCKERS

I stand so I'm shielding Alok and lower my voice. 'He only found out recently, which means he has already suffered alone for an unimaginable length of time . . . Regardless of what your opinions are, you need to be careful about how you react to this, because he is your son, and right now, he needs you.'

Oliver shakes his head. 'I . . . I don't . . .'

'You need to go, before anyone else sees you,' Sanse says to me, when sirens begin to approach.

I keep my eyes on Alok. 'But—'

'Now, Gabby. *I* will handle this.'

Maria pulls my arm. 'Come on, babe.' She lowers her voice. 'You do *not* want to piss her off, trust me.'

'Fine.' I turn to Alok. 'I'm here if you need me.'

He only nods before he releases my hand.

Chapter Thirty-Three

Maria and I shiver violently as we walk along the beach and back to the street, so Grandma can pick us up. We came down here to wash the blood off us, but by the time we arrived, I couldn't have cared less.

Maria wasn't supposed to be staying at my house tonight, but after she called her parents to let them know what happened, they encouraged her to. I'm so proud of her for how she coped with tonight, especially when we got covered in blood, and I told her so; but apart from that, I feel nothing.

I'm numb.

Because how do I even begin to process what's happened?

'I wo-nder wh-at O-liver and Sanse w-ill ta-lk about,' Maria says, her teeth chattering.

I resist the temptation to shift so I can warm myself and her up.

'Hopefully they'll find a way to work together. If not, they'll probably ask you to hypnotise him, too.'

'I wouldn't mind. It was kinda nice to be able to use my abilities for something meaningful.' She sighs when we reach the steps. 'When are we going to talk about the elephant in the room?'

I spot Grandma's car parked at the side of the road. 'I'm sure you won't be waiting too much longer.'

Grandma gets out of her car and rushes towards us, but I resist her hug when she attempts to give me one. 'I don't want you getting wet.'

'Nonsense.' But she doesn't try again. Maria lets her hug her, though. But then Grandma gasps when she notices my wounds. 'Gabby—'

'They're almost healed. Can we go?'

'Of course.' She hurries us into her car. 'The heating is on full blast. We need to get you out of those wet clothes . . .'

That's the least of my concerns.

The drive back to the manor is made in silence, but not from Maria's lack of attempts to get me to talk. She tried to bring up Ethan several times, but I just stared out of the window. I won't be able to run away from the conversation for much longer now that we've both been made to have hot showers and put warm clothes on so that we can join Grandma in the living room by the fire.

'Here you go,' she says, handing us both a mug of steaming hot chocolate. 'There are biscuits on the table, too, if either of you are hungry.'

Maria gets some for herself, but I just cup my mug in my hands. I'm not cold any more, but I'm still shaking.

Maria holds my wrist. 'Babe?'

I look up to find Grandma staring at me from the chair opposite ours. 'Sorry, what did you say?'

'I asked if you wanted to talk about what happened, dear?'

'Why? I've already told you. All we can do now is wait.'

'You're blaming yourself, aren't you?' Maria says, softly.

I scoff. 'How can I not? You heard him. He let them change him so he could be with me.'

He must've gone to The Coven . . .

'Gabrielle . . .' Grandma's expression saddens. 'Ethan made that decision on his own. You didn't make him change who he was. Being a vampire wasn't the only reason you had for not wanting a relationship. You had every right to say no.'

'But it was the main one.' My chest aches. 'I've ruined his life. God knows what will happen to him now. He could be anywhere . . .' *Still hurting people.*

'Hey,' Maria says, rubbing my back, 'they'll find him, and they'll get him the help he needs. He can live normally again. We all know Ethan isn't bad. Even Oliver knows that. He's known him for years.'

'Maybe you're right, but I still played a massive part in this.' I try not to cry but I can't stop myself. 'I didn't want him to get hurt.'

Grandma kneels at my feet and, after taking my mug away, holds my hands. 'We know that. This isn't your fault.'

'Even if that's true, Alok was outed to his dad because I asked for his help. What if he doesn't accept him? I didn't want him to be alone with finding out what he was, but now his parents might disown him, and that's . . . that's even worse. I've ruined his life, too. I'm ruining everybody's lives.'

'No, you are not,' Grandma says, raising her voice. 'Stop this. I won't have it. You have not made either of those boys do anything they've not wanted to do. They're both adults, and they're both responsible for their own choices.'

'I agree with your grandma,' Maria says. 'It's not like their lives are over, and you should know that. Ours aren't because of what we are, are they?'

'No, but—'

'No buts, babe. Alok was born the way he is, and if his parents can't accept that, they don't deserve him. And Ethan *chose* this life. He knew what he was getting himself into, at least to an extent, so you can't feel bad for him or blame yourself for what he did.'

Grandma agrees with her, too. 'We've had this conversation many times now, dear, but I need you to *listen* to me this time. You cannot continue to carry people's burdens as your own. Don't lose your ability to be empathetic towards others, but their problems are not yours. You can only be there to support them if they need or ask for you to be.'

'Sorry,' Maria says, 'I'm not trying to tag team your grandma, but she's right about that, too. Don't get me wrong, I love you for it, but over the past six weeks, I've gotten to know you quite well, and as much as I love how much you've tried to be there for me, you need to be there for yourself first. You can't fix other people's problems to avoid dealing with your own. Eventually, you'll have to stop running and face them.'

Her words cut me. 'Don't hold back.'

'I'm not trying to upset you, but you asked me to be real, so I have to be.'

I sigh. 'You may have a point.' I don't have to like it, though. *Do I run from things?* I guess so, but I've also tried not to . . .

Grandma pats my hands before getting up. 'Drink your hot chocolate while it's warm, and then you should both get some sleep.'

I don't know if I will when I've just been called out like that.

I can't sleep. I've been staring at my bedroom ceiling for hours, replaying every single moment of the night. I'm so worried about Ethan and Alok, and while I know what Grandma and Maria said, it's just . . . How can I *not* be to blame for this?

I sigh in torment as I roll on to my side, but then I quickly sit up when I see a face peering through my window. 'Alok?'

He motions for me to let him in, so I rush to let him. He's wearing clean clothes, a T-shirt and jeans, so he must have been home. *That's a good sign, right?*

'What are you doing here?' I ask, closing the window. 'Are you okay?'

'I'm fine. I wanted to make sure you were okay.' He holds my arm before checking out my shoulder, visually and audibly relieved when he sees I'm no longer wounded. 'I wanted to kill everyone there when I saw you bleeding. Even my dad.'

'Alok . . .' I step forward to hold him. 'Thank you for trying to protect me.'

He tightens his arms around me, too. 'Always.'

'What did your dad—'

'I don't want to talk about him.' He lifts his head. 'I'm tired.'

'You don't want to be at home, do you?' I ask knowingly.

He shakes his head.

I pull him over to my bed, and then we lie facing each other in silence. I feel a surge of protectiveness when I think of what his parents might've said to him, remembering how vulnerable I'd felt after I crashed through my bedroom window. *It feels like years ago now.*

SUCKERS

I hold his hand when I feel him searching for mine, and my heart aches when he sighs with relief.

'I can still smell your blood,' he says, quietly. 'When you got hurt, I felt so many things . . . I feel bad for some of them. Since our kiss in the woods, it's all I've thought about, and then when I came here the other day . . . I wanted to bite you so badly.'

My mouth is suddenly dry. 'I almost bit you,' I confess. 'Both times.'

His gaze falls to my lips, and I close my eyes briefly when his hand releases mine to trail my hip. 'I wish you had.' His hand tightens around my waist. 'I still want you to.' He pulls me closer, and I gasp. 'I need to know how you taste.'

I inhale his scent, shuddering when his arm tightens around me and he feathers kisses along my shoulder. His lips trail my ink, the thorns that lead to my neck.

'I've never done this before.' *I'm trembling so badly . . .*

He pauses. 'Do you want to?'

'Yes . . . but I'm scared that I won't stop.'

He lifts his head, his eyes reflecting the same fear. 'I trust you.' He lifts my chin. 'And you trust me, right?'

I nod my reply because I can't speak it, but no more words are needed.

Alok kisses me so softly, gently coaxing my lips apart as his fangs scrape them. The feeling is nothing like what I expected, but the way my body reacts to it is. The anticipation of whether he'll bite my lip or somewhere else has me wild with arousal. *Will it hurt, or . . .*

The pinch to my bottom lip causes me to moan with mixed pain and pleasure, but when he sucks, I can barely cope with the desire that rushes through me. His groan of satisfaction only heightens it, and I've sunk my fangs into his lips before I've even realised what I've done.

When his sweet, coppery blood hits my tongue, I lose my mind and my body to ecstasy. I pull him closer, gasping between moans and gulps, gripped with a passion that turns me almost feral.

And he mirrors it all.

He applies more pressure to his caresses of my body, more fervour to his kiss, and when he leans over me and sucks again but harder, I almost . . .

He lifts his head, lips dripping with our blood, and then his hand slips lower. 'Gabby . . .'

I part my legs so he can slip his hand beneath my nightdress, and my skin *burns* when he touches me there. I reach a hand beneath his T-shirt, too, wishing there wasn't anything between us.

'Your skin is so soft,' I whisper.

He quickly sits up to pull off his T-shirt, and the rest of his clothes, and then he helps me out of my nightdress before his gaze darkens and his hands return to me. He moans when he licks the blood off my chin, and so do I when I return his eager touch and feel how aroused he is.

'I want you,' he says, before groaning again and scraping his fangs across my jaw. He inhales sharply when I tremble against him. 'I want you so badly.'

I gasp as my thighs clench around his hand. I've never felt anything as intense as this. 'Alok, I . . .'

He kisses me as the pleasure I feel intensifies, and when I taste smoke again, I'm not sure if it's his or mine. I'm not sure of anything after that either, because I experience the most intense climax of my life.

'I was scared you were going to catch fire again,' he whispers in my ear when I finish shuddering against him. 'I'd survive it, but I don't think your sheets would.'

SUCKERS

I blush as I open my eyes to see him smirking. 'You just can't help yourself, can you?'

His expression turns serious when he glances down at my lips. 'Not with you.'

My heart flutters with that answer, but then I pull him closer before I taste our blood on his lips. 'I can't seem to either.'

'Then don't.'

I slowly nod when he lifts his head to look down at me, caught in a haze of lust, but before I completely lose my mind to him and this moment, I get up from beneath him to find a condom in my purse.

Alok helps me back into bed after he takes it from me, and my heart thumps hard as hell while his gaze leaves mine. As soon as his eyes return to mine though, and the side of his firm, powerful body rests against my side, the last of my nerves about doing this with him fade away.

He bites me again, this time on my shoulder, and then he settles between my thighs. His skin is as warm as mine, and if I wasn't so afraid of setting my entire bedroom on fire, I'd be in flames.

My lips part when he lifts his head this time, his eyes as dark as the blood on his dripping fangs, but then I close mine because what I feel next is nothing short of life-changing.

I cling to his tensed arms as he rocks into me and groans. My senses are in overdrive now, and with each gasp he causes me to make, I'm consumed by his sweet scent. 'Oh god, Alok . . .'

He rests his head against my neck and whispers, 'Gabrielle . . .'

The sun shining through the window makes Alok almost glow as he lies beside me. We've both been awake for a while now, but we haven't said much.

His eyes, however, have said plenty. As, I'm sure, mine have, too.

Neither of us got carried away last night – not when it came to drinking each other's blood anyway, which is a relief. If anything, Alok was the one who stopped me from losing control. It makes me wonder if it's because he's been a vampire longer than I've been, or if he was just afraid he'd hurt me.

'I should go before your grandma wakes up,' he says, after sighing heavily. 'I need to face some shit, too.'

I don't ask what because I don't want to spoil his mood before he leaves here, but he can only be talking about his dad. 'It's okay. I need to deal with some myself. Maria's here as well.'

'I can't believe she's like us. When she told me in the surveillance room, I thought she was joking at first.'

I smile. 'She's amazing, isn't she?'

He nods. 'Explains a lot about her, too.'

'Yeah.' I close my eyes when he rests a kiss on my forehead, and then I sit up to watch him get dressed. 'Can you let me know you're okay later?'

He turns after he pulls up his jeans. 'I will, but don't worry about me.'

I nod. *If only it were that easy . . .*

After Alok leaves, I take a shower before going down to Maria's room to get into bed with her. I don't regret what I did with him last night – it was incredible – but I feel as though I'm now carrying around more guilt.

Ethan's currently on the run after becoming a vampire to be with me, and here I am, sleeping with his enemy . . .

Maria doesn't wake, so I watch her while she sleeps, her words from last night replaying in my head. I'd hated some of the things she said last night, but the worst part is, she's right about a lot. Emotions are a big part of what I am now, and I really need to stop running away from them. I can't keep distracting myself from facing the truth of things, either. I need to grow up.

I carefully sit up and unlock my phone. There are no messages from Ethan, and when I start typing one out to him, I delete it. He must be going through so much right now . . . I need to give him time. And as much as I wish I could, I can't solve his problems.

However, I can solve my own, and there's one that I can't put it off any longer.

Me: Hey, it's Gabrielle. Mum said you came by the house looking for me?

I hit send on the message to Kyle before I can delete it, and then I hug my phone against my chest and sigh.

'That sounded heavy. You good, babe?'

I look down at an awake Maria and nod. 'Yeah, are you?'

'Yeah.' She sits up against the headboard and pulls my arm down so she can hold my hand. 'I'm sorry if I hurt your feelings last night. I just . . . You're my best friend too, and I want the best for you.'

'I know. I asked you to be real, and I meant it. You were also right with a lot of what you said . . . I run from how I feel. I make excuses . . . I think I need a new journal.'

She smiles. 'You do. Wanna go to town? We can get coffee.'

'Yeah, sure . . .' I think about Ethan again, and Alok, and I feel sick to my core.

I've gotten myself into such a mess with them.

'Nope, you're not doing that,' Maria says, getting out of bed. 'I know you too well. Up. Now.'

I exhale deeply before pushing back the covers. 'Okay.'

Maria insists on coming back to the manor after our visit to town, and I give her a tour of the place while Grandma cooks for us.

'I wish I'd come sooner. The only reason I didn't is because I thought the place was haunted. Vampires I can deal with. Ghosts, not so much.'

I chuckle as we make our way back to the kitchen. 'I feel you on that. Need some help, Grandma?'

'Nope, it's almost done.' She turns from the stove and looks at her phone on the table. 'Sanse called me while you were in town.'

'And?' I ask, eager to know what they talked about.

'She's coming to see us.'

'When?'

'Tomorrow evening.'

'Okay . . .' I sit down at the table because my legs are suddenly weak. What's she going to say? Why couldn't she just tell Grandma on the phone? Oh god . . . it must be bad.

'Babe? You good?'

I nod at Maria, but I'm really not.

'It will be okay. She's come to my house plenty of times, and not all of them have been for bad reasons.'

I try to find hope in that but it's futile.

'I can come over for when she's here, if you want?' Maria says, reading me well. 'Would that be okay, Noemie?'

'Of course,' Grandma answers her. 'It will most likely save her a trip. You were there last night, too.'

I smile at Maria, feeling much better already. 'Thank you.'

Chapter Thirty-Four

'Hello?' We hear Sanse call from the hall.
Grandma walks over to the door to shout, 'In the kitchen, like usual.'

I almost throw up waiting for her to appear. I've done nothing but obsess over her visit since I woke up.

She smiles at Grandma and gives her a warm hug before greeting Maria and me at the table. 'How are you, girls?'

'Good,' Maria says. 'Gabby's up and down, though.'

Sanse nods understandingly, and I wonder what she knows.

'I can imagine.' She sits down next to me and strokes my arm. 'Saturday night must have been quite upsetting for you.'

'I feel bad,' I blurt out.

She frowns. 'Why?'

'Because Alok was seen by his dad—'

'Alok,' she interrupts, 'is fine.'

I sigh with relief because I haven't heard from him since he left here, but . . . 'Ethan—'

'Will be, too, as soon as we find him.'

'But how will you?' I ask, tormented. 'He could be anywhere.'

Her expression turns grave. 'He hasn't gone far. He's been spotted at The Coven.' She sighs then. 'It seems he's latched on to the vampires there.'

I had a feeling, but . . . *Oh god* . . .

She contemplates her next words. 'Two weeks ago, Ethan met a priestess at The Coven who agreed to transform him into a jiangshi vampire. However, the deal that was made means that Ethan needs blood or something known as "qi" to survive.'

My heart feels like it stops completely then. 'So he can't live without it?'

She shakes her head gravely. 'No, which is why he's acted the way he has. Every time he resisted, his survival instincts were triggered, resulting in him attacking someone to get what he needed.'

'But he's still the same person, right?' Maria asks.

'Oh, absolutely, but in order for him to return to the life he knows, he needs to learn how to siphon small amounts of energy from multiple people he meets throughout his day in order to keep his life.'

'So people won't notice he's doing it?'

'No, not once he's learnt how to do it. Which is why we need to find him so we can help him. I hope the vampires at The Coven are doing that, but . . .' She shrugs.

I've never felt so hopeless. 'You don't think they will, do you?'

'I honestly don't know. The rites performed on Ethan are a very powerful kind of magic, and not many exist that can teach him what he needs to learn. Jiangshis are rare, because not many survive the transition.'

'Do you know any others?' Maria asks.

'Yes, Lani.' She gives us both a look. 'If he approaches any of you, please tell him that. It might help him change his mind about running from us.'

'We will.'

I hope he does come find me. But after how hurt he looked after I asked him why he'd choose to become one of us, I start doubting that he will.

Sanse gives me a long look then. 'I'll make sure to give you my number before I leave, just in case you need it. You're still returning to London next weekend?'

I nod. 'Uni starts soon.'

'Ah, yes, I remember. Are you looking forward to it? I know you were concerned that you may have to take a gap year when you first arrived.'

'Yeah . . . mostly. I feel ready.' Or at least, I did.

'Well, if I do say so myself, I think you have done incredibly well to have mastered your soucouyant side so quickly.' She smiles at Grandma. 'She's a credit to your family, Noemie.'

'She is. I'm very proud of her.'

'As you should be. Would you like the information for the group in the south, Gabrielle?'

I hadn't thought about that. 'Where is it?'

'There's one right in the heart of Brighton.'

'Oh! Okay, sure. Thank you, and thank you for all your help while I've been here, too.'

'You're more than welcome. However, for your future safety, and others', please don't try to investigate vampire attacks yourself again. As soon as you knew there was trouble last night, you should have gone straight home. Not put yourself in danger of being attacked, or revealing your true identity by shifting in a very public place.' She looks at Maria then. 'Your gift helped us tremendously and we are all grateful, but it could have gone horribly wrong.'

'Sorry,' we both mutter.

Sanse's look is knowing, but then she and Grandma smile at each other.

'Oh,' Sanse says, 'and before I forget. Maria, Kesa wanted me to pass a message on to you.'

Maria sits up. 'Me? Okay . . .'

'She said you'll no longer be under surveillance, as long as you continue with the plan we've made.'

'Really?'

'Yes, really, and I must say, I'm thrilled for you.'

'So does that mean no more staying behind at group when attacks happen?' I ask.

Maria nods excitedly. 'Yep.'

'Babe. That's amazing news.'

'It is,' Sanse agrees. 'It seems you two have been brilliant for each other. It's been lovely to see Maria so happy at group. She told me you encouraged her to start taking regular blood——?'

'Me and my grandma, but I think she was on her way there herself.'

'Well, either way, I'm glad. Will you two be staying in touch?'

'Hell, yeah,' we both say in unison, and then we laugh.

'She's not getting rid of me now,' Maria adds. 'I've already planned my first visit to see her at uni.'

I smile at her. 'You're not getting rid of me either.'

That girl's my sister now.

* * *

SUCKERS

I see Sanse to her car and she gives me her number before she leaves. She also reassures me again that Ethan will be okay. She sides with Grandma and Maria, too, by insisting that it's not my fault when I tell her how I feel about him.

They can all say that, but I think there will always be a part of me that disagrees.

'I'm gonna go now, babe,' Maria says, after Sanse leaves. 'Dad's picking me up.'

'Okay.' I hug her tightly. 'I'll see you this week though, right?'

'Of course. I'll see if the others are free for a meet up, but if not, keep Saturday night free, okay? I want to spend your last night here with you.'

'I will. Thanks for everything.'

'You know I've got you, girl. No matter where you are.'

'And I've got you, remember.'

'I know.' She shouts goodbye to Grandma before she leaves, and then I go back to the kitchen.

'Everything okay?' Grandma asks.

'Yeah, I think so. I just . . . I hope they find Ethan.'

'They will. They've tracked down many a vampire before, and if he's been spotted at The Coven, it's only a matter of time.'

Yeah . . . 'I'm going to write for a bit.'

She smiles knowingly. 'All right, dear.'

I check my phone on my way up to my room, and the sickness I already feel intensifies when I see a message from Kyle.

Can you meet in Camden one day next week?

I think about ignoring it, but Maria's advice repeats loudly in my head.

Me: I can do next Sunday night?

Kyle: That's cool. Blues at 7 okay?

Me: Sure.

Something else to dread . . .

'All he does is complain about Ethan quitting and leaving him in the lurch,' I tell Maria when we walk along the beach on Tuesday afternoon. 'It's doing my head in.'

Maria chuckles. 'Can't blame him, though. Is he going to hire someone else?'

'Apparently so. I'm just glad I'm not going to have to listen to it for much longer. I feel bad for Grandma, though.'

'For real . . .'

We sit on the sand to watch the waves, silent for a while. I think we're both feeling it now, my soon-to-be departure. Mum and Dad are coming to pick me up on Sunday so I can pack for uni. I'm meant to be moving into my shared house in Brighton the weekend after.

Time is going so fast.

'Have you heard from Alok yet?'

I shake my head. 'Not a thing.' I caved last night and texted Alok and Ethan the same thing.

If you need me, I'm here.

'The boys haven't either, and Alok hasn't been at work. Do you think he's okay?'

'I really hope so.' He definitely saw my message, so it's up to him to contact me now. Ethan is still on the run, too, and as far as I know, no one's seen him again. 'Has Sanse said anything to you about either of them?'

Maria shakes her head, appearing just as gutted as I am. 'I've not heard a thing from her. Not that I want to complain about that after the last few weeks of mayhem we've had, but it would be nice to be kept updated about our friends.'

'Right. Do you think they're intentionally keeping us in the dark?'

'Probably.' She gives me a look. 'Gabby . . .?'

I sigh, already knowing what she's going to bring up, but I'm still not prepared for it. 'Go on . . .'

'I don't want to upset you, but . . . how are you feeling about everything to do with Ethan now? I mean, I still stand by what I said about him choosing this life, but . . . he must really care about you.'

My heart aches. 'He told me he loved me at the lightboat house.'

'Wow . . .'

'I know. And . . . I . . . I love him, too, but . . .'

'Alok.'

I hold back tears when the guilt threatens to tear me apart. 'I didn't want to get involved with anyone when I came here. Learning everything I had to was my focus, and I tried to resist . . . But I've screwed up so much.'

'Hey, I understand, babe. A lot has happened this summer, in this town, with you, with them, with all of us. Everyone's emotions have run high, and you know how complicated those can be when you're one of us.'

I close my eyes briefly. 'I wish they weren't.'

'So do I, believe me, but think of what your grandma would say. Everything will work out.'

I breathe a laugh. 'She would say that, but I don't know if I believe it.'

She smirks. 'Yeah, I guess. Do you know what you're going to do about them?'

'I have no idea, and if I don't see them before I leave . . .'

'I hope you do, for your sake.'

'Me, too.'

We sit in silence again for a while after that, until she suddenly takes my hand.

'I don't want you to go,' she whispers.

That makes me tearful. 'I don't either. Or at least, I wish I could take you with me.'

'Girl, don't even. I'll start looking at the degrees they offer down there.'

'Well, if you do, we can house-share together, and we could study together—'

'Stop.' She holds her hand up. 'I'm so serious.'

'So am I.'

Her eyes light up. 'Maybe next September.'

'Don't get my hopes up,' I say, resting my head on her shoulder. 'I'm going to text you every day.'

'So am I.'

'And if you ever need me—'

'I'll text you.'

'You better.'

'And if you ever need me—'

'I'm calling you.'

'And I'll answer, no matter if it's day or night.'

I lift my head and smile at her as an idea suddenly occurs to me. 'Let's get matching tattoos.'

She gasps. 'Are you serious?'

'Deadly.'

'What should we get?'

'I have an idea . . .'

I quietly strum my new, matt-black electric guitar that Maria encouraged me to buy while we were in town, still surprised by just how right it feels to be playing six strings again instead of four. No, she's not as deep and sultry as my bass, but I can play anything I want on her, which means I don't need a band around me any more.

I got it from the same music shop Ethan took me to, and the memory of us there – paired with passing by The Coven – has had me in my feelings since.

I don't want to leave here without seeing him . . .

I remember what happened after I bought this guitar, though, and I can't help but smile down at my new wrist tattoo of a snake wrapped around a ball of fire. I'm so in love with it, and so was Maria with hers. It's a piece of ink I'll never regret either, because I'll never regret meeting Maria.

I love her to death.

I mess up the chords on one of the new songs I've been practising the last couple of days, so I start again. The lyrics aren't set in stone yet, but once I started writing in my new notebook, I was inspired by the words that came out, and here we are.

The songs I've been writing are much slower than I'm used to, and a little depressing, I won't lie. They make me cry a lot because they're deep and mostly about everything that's happened since

I've been here. Grandma said tears are good when she caught me crying in here yesterday, because I'm letting the emotion flow.

I just feel like there'll be no end.

A loud knocking on the manor door puts a halt to my playing, so I get up to go and open it.

'Alok?'

He shows off his dimple. 'Hey.'

I quickly step forward to hug him. 'Thank God you're okay.' I close my eyes, comforted by his scent. 'I've been so worried about you.'

He strokes my locs. 'Sorry I didn't text you back, but things have been a little crazy. I'm good, though.'

I step back. 'Does that mean your dad . . .?'

'Yeah, he's fine. Wasn't at first, but he's getting there.' He leads me to sit on the steps with him, and then he tells me how his dad didn't speak to him for two days after he saw him shift. 'Mum said she didn't care what I was, so I was lucky with her. Dad, though – it was a lot for him to come to terms with. It wasn't until after Sanse came to speak to him again last night that he started treating me normally again.'

'Do you know what they talked about?'

He shakes his head. 'I heard Sanse raise her voice a few times. Mum was trying to listen through the door, too, but she didn't hear much. They're working together now, though. I don't know if you know that.'

I gape at him. 'No. Sanse hasn't told us anything. How?'

'Dad's going to keep running his rallies, but they'll be more about educating people on the traits of vampires so when attacks do happen, Sanse and Dad can work together to catch them.'

'Wow . . .' I release a heavy breath. 'I wasn't expecting that.'

'Dad also apologised . . . because I couldn't tell him.'

'As he should.'

'Mum's given him a hard time, too. She was so angry when he wouldn't speak to me.'

'So would I be if that was my child. Parents are supposed to love their children unconditionally.' I shake my head. 'I can't believe your dad and Sanse will be working together. I mean, I hoped for it, but I didn't really think it would happen.'

'You're not the only one.' He gives me a look. 'Do you know about Ethan?'

My stomach twists. 'Yeah. I'm guessing you do, too?'

'Yeah . . . It's kinda fucked up . . . I hope they find him soon.'

'Same . . . I'm glad things have worked out with you and your dad,' I say, trying to steer the conversation away from that topic, 'but I still feel like I should apologise. If I hadn't asked you to help me, you never would have been found out.'

He shakes his head. 'Nah, it's not your fault. I wanted to help. And really, I should be thankful, because I never would have told him. It's a relief not having to hide it from them any more.'

'Well, I'm happy about that.'

'Sanse told me about the group.' He smirks then. 'I still can't believe Maria's shift is a snake.' He chuckles. 'I honestly never would have guessed she was one of us.'

I immediately smile and show him my tattoo, at which he balks.

'Don't be a hater. Just because you're too scared to get one.'

He laughs. 'I will, eventually. I'm not surprised you two did that, though.'

'Maria is special in so many ways. I'll never forget the day I saw her shift for the first time. It was my first time at the group, and a guy there called Lorenzo had to shift into a giant bird and strike her with lightning to stop her from scaring me.'

His eyes widen. 'Shit, well, I don't know if I'll go, but I'm glad to have someone else around like me, especially because you won't be here.'

'So am I.' I turn to face him. 'I've been so stressed over leaving you. *Seriously* stressed.'

He slips his hand in mine. 'I know I didn't want to accept what was happening, but I want you to know how much I appreciated you nagging at me. If it weren't for you . . . Shifting in front of you in the woods terrified me, but it also made everything I'd been trying to ignore real. I don't know if I would've gotten through everything since if you hadn't been here.'

I hold his hand tightly. 'I'm glad I could be here for you . . . I care about you a lot.'

'I care about you, too. *Really* care. The other night . . . everything we've done— I don't want you to think—'

I shake my head to stop him. 'I don't feel any way. That night was emotional for both of us, and there wasn't anything that happened that I didn't want to do.'

He sighs with relief. 'Okay.' But then his gaze is longing. 'I don't want us to go back to being strangers when you go home to London.'

'We won't be,' I insist. 'I'll be back to visit, too, and you have my number. I meant what I said. If you need me, I'm here for you, okay?'

'Yeah . . .' He releases my hand and dusts off his jeans before getting up, and then he helps me up. 'I'll see you before you leave, all right?'

I nod, suddenly feeling sad. 'You'd better.'

'I promise, I will.'

Chapter Thirty-Five

I fidget with the lace armholes of my black midi dress as I follow Maria into the Crafty Cove gift shop in the town centre. She made me bring my new guitar, and I'm holding the case firmly against me. 'What is all this about, babe?'

She smiles mischievously while holding the door open for me. 'Just wait and see.'

I go inside the shop, which had been selling everything from snow globes to wind chimes when we visited on our shopping trip earlier in the week, but is now . . . 'Oh god.'

A huge crowd starts cheering as I look around at the 'Goodbye Gabby' banners adorning the red brick walls and a small stage set up at the back. Everyone from the cove is here, everyone but Ethan . . .

There is also a mass of people I don't know, but who seem to know me.

I briefly close my eyes and laugh. 'You did not do this, Maria.'

She holds me around my shoulders. 'I figured you needed a little push. You can't keep talking about things and not doing them, girl.'

I groan, but I don't have much time to dwell because everyone that I do know comes to hug me.

'I can't wait for this,' Willow says. 'I've been dying with excitement since Maria told us about it.'

'I wish she'd told me.'

Maria smirks before leading me to the back. 'Play first, goodbye drinks after. Your amp is here, and the owner says he'll do the lights. There's a little room out the back, too, if you need a few minutes—'

'I definitely need a few minutes.' I put my guitar beside the stool and mic, and she follows me to a small room with worn grey carpet and not much else.

As soon as the door closes, I begin to panic.

'I should've worn something else,' I mutter as I breathe deeply to contain my nerves. Playing solo in front of people I know is one thing, but in front of strangers . . .

'Huh? What do you mean? You look incredible.'

I turn to face her. 'I don't think I'm ready for this.'

She looks at me like I'm crazy. 'Babe, you're going kill it. Can you not freak out?'

I roll my eyes. 'What do you think I'm trying to do?'

'What are you scared of?' she asks, coming to hold my shoulders. 'Because, I mean, gigging is what you do, girl.'

'Yeah, but this isn't a heavy metal gig with a bunch of screaming headbangers off their faces. It's dark out there, intimate, with a spotlight on only me, which means all eyes will be, too, and everyone will hear if I screw up a note, or a chord . . .' My new music is unforgiving to even the slightest mistake . . . 'God, I don't even know what genre I fall under any more. Sad, morbid, rock soul?' I groan. 'I really don't think I can do it.'

'Yes, you *can*.'

'I—'

She suddenly frowns. 'When's the last time you shifted?'

'Last Saturday. Why?'

Her eyes widen before she steps back. 'No wonder you're stressing out over such a minor thing. That flame of yours is probably screaming to be let loose. Shift now. Trust me, you'll feel much better – and chill the hell out.'

I close my eyes and let my flame consume me, rising a little so as not to burn the carpet beneath my feet. The heat makes me shudder before it settles, and then, once the flames are steadily dancing across my skin, relief hits.

'Why haven't you been shifting regularly?' I hear Maria ask before I open my eyes.

I shrug as I feel my emotions calm. 'I just haven't felt like it. My thirst hasn't been triggered either.'

'Because you've been in your feelings,' she accuses, but then she smiles. 'Girl, you look so sick right now. Shame you can't perform like this.' She reaches her hand closer but quickly pulls it back. 'Yeah, definitely not.'

I chuckle. 'I do feel better now.'

'Good, now shift back. Your first audience as a soloist is waiting.'

'I can't believe you did this,' I mutter as the flames die out.

'You'll thank me after you realise how much sooner you should've done this.' She links her arm in mine as we return to the stage, but when we reach it, she holds both my hands. 'When you sang for us at the cove, I knew right there and then that this is what you were born to do, so don't fuck it up. Believe in yourself like you tell me to. Got it?'

I nod, surprised by how fiercely she tells me that. 'Okay.'

'Okay. We'll all be at the bar, so just look at us if you get nervous again. We all love you.'

'Thanks, babe.'

If only Ethan was here, too.

But I suck it up and take a deep breath. Shifting definitely seems to have cleared my head a little. I need to make sure I do that more often.

I can't believe I'm actually about to sing my own music with a guitar and not a bass . . . Not that I have a choice. *I can't let the cove crew down now.*

Let me just check she's in tune . . .

I make a few adjustments, closing my eyes briefly when every chord hits, and then I take a deep breath before picking Maria out from the crowd at the bar, and smiling.

She's right.

This is what I do.

The spotlight blinds me momentarily as the owner adjusts it over me, and then the chatter in the entire place dies out and is replaced by applause.

Oh god . . . Really doing this, alone . . .

I hop up on to the stool and pull the mic closer to me, tapping it lightly to make sure it's on. 'Hello, everyone, for those that don't know, my name is Gabrielle, and I want to thank all of you for being here. I usually have a band around me, so I'll be honest and say I'm just a little bit nervous, so I'll try not to screw this up.'

Everyone chuckles, and so do I when I hear Mikey yell, 'You've got this, gal!'

'Thanks, Mikey.'

The light is dimmed a little more when I begin the intro to my own version of 'Nothing Else Matters' by Metallica, and then I close my eyes to settle into the song. As Ethan's not here, I figure I'll dedicate this to him as a warm-up.

I couldn't play it fully on my bass when he requested it, but it was the first thing I played when I got my new guitar home, and I cried my eyes out.

Girl, please don't do that here.

I breathe as I begin to tap my foot against the bar on my stool, smiling when I remember Ethan doing the same in the hall . . .

The audience cheers, but I begin to fade them out as I become one with the song. The nerves fade, too, and that's when I know for certain that everything truly does happen for a reason.

There are a lot of knowing looks from the others when I finish my set and join them for drinks. I expected them, though. They've all inspired the songs I've written in some way, and although I didn't play some of my deeper songs, there were a few things that I did let slip . . .

'I'm coming to every single one of your gigs,' Willow gushes when I sit down next to Maria. 'I recorded it, too. I'm going to play it over and over again.'

I chuckle. 'Thanks, babe.'

Everyone around me says how good I was, but I think the best compliment comes from Alok when he corners me at the bar, especially after the shit he gave me at the cove the first time I played.

'Interesting song, that third one.'

I laugh. '"Community Service"?'

He shows off his dimple. 'Uh-huh. I'll get hers,' he says to the barman, 'and I'll get a beer, thanks.' He looks back down at me and smirks. '"I hated you at first but grew to love you in my own way"?'

'You memorise lyrics pretty fast, well done.'

He laughs, and so do I. 'Always funny. Seriously, though, you killed it. But I'm still going to tell people I don't think you're that good. Can't be ruining my "mean guy image", as you called it.'

I roll my eyes. 'Oh, stop it. Everyone knows you're not an asshole any more. Sorry to be the one to break it to you.'

'Maybe . . .' He passes me my drink after the barman hands it to him. 'It's because of you that I'm not like that still. You know that, right?'

I weaken when he tells me that. 'Maybe I had a part to play, but that was all you.'

He refuses that idea. 'If it wasn't for you . . . Things seem so much better now.'

'And I'm really glad they do. You deserve it, Alok.'

'I think I'm starting to believe that now.' He swigs his beer, but just as I feel like he's about to tease me with something else, Maria comes to excuse me from him.

'What's wrong?' I ask, as she leads me back to the stage.

'Ethan's here,' she hisses before looking me in the eyes. 'I won't tell Sanse, but . . .'

My heart races. 'I understand.'

She nods before returning to the others, and I can barely breathe as I go to find Ethan.

He turns around when I close the door to the back room, and I inhale sharply. He's dressed in black and his hair's a little dishevelled, but when his eyes meet mine and he smiles, I'm flooded with relief.

'Hey, Gabby.'

'Ethan . . .' I take a few steps closer to him, but he comes the rest of the way and holds me tightly against him. 'I'm so glad you're okay.'

'Yeah . . .' He holds me tighter and sighs. 'I've wanted to come and see you so many times, but I wasn't sure . . .'

I step back so I can look up at him. 'Wasn't sure of what? That I'd want to see you?'

'A little. After what happened – what you said . . .'

'I—' I swallow down a new wave of guilt. 'I reacted the way I did because I was in shock, Ethan, and if you hadn't run away when Sanse and the others were trying to help you, you would've—'

'—*Help* me? Is that what they told you?'

'Yes, and it's the truth. They're worried about you. We *all* are.'

He laughs coldly. 'The truth . . . like the truth of you leading me on while falling for Alok-the-blood-demon? Or maybe you've just liked playing us both.'

I blink. '*What?* I've never led you on.'

'Yes, you have. I saw you and Alok at the bar, but there have been so many other moments . . . Any time we got close, he'd come and fuck things up between us, and you *let* him.'

'It's not like that.'

'What's it like then? Because I told you I loved you on Saturday night before we kissed, yet when you had to choose between two vampires, you chose him.'

'I didn't choose anyone! Alok was helping me get to you so I could protect you. Help *you*. You're the one who ran—'

We turn when the door flies open, and Alok comes in.

Alok glares at me before his eyes glow red at the sight of Ethan. 'What are *you* doing here?'

Ethan's jaw clenches. 'I came to see Gabby.'

'Not with your little crew from The Coven? We know all about that, bro. But just so you know, you picked the wrong side.'

Ethan's eyes darken. 'Stay the fuck out of my business, *bro*.'

I hold my hands out when both their scents begin to heighten. 'Please—'

'Oh, look, protecting Alok again.' Ethan throws me a look before heading to the door. 'Safe journey back to London, Gabby.'

'Ethan, wait—' But I stop following him when Alok grabs my arm.

'You kissed him Saturday night?'

I shrink away from him. 'It's not what you think. He told me he loved me, and then he kissed me—'

'So that's a yes.' He laughs bitterly. 'So did it mean anything to you that it was me you were with, or was I just a stand-in for the guy you really wanted in your bed that night?'

I gape at him. 'How could you even think that, Alok. I just told you—'

'Y'know, maybe Ethan's right. Maybe you have played us both, and enjoyed it.'

I clutch my chest as tears sting my eyes. 'I care about you both.'

The hurt in his eyes wounds me before he storms out of the door, but I don't follow him. I fight back tears while my heart feels as though it's burning to ash inside me.

'Babe?'

I look at Maria when she rushes to my side, and as soon as her arm's around me, I burst into tears.

'Shit,' she says, stroking my back. 'What the hell happened?'

I choke out a sob and shake my head. 'They hate me.'

Chapter Thirty-Six

I throw on a pair of ripped shorts and a Nirvana T-shirt before checking my fit in my bedroom mirror. I look good, but there's no hiding the dark circles around my eyes or the haunted look they give me. I tried hiding them with make-up, but I gave up.

I don't even want to leave the house.

I got back to London a few hours ago and have been in bed ever since, dwelling on my arguments with Alok and Ethan, making it hurt more and more and more . . .

I deserve it.

So much time was put into mastering my thirst and shift while I was in Whitby, that I forgot my emotions are just as important, and I let them run wild.

I was on such a high after my solo performance that I was *close* to taking the gap year I'd been considering for weeks now. I thought maybe I'd stay with Grandma, do more gigs, help the town with any more attacks, because I know there are still rogue vampires out there, lurking. But after what happened . . .

Since I became a vampire, no matter how hard I try, I can't stop hurting the people I care most about. Kyle was the first, and now there's a long list of people I've hurt either directly or indirectly.

Me going to Brighton will keep them all safe from me.

I kiss Mum goodbye in the living room. 'Wish me luck.'

She smiles sympathetically from the couch. 'It will be fine, but if you need me—'

'I'll call,' I say, as I head to the door.

Please don't let me miss the bus.

I make it to the bus stop with a minute to spare, and while I stare out of the window waiting for my destination, I think about how much I've *not* missed this.

Being back in London makes me sad. I'm going to miss waking up to the rustling of the birds in the manor's roof, the scent of the fresh Whitby air, and the lazy mornings with Grandma.

I send her a text, knowing she'll be missing me, too.

Miss you already, Grandma xx

I text Maria after.

On the bus to meet Kyle. Wish me luck. PS London sucks x

Maria: You'll be back by the sea in no time. Good luck and call me when you get home x
I will.

SUCKERS

I use my thirst-taming techniques to settle my anxiety, but those don't really help me. It's the man in front of me that clearly forgot to put on deodorant that manages to take my mind off it.

Why did I have to screw things up so badly back in Whitby?

That thought echoes through my head when I get off the bus and begin the five-minute walk to Blues in Camden. The busy pavements and litter strewn everywhere grates on me, too.

I stand across the street from the music bar, trying to spot Kyle inside so I can attempt to gauge his mood. I'm not sure if I'm just overly cautious these days, but a part of me doesn't trust this.

What if he's setting me up?

I frown. What's Mads doing here? And Fallon?

He brought the entire band?

This can only mean one thing, surely, but then, I expected this, didn't I? I've already come to terms with them kicking me out. And if they all confront me about biting Kyle, I'll deny it.

No, I can't do that. But I can run.

God, I really need to stop playing out scenarios in my head. I take a deep breath and walk across the street. *I need to just get this over with.* Be a big girl. Face my fears . . .

For once.

I enter the red-brick building reluctantly, praying I don't end up being chased back out, but no sooner have I taken a handful of steps than Mads runs up to me.

'Where the hell have you *been*?' She hugs me tightly. 'We've been worried sick about you!'

'Um, sorry?'

She scoffs. 'Sorry? Is that it? We had to cancel gigs because of you. What happened?'

'Gabrielle!' Fallon yells, waving me over to him and Kyle.

'I'll explain,' I say, as we head over to the table, but I have no idea how I'm going to. This was not the welcome I was expecting.

Kyle immediately gets up when I reach the table. 'I'm sorry, Gabby. I was way out of line.'

I frown. 'Okay . . .'

'And the rest,' Fallon grunts.

'You were right to do what you did,' Kyle continues, remorseful. 'I crossed a boundary, and I knew you'd had some shit going on — we all knew. I fucked up, and I'm sorry.'

'Hold up,' Mads says, sounding as confused as I am. 'What's going on?'

Fallon throws Kyle a look. 'Pretty boy here tried it on with Gabby at the party — which was the real reason why he had a busted lip — and she ran off. Isn't that right, Kyle?'

'You dick,' Mads yells. 'You said some random punched you in the face! And we were so worried. And I've just given her a hard time.' She looks up at me. 'I'm so sorry, hun. I had no idea.'

I stare at Kyle, then at the others, speechless, until I kick my brain into gear. 'Um, honestly, it wasn't like that. Kyle did nothing wrong. I just overreacted.'

'Sounds like you underreacted to me,' Mads spits out. 'I would've kneed him in the bollocks.'

I snort out a laugh but quickly compose myself. 'Really, Kyle, I'm sorry for what I did. I honestly don't know what came over me. You don't need to apologise. I ran off because I was shocked about the whole thing, and then my grandma offered for me to go and stay with her up north, so I thought maybe I could clear my head there. I'm sorry for worrying you all. I thought you'd kicked me out from the band ages ago. I'm shocked to see you all here.'

'We'd never kick you out,' Fallon says, evidently surprised I've said that. 'We thought you'd ditched us.'

'No.' I shake my head.

I'm so confused right now.

'So you're not mad at me?' Kyle asks, sitting back down.

'No, not at all.' I sit down beside Mads, but I stay on the edge of my seat. I also feel awful because Kyle sighs loudly with relief, so I apologise again. 'I really am. Mads said you had to cancel gigs?'

Fallon nods. 'Not that many – we got a fill-in for most of them.'

'Who was shit,' Kyle complains. 'Are you back for good now?'

'Yeah, but I'm leaving for uni next weekend, still.'

'But you're planning to come back for gigs, right?'

'Uh, did you want me to?'

'Hell, yeah!'

I look nervously between them all. 'Okay, well, I suppose I should tell you that I started playing the electric guitar and solo gigging. I've been writing songs.'

'Well, shit,' Fallon says. 'You've been busy.'

I laugh at that. 'You have no idea.'

'We gonna get to hear these songs?' Kyle asks, still cautious to talk to me.

'Maybe, once they're a bit cleaner. I want to perfect them first. You know me.'

Fallon gives me a look. 'I'm sensing some hesitation, Gab. Do you need some time to think about coming back? I don't want to force you.'

I open my mouth to say I'm good to, but I can't. 'Yeah, I do, but I won't take long to decide.'

Not long at all.

* * *

'What the hell?'

'I know,' I say to Maria on the video call. I reposition her on my dresser while I oil my locs. 'It was the craziest shit. He even hugged me before I left and apologised again. Said he panicked after I bit him and knew he screwed up. I feel bad.'

'Girl, please stop. If anything, this has just taught him not to try it on with girls without their consent again.' She rolls her eyes into the phone. 'Seriously, I think you're too nice sometimes.'

'I'm not.'

'If you say so. Anyways, apart from you overthinking it, you must be feeling better now you've got that off your mind?'

'I do . . . I told them I was going to do my own thing, too, and they were super supportive.'

'As they should be, if they're really your friends, which it sounds like they are. Did you tell them you've gone to the other side yet?'

'No . . .' I smile, biting my lip. 'I'm still in denial myself about my transition to soft rock.'

She snorts. 'You haven't gone soft, you're just exploring yourself, and as you know, I'm a big encourager of that.'

I sit back in my chair. 'Really?'

She nods, wide-eyed. 'Really.'

I chuckle, and it feels good to, after how shit I've felt.

'You finished unpacking yet?' she asks, applying some eye shadow.

'Almost.' My heart sinks when I look at the clothes piled on my bed. 'I hope I find some decent people at uni to hang with – maybe even at the group in Brighton that Sanse gave me details for.'

'They'll never be as good as us, and *I* can't ever be replaced,' she retorts.

'Trust me, I know.'

SUCKERS

Maria leans closer to the camera and sighs. 'I hate seeing you like this, babe. Tell me what I can do.'

'There's nothing.'

'Have you heard——'

'No, not from either of them.'

She's visibly surprised by that. 'Well, just focus on your new life in Brighton. The fresh start, like you said. That's got to be a little exciting.'

I scoff. 'I'm excited about being by the sea again, but I'm dreading all the work.'

She tsks. 'Don't put me off. I'm still looking for degrees for next year.'

I smile. 'Sorry. Yes, I'm excited. I can't wait to get stuck in.'

'That's better . . . Right, I have to go.' She pouts. 'I wish you were coming. The cove isn't going to be the same without you. They're already missing Ethan. Alok said him disappearing off the face of the planet is all the others talked about last night before we got there.'

'I don't blame them for questioning it.' My heart aches all over again, but even so . . . 'I wish I could come, too.' She couldn't even begin to understand how badly I wish for that. 'Have a good time and tell everyone I said hi.'

'I'll video call you later. You can tell them yourself.'

'Okay, babe.'

I hang up, tears welling in my eyes as I open my journal.

I know I made the right decision to come back here, but why does it hurt so much?

Chapter Thirty-Seven

A month later

Whitby Gazette

Whitby town mayor, Oliver Shaw, has spoken at a planned, peaceful protest outside the town hall today, concerning recent suspicious attacks on local residents. He shut down rumours of another curfew being put in place, and has urged for calm amongst the community.

'We are investigating a number of leads and hope to give you all more news as we have it. In the meantime, we would like to ask for your help to find a missing member of our community, Ethan Zhou. Many of you will know his mother and will be as concerned for his wellbeing as she is.

He was last spotted outside Mister Cooper's Coffee House. Any recent sightings of him would be beneficial for us to be made aware of, so please contact the local police or myself if you can help us with this in any way . . .'

ACKNOWLEDGEMENTS

Firstly, I'd like to send a huge thanks to Jessie Botterill for name dropping me for this project. You have no idea how much I appreciate you!

To Hachette Children's Group and Anne Marie Ryan, thank you for giving me this opportunity. I won't ever forget how amazing it felt to receive that email.

Nazima Abdillahi, thank you for pushing me the way you have. Yes, at first, I may have been in my feelings – haha – but if it wasn't for our video call, this book definitely wouldn't have been as good.

I'd also like to thank the brilliant Charlie Bowater for the beautiful cover for *Suckers*. It was everything and more than I hoped it would be. To Laura Pritchard, Belinda Jones, and everyone else behind the scenes who worked their magic with this story to make it the best it could be, thank you for your time and effort.

You've all been such a pleasure to work with, and I'm grateful for all the guidance and support I've received through this incredible journey.

LeeSha Shay released her first book in 2012 and currently writes African American Urban Romance, Paranormal, Fantasy, Sci-Fi, Romantic Comedy and Contemporary Romance. With more than 50 books published to date, representation is important to her, so you will always find positive depictions of black men and women in her books, with a focus on family bonds, growth, and above all, strong, fiery heroines.

Writing novels that make her readers 'feel' is her mission. As someone who has lived through many up and downs in her personal life, she uses those experiences in her stories, priding herself on the realism in her work, regardless of genre.

As a mother to four children, LeeSha enjoys her spare time caring for her family, helping others discover self-love through her wellness blog and social media, binge reading, and watching food review shows on YouTube.